The Celeste Experiment
Copyright© Omar Imady, 2022

For information, contact:
Villa Magna Publishing, LLC
4705 Columbus Street
Suite 300
Virginia Beach, VA 23462
www.villamagnapublishing.com

ISBN: 978-1-940178-59-2
Cover Design: Noel Hagman-Kiziltan

Also by Omar Imady

Fiction

The Gospel of Damascus: The Golden Scrolls

When Her Hand Moves

Nonfiction

Historical Dictionary of Syria

The Rise and Fall of Muslim Civil Society

The Syrian Uprising: Domestic Origins and Early
Trajectory

Syria at War, Eight Years On

When You're Shoved from the Right, Look to Your Left:
Metaphors of Islamic Humanism

Coming in 2023:

Fiction

Catfishing Caitlyn

Erasures

The Weight Of Waiting

Nonfiction

An Inside Story of Modern Syria: The Unauthorised
Biography of a Damascene Reformer

About the Author

Omar Imady is an uncommon collection of many things – poet, historian, novelist, Syrian, American, exile, Sufi, 'Alan Wattsian', cat lover, avid coffee drinker, insatiable gastronome – all of which find expression in his growing repertoire of eclectic fiction. He is the author of multiple books, including The Gospel of Damascus, a 2012 Book of the Year Award finalist, and When Her Hand Moves, a collection of three controversial, thought-provoking novellas. His forthcoming novels dig ever deeper into the human experience of alienation and the quest for meaning in a world increasingly hostile to answers.

Acknowledgement

No book comes to fruition without the sustained and dedicated effort of a publishing team. I consider it my great privilege to work with the team at Villa Magna Publishing. My sincerest thanks and appreciation I extend to each of them - Giovanni Donatelli, Noel Hagman-Kiziltan, Rocio Txabarriaga, and Starla Keith - for their faith in, commitment to, and unending enthusiasm for my work.

Table of Contents

THE
CELESTE
EXPERIMENT

"The master's tools will never dismantle the master's house."

Audre Lorde

They rustle in his ears. Pages chasing pages. Paper thirsty for ink. Books thirsty for titles. The sounds morph into an incantation.

Write. Write. Write.

"Who," he responds contemptuously, "would be in the least interested in reading words written down by me?"

A white heterosexual male living in one of the decaying urban voids of the third millennium. The legitimate heir of countless centuries of racism, misogyny, and random violence. Everything about him disqualified him. He came from a geography genetically tainted with the likes of Harvey Weinstein, Jeffrey Epstein, and Keith Raniere. Those of them who manage to escape their intrinsic inclination to desecrate, invariably end up like Ernest Hemingway, Anthony Bourdain, and Robin Williams, constantly struggling, and ultimately failing, to steer away from the hypnotic sirens of the abyss. They may depart in less dramatic ways, but they are acutely aware of the irreparable faulty wiring they are trying to escape.

This much he knew. If the ink flowing in his brain was to ever make contact with paper, he would first have to find a pen. A pen that was everything he wasn't.

Female. Of deep colour. Indifferent to sexual classification. And a survivor of one, or more, of the hopelessly sexist belief systems that triumphantly claim over eighty percent of eight billion humans.

A daughter of millennia of women who were barred from temples, chastised in churches, and disciplined in mosques. Women who had their heads shaved, their feet bound, their genitals mutilated. Women who were cursed for bleeding, dehumanised for breeding, and reduced to feeding. Women who were attacked with acid, lashed with whips, and stoically stoned.

A woman with a personal vendetta, a grievance strong enough, relentless enough, lethal enough to stand up to pujaris, monks, rabbis, priests, and imams. And to do so not as an external critical observer, but as a Trojan horse, a bomb implanted at the very core of the power source.

Tick tock. Tick tock. Tick tock.

Boom.

1

Paris smelled like piss. Michael Sergeant had always admired its extreme juxtaposition of splendour and decay. Of life and death. He had not been to Paris in a decade. A whole tenth of a century. What had there been in Paris that could have helped him in that period? Paris was not a place of faith, it was the antithesis of religion, it was where one came to celebrate oneself. To smoke, to spit, to drink, to drown, to feast, to fuck. Paris was not a place of faith. But Paris was where he would find Professor Dufort, foremost authority on the psychology of religion.

The last time he had stepped out into Paris, Michael had been hand in hand with Celeste. They had escaped their hotel reception in London, fled like teenagers stealing away from a house party, and made their way to St Pancras. They'd slept on the train, hazy from the wine, tired from the dancing, at peace with each other's presence enough to lean their heads back against their seats, interlock their arms, and sink into blissful open-mouthed oblivion. The first sleep of their married lives they spent underwater. Celeste thought it was quite poetic. She loved poetry, and Michael loved everything she loved. Fiercely. Indefatigably.

Celeste loved the Eiffel Tower. Most people visit, tick it off their list, and never visit again. It is something to be seen from a distance, rather than experienced. But Celeste loved the experience, the ascent, the changing of the lifts, the suspense, the sight of Paris spreading beneath her feet. She loved the view and the scale, how something that usually looked so small suddenly seemed so big, and how everything else that had seemed so big slowly shrank. It was monstrous and magnificent.

Michael bought her champagne and oysters at the summit. Celeste loved food. She was mad about food. Everywhere they'd travel they would eat. But she'd always come back to Paris hungry. Hungry for the meat that melted like butter, for the brioche that melted like spun sugar, for the fruit on the sides of the road, the figs that fell apart and the strawberries that sang on the tongue.

It was through her travels, led around the world by work that she'd inherited from her father, that she had met Michael. He'd been her pilot. It had been difficult to get the job of flying a private plane, but he had been determined to quit commercial flying. The schedules were brutal and he had seen enough of the insides of hotels. She'd asked to come and sit in the cockpit. No one had warned him she would, but she told him she'd done it since she was small. Whenever her father would take her on trips with him, he'd take her into the cockpit and let her look out of the window. It was the closest they'd be to heaven, he'd told her. She loved looking out of the window. Not down. But up. Perhaps she'd hoped to see heaven. Michael loved to watch her, the slope of her smooth neck, the intensity of her gaze, the way her earrings would lean backwards as she tilted her head, the way her hair would slide off her shoulders. She loved turbulence, she told him. It made her feel alive, at the mercy of the elements. She loved Vivaldi's Spring, cheap cigarettes, and the smell of nail polish. She loved dancing, to anything at all, she loved the taste of vinegar, dark rainy days when sunset seemed to arrive early, and the feeling of making love on carpet. She loved being touched at the very top of her cheek and across her bottom lip. She loved museum ceilings, psychological thrillers, and white chocolate. Celeste loved life. And Michael loved everything that she loved. Which is why she had to live.

The doctors were not sure how long she had. The cancer was advanced. There was little they could do. So, they went to another doctor. And another. And another. All you can do is hope and pray, they were told. All the money they had would not help them find a cure in time. Or even find a cure necessarily. Modern medicine could not help them. So, Michael prayed, and he hoped.

He had not been raised a practising Catholic, but he knew enough to kneel that night. The next day he bought a Bible. He read it over a period of three days. And each day he prayed. Celeste had watched him the first day. On the second day, he had asked her to join him. She had smiled and closed her eyes, her head still on her pillow. On the third day, he pleaded. On the fourth day, he insisted. This was their only hope. On the fifth day, he sought out a priest. They must be baptised. Michael had been christened at two weeks old in a small stone font in a nondescript church in a village in Sussex. But Celeste had not. So, they travelled to Italy. If they were going to do this, they would do this right. If Celeste was going to live, they would do this right. If they did this right, Celeste would live. She was baptised in a pool in the Sistine Chapel in the Apostolic Palace in the walls of the Vatican. Michael should not have been surprised by the lubricating effect of a well calculated donation.

As he prayed, he could not help but let his gaze wander to the image of Eve, her arm extended to Satan, to the reclining image of a nude Adam, barely making the effort to reach towards the outstretched arm of a leaning God. He wondered whether Michelangelo had meant to make Satan look so much like a woman. And why if covering one's body was an indication of sin, God was the only one clothed. Then he looked down and repented of his wandering thoughts.

17

They attended Mass together. Read litanies morning and evening. They had converted one of the many rooms in their home into a chapel. Celeste had chosen the paintings carefully. Michael had chosen the words. Painstakingly selected, consulting bishops and priests the world over for the supplications, invocations, recitations that would reach the heavens and be unequivocally heard. And they confessed – all the secrets they dared not tell each other – to the priest behind the screen, the identity of whom they knew but suspended for the seconds, minutes, sometimes hours they would spend purging their souls of past guilt.

Celeste confessed to two abortions, for which the penance was great. God was forgiving but he required payment. Michael confessed to knowing and to wanting them. He confessed to the years he had spent away from God. He confessed to the sins of lust, of gluttony, of pride. Of a greed for life. He confessed to being tired. In the week after their third consultancy meeting, he confessed to impatience. After their fourth, he confessed to anger. After their fifth, he confessed his apostasy. And then he turned to the Torah. What was Christianity anyway but a bastardised version of Judaism? They had to return to the source, the burning bush, Mount Sinai, not the words of men who wrote about a man. The words of God. Commandments. Jerusalem. The cradle of faith.

The word *orthos* in Greek means correct; *doxa* means practice. They would do Judaism right. They would become Orthodox Jews. No other way was correct. In order to convert, candidates are required to study Jewish law for ten months. Celeste may not have ten months. Michael made calls, pulling on the threads of every contact Celeste had made through work and her family's extensive social network. They could expedite

18

the process, fly to Israel, be immersed in the *mikveh*. For a second time, Celeste was submerged into water with the hope of emerging anew, reborn, without the illness plaguing her gradually diminishing body. Our Father had become Elohim, and Michael became Mikha'el, and Celeste became Miriam. Her father became upset. It was one thing to take a familiar religion to its extreme. Mass he could understand, charity, even fasting if he saw it through the prism of health and wellness. But this was unwellness. Not of the body, but of the mind. For who in their right mind would travel to the centre of an everlasting warzone to stand at a wall and wail for a cure? He would ring daily, plead with Celeste to come home. They would enjoy the rest of the time she had left together, there was so much left to live. She would listen. Michael sat beside her on the bed in the apartment they had rented as close to the Western Wall as Israeli authorities would allow them. Watching her slip deeper into her silence, observing the doubt pass over her eyes, he would take the phone from her hands, and in words befitting a pulpit he would inform his father-in-law that they knew what they were doing, and that it was not enough to have faith in medicine, they needed to have faith. He would put down the phone, take Celeste's hands in his, and together they'd pray.

It was explained to them by the doctors in Tel Aviv that chemotherapy could buy them some time. No doctors back home had offered this lifeline, if it could be considered that. Michael saw it as a sign. There was hope. The pills they suggested would target cells that reproduce rapidly. Cancer cells reproduce rapidly. So do hair cells, and the cells of fingernails. There are ways to prevent hair loss from chemotherapy, but why bother, Michael insisted. God was making this easy. Celeste would need to shave her head anyway to cover it with a wig, or at the very least a *tichel*. And she would look so dignified, he said, with a silken scarf wrapped around her head and fastened at the back. Michael never allowed himself to think about the fact that his wife wore another woman's hair, or that the wound from his circumcision had taken three weeks to fully heal. It coincided partly with Celeste's period, during which he could not touch her intimately anyway.

He would lie beside her at night as she slept, fighting the flood of sacrilegious memories from days that could have been better spent. What might have been? Was the suffering a punishment for the way they had lived? They had not hurt anyone. Not on purpose. But they had not helped either. The money they had spent on themselves, the holidays, the furniture, the paintings, the food, the parties. The price of their wine alone could have built an orphanage. Were you punished for what you didn't do as severely as for what you did? Was there enough time left to make amends? God was forgiving, but he required payment. They had made donations, contributed to schools around Israel, Jewish schools around the world, clasped the hands of beggars stuffed with notes, funded hospitals, homeless shelters. The chemotherapy was a sliver of the promise of salvation. So, they gave more. Michael watched his wife's chest rise and fall and fought the urge to touch her. It was the sabbath and intercourse on the sabbath was encouraged. But he had two days left until she was pure again, and he was still sore. And her life was at stake. He turned his pillow over and threw back half the sheet to allow the breeze from the open window to brush over him.

I shall drink this water
From the well of the lady,
Of Miriam, the prophetess,

Who heals from all afflictions

And from all evil that may befall us…

He had heard from the rabbi that the well of Miriam contained waters of healing. It was peripatetic, roaming the world like a wandering saint, waiting to be found by those who were seeking it. He had heard it was customary to draw water from the wells on Saturday nights and that if found, the water would heal all it touched. Tomorrow, he would draw water from the wells. He pulled the blanket back over him. Tomorrow they would drink from the well of Miriam.

*

The waters did not work. The months of prayer, of pilgrimage, of endurance did not work. The pills did not work. In fact, they worked against her. Michael and Celeste moved east, at least theoretically. Back in California, one of the many places they had called 'home', whatever home had really meant to them outside of their experience with each other, they joined an ashram. Michael had spent months researching holistic cures for the disease. They needed somewhere pure, unadulterated by the pollution of attempts at modern life, free of toxins, of noise, of anything mass produced. They did not need words, they needed silence. They did not need rules, they needed respite. And real medicine. Not the chemicals Michael had allowed them to pump into his wife's body. How could he have permitted them to give her drugs that were essentially killing healthy parts of her? He would fix this. Ayurvedic medicine would fix this. It would replenish what had been attacked and fight the disease by depriving it of all the negativity it fed from.

The swami did not speak English, but he had an interpreter. He told Celeste, through his medium, to take his hand. Michael nodded to her to close her eyes as the swami had. He closed his eyes too. Her *doshas* needed rebalancing, the swami said, or at least his medium told them. He prescribed a series of treatments to alleviate her symptoms and restore harmony between her elements. No meat, no fish, no cooked foods, no dairy, no white foods, no black foods, no foods which were grown with chemicals. She would eat what they provided her, no more, no less. Ginger, garlic, ginseng, turmeric; everything was pungent. It would drive out the disease, the swami said with the authority of millennia of authorities who had handed him this right. And to cleanse the mind, they would meditate, in silence, for an hour in the evening and an hour in the morning. Between they would help on the farm; connection with the earth was vital for the health of the body. It was where they would all return. But not yet, the swami told him. First, they would cure Celeste.

Once a week, the swami would meditate with them. Or rather, they would meditate with him in a large room in the middle of the ashram, the incense swirling up above them, clinging to the draped fabric that hung off the walls and off their bodies. Meditation always seemed to be the loudest part of the day for Michael. Though he would hide it from Celeste, he would need to summon every part of his energy to drag himself from his bed to the woven mats in the morning, and then to draw upon reserves he did not know he had to ignore the stream of thoughts that seemed to know that this was the only time he was not supposed to be thinking. The struggle is part of the healing process, the swami told them, after three minutes of sightless silence. The disease does not want to leave, and it will fight.

Celeste had initially taken to the place. It was so unlike anything she had experienced before, and she loved the experience of experiencing – the newness, the emphasis on life. Michael had noticed colour in her cheeks as they lay on their low beds that smelled faintly of orange blossom on the first night they arrived. He took it as a sign – life flowing back into her. It became his nightly ritual; to scan her face for signs of life. There were nights when he thought he saw it, just beneath her skin, usually on her cheeks, sometimes around her mouth. He'd want to touch it but was afraid of frightening it. He looked for correlations, for things she'd done that day that might have coaxed it to come out, to rise to her surface, and wondered what he might do to help it. He threw himself into the rituals in the hope that the stronger he seemed, the more committed he became the more life he would have, and the more he could encourage it to live in his wife.

But as the months passed, the signs of life in Celeste diminished. She was tired. Her appetite became a memory. The silence of her meditation seemed indistinguishable from the silence that permeated the rest of her day. She would smile. She would laugh quietly when she felt Michael needed to hear it. And she would listen. But the little life she seemed to have left she used in concentrated doses.

Her light wants to leave, the swami told him, when Michael sat with him after their weekly meditation. What could be done? Nothing. When the light desires another home, there is nothing they could do to stop it. Michael had flung the small table in front of the swami across the room, scattering the incense and smashing the vases that had adorned it. He had cursed the swami with words that did not need interpreting. By then, the medium was mute anyway.

By the time they left the ashram, Celeste had made the transition from living to dying. These were not states which could exist together in one person. A person was either engaged in the process of life or the process of death. One could not do both. Michael knew this and refused to know this. To give up was to be defeated, he had never been defeated. He had battled the elements in all their intensity sheltered only by a cage of thin metal suspended thousands of feet in the air. The very sky had turned against him, and he had won. The forces of modern medicine, Jesus, Yahweh, the Lamb and the Lord, the saints and swamis of the east, the earth and all her bounty, had all turned against him but he would not be defeated. There was hope, there was always hope. There was something out there. Celeste was too young to die. And he was too old to live without her.

He spent his nights now not searching for signs of life in Celeste but promises of life online. He scanned webpages, videos, forums, read articles and blogs from anyone who said anything about a cure. He read until his eyes itched and his head swam. What had he done wrong? He had started with what was familiar, that had been his first mistake. He had moved backwards, not forwards, that had been his second. And then he had left 'God', that had been his third he now realised. What he needed was something that was unfamiliar, new and God-oriented. The perfect formula, the elixir. They would embrace Islam. But he could not bring himself again to inflict upon Celeste the rules they had abided by, she was too weak. Besides, rules were not what they needed, they needed the spirit. To reconnect with the spirit of God in the hope, in Michael's certainty, that he would revive them. He would find this spirit in Sufism.

Celeste covered her head once again as they sat in the courtyard of the mosque. After the brief ceremony, the imam's wife led her to the women's quarters. Michael remained with the imam. Prayer was to be performed five times daily. Celeste could sit if she could not stand, lie if she could not sit. Michael appreciated the mercy of these mitigations. God was the All Merciful, he was told. There had been miraculous recoveries, he had read about them. It was just a matter of persistence, of not giving up or giving in to the despair. They should never despair of God's mercy, the imam told them. God was All Merciful. Surely, there was enough mercy for Celeste.

Michael prayed, with Celeste sitting beside him, her still hairless head covered. They bowed, they prostrated, they read their invocations, they repeated their remembrances. When Michael finished and looked up at Celeste from his kneeling position, he noticed she had fallen asleep. To despair was to disbelieve, the imam told him. Michael spent his nights in ardent supplication, fending off the gravitational pull of despair that seemed to orbit him. He distracted himself by reading through books of prayers for health and healing. He read over water and gave it to Celeste to drink. He summoned faithful believers to recite prayers in Arabic over her as she slept. Through it all, Celeste smiled, when she could. She would hold her prayer beads, slowly moving them when she noticed Michael was watching. He'd hear them fall to the floor as they slipped from her hand when she drifted off to sleep.

She needs medicine, the imam told him. The pain had started in the night. Celeste had awoken with sharp breaths, struggling against her sheets as if even the slightest pressure upon her body made it harder to breathe. She was supposed to be getting better. God was supposed to cure her. They had done everything right. Everything. Sometimes, the thing we hate is the thing that is best for us, the imam told him. Michael had thrown the prayer beads in his face. The paramedics had pulled him away from the man before he could inflict any serious damage.

They ended up where they started. Modern medicine. Not for the cancer. There was no hope. But for the pain. They could numb the pain in a way that all the prayers in the world could not. Michael only wished he could inject himself with whatever they were giving his wife. He gave in to the despair and gave up on belief. There was no hope, there never had been.

It has been said that three things must happen before a person dies. The first is that they seem to recover. It is as though death allows them a final foray into life. It loans them a veneer of colour and energy, a final visit before their final departure. It is a kindness and a cruelty. Not long before she left, Celeste sat up slowly in her hospital bed and placed her hand on Michael's who had fallen asleep with his head on her mattress. He stirred and then seeing her through his bloodshot haze sat up in shock. He reached forward to touch her face, tears that he had not allowed to fall in grief welling up in surprise. She laughed gently at his speechlessness and filled the breathless silence with his name. She asked him to tell her things, things she had missed in the days and nights she had drifted in and out of the entrance hall of death. He spoke to her of all the memories he had revisited, the time before the age when they had regretted those moments. He spoke mostly of the times they had spent alone, the times they had spent with people had always seemed shared, diminished somehow by the presence of others, the splitting of themselves to distribute around a room. He spoke of the moments they had touched in unlikely places, laughed inappropriately, cried for no reason. They touched, laughed, and cried, and that night Michael slept for the first time in weeks. He would not allow himself to think that hope had returned though he felt it. Perhaps his pain - the unnameable, indefinable, unbearable anguish he kept barely at bay - had been witnessed. Perhaps this was the salve for him, the relief the doctors in the hospice could not provide. Perhaps, just perhaps, this was the mercy he had been waiting for.

It was four o'clock in the morning when Michael awoke to the sounds of Celeste moaning. He slammed his hand on the buzzer to call for the nurses. Her moans were getting louder, they seemed to come from a place in her throat he had never heard before. Her eyes were closed tight, her forehead tense with the concentration of one attempting to overcome the insurmountable. She did not respond to her name. She brushed aside his hand when he tried to stroke her, to soothe her. The nurse pushed an injection of fluid into the tube in her hand. Gradually, Celeste stopped moaning and turning her head. Her breathing steadied and she seemed to be asleep.

It did not take long for the panic in Michael to subside, not into relief, but into the deepest well of anger known to man. Betrayal. He pushed open the door of the ward and headed to the car park, to the only place he could be sure he was alone. He found his car parked under a tree at the far end of the parking lot. Opening the door, he slid in. He ran his hands around the steering wheel and then dug his nails into the leather. Turning every ounce of his might skywards, Michael let out a sound that it occurred to him later came from the same point in the throat as Celeste's moans. With this wordless sound, he cursed the heavens. He cursed every notion of the divine man had ever believed in. He cursed faith, and he cursed hope. When the sound finally left him, a strange calmness came over him, as though he had emptied a space inside of himself. He picked up a jacket he had left on the passenger's seat and headed back into the hospice.

The second thing that must happen before a person passes is a search for something that isn't there. In the days after the betrayal, Celeste showed very few signs of consciousness. She roused briefly perhaps once a day, each time to ask to see her father. He isn't here, Michael would remind her. Her father had died whilst they were in California. Though he would not admit it, Michael was glad to have been able to use Celeste's illness as an excuse not to go to the funeral. There would have been questions, persuasions, petitions for them to come back home. They had barely spoken to him after they had left Jerusalem. He had not given up his attempts to get his daughter back, but they had become more subtle. Michael suspected her father's own illness had been an attempt to play on Celeste's feelings of loyalty and guilt, though his sickness turned out to be genuine. He had sent her a letter. Michael had thrown it away before Celeste could see it. He had wanted to save her from the anguish of doubt. These were not memories he revisited but which visited him.

Celeste asked for her father. Papa, she had called him. She would repeat it. They must find him, she would insist. There was something she needed to tell him. Where was her papa, she would ask, over and over, her eyes barely open. Michael would take her hand and try to tell her that her father wasn't here anymore, but she would persist. Fighting the terrible urge to scream at her that her father was dead, Michael finally told her that her papa was coming. He's coming, she repeated. And her breathing slowed, and the beeping of the machines settled.

The third and final thing is the apology. On the morning of the day she died, Celeste opened her eyes. Michael, who rarely moved from his seat by her bed, sensed her stir. He saw her lips moving ever so slightly and leaned forward, cradling her hand in his. Her words emerged in the slightest of whispers. I'm sorry, she said. I'm sorry, Michael. There was nothing to be sorry for, he told her. In fact, he was the one who should be sorry. For all of it, for everything. He opened his mouth again to beg for her forgiveness with the words he had repeated over and over as he watched her lie there, the only signs of life apparent on the screens around her and in the almost imperceptible rise and fall of her frail chest. He felt her fingers press against his hand. He damned the desperate flow of regret and remorse he was about to flood her with. Celeste needed to speak. He lowered his ear to her lips to hear the words he knew he could never repeat to another soul.

There have been books written in almost every language about what happens to the dying at the moment of death. But Michael had never read one that told him what happens to those they leave behind. In the coming days he would wander through shock, sadness, guilt, regret - grief in all its guises. But in that moment, Michael experienced an extreme and overwhelming sense of aloneness, as though a cavern had opened up inside him and he found himself standing in it, completely and utterly abandoned. Had he screamed then, he would not even have heard an echo. This was not the same as loneliness, for with loneliness one is at least aware of the possibility of the presence of another. In the moment Celeste died, Michael knew, completely and absolutely, that he was utterly alone.

The next thing he felt was an intense and burning conviction. And that was why he was in Paris.

2

"Professor Dufort?"

"*Oui*. You are Michael," replied the tall man in the worn beige trench coat. He was standing hunched under the maroon awning of the bistro upon which the rain was hammering. Cars drove by sending great sheets of dirty water up onto the pavements. Pedestrians scurried past trying to avoid the tidal waves that washed over their feet. The man extracted a hand from his deep pocket and shook Michael's vigorously before turning quickly and heading through the dark mahogany doors. Michael closed his umbrella and followed him inside.

The small restaurant was warm and slightly muggy, as though the moisture from the damp customers had risen from their sodden clothes as they warmed themselves on coffee and hot food. The two men were seated in the corner of the room by the large window overlooking the flooded street. Small droplets of condensation ran down carving rivulets of transparency along the steamed pane.

"Thank you for meeting me."

"*Je vous en prie*. It is my pleasure. I was sorry to hear of the passing of your wife. I read about it in the paper."

Michael nodded and lowered his head to sip his coffee. He was not sure he would ever find the correct response to condolences. Professor Dufort broke the silence.

"How is it I can help you? Your email seemed urgent."

Michael leaned forward, the teaspoon in his hand. "I need an expert, Professor Dufort. I have scoured the internet for the foremost thinker, and yours was the name that kept coming up. I have read your books, your articles, I have watched your videos, your debates. They're impressive."

It was Dufort's turn to nod in silence.

"You are the world's leading expert on the critique of religion. You are the loudest voice out there calling for the end of the age of faith. And I want to know, how can it be done?"

With each of these last words Michael drummed sharply on the table with the end of the spoon.

"How can it be done?"

"How can religion be decisively and categorically disproven? What is left? I will fund it. You are the expert, and I am the heir to over a billion pounds. Together, whatever is left, we will do it. I will fund research, think tanks, conferences. You name it, I will fund it."

Michael had anticipated shock, gratitude perhaps, hesitance maybe. It was an overwhelming offer, after all. Limitless resources to fund what had essentially been this man's life's work. But to Michael's surprise, Dufort sat back in his chair and laughed.

"Research? Conferences? *Vous ne comprenez pas, mon ami.* You do not get it." Dufort shook his head. "It will not work."

"But your research... on the science of spirituality, the brain functions associated with religion, your theory that there is no part of the brain solely associated with faith. The overlaps between religion and hallucinatory experiences. That the same – what are they called? Circuits? – the same circuits are activated by drugs and sex. It was so compelling."

Dufort had opened a packet of sugar and was pouring it into his coffee. "You want to know what the faithful said when I published my findings?" He tore open another sugar sachet and tipped it slowly, looking up at Michael. "They said, 'So what?'" He laughed again.

"So what?"

"So what? God designed the brain to be like this, of course there is overlap. Reward is processed in the brain, so of course religion is too. Religion is rewarding. You have proven nothing."

"That's what they said?"

"*Oui.*"

"But all their ridiculous claims, there are so many that have been shown to be mumbo jumbo. Complete and utter bullshit. Claims about the solar system, and other natural phenomena. And…" Michael threw his hands up in the air as if grasping at his own thought, "and their abuse of women! Everywhere you look there's another justification for beating them, depriving them of their rights, making them cover up."

Michael felt a pang of guilt that somehow managed to affect both his head and his stomach. He swallowed and shook away the regret.

"Have you ever been to a magic show, Michael?"

"A magic show?" What was this man talking about?

"Yes. They have the magician, he shows you one thing, you look, you look away, it becomes something else. Or those paintings, you look at it from this angle, it is one image, you turn your head, it is something entirely different. They are magicians. You look at the text, you tell them this is what you see. They take the text, they flip it upside down and tell you, 'No, you fool, it was this all along'. And the reason you cannot argue is because they speak in symbols. And symbols do not conform to the realms of fact. Symbols morph, they can be re-read, re-seen, re-presented. All depending on who is the reader. Go to a sermon, it is far better than any magic show you will have ever seen."

Michael shook his head again. He was finding this inordinately frustrating. He had not expected to come here to convince the man to take his money. "Fine, but what about the research into the origins of the scriptures? The council you headed investigating the validity of passages of the Quran? You proved that they contained references to areas outside of Mecca, where they were supposedly revealed. Lands in the North? That surely undermines the entire history of the Islamic faith. If Muhammad was talking about a place that was not Mecca, then..."

"Then what?"

"Then what? Then the whole religion is flawed!"

"*Vous ne comprenez pas,*" he repeated. "I was like you, my friend. I was convinced I could use the scientific method, logical reasoning, sound argumentation to unravel these religions and show to the world that they are ridiculous."

"Not just ridiculous, fraudulent and dangerous," added Michael.

"All of it. But you see, this is what I realised. These religions, they are, *comment dites-vous*, how do you say...? Impervious. They are impervious to these arguments. They are like mercury. You attack them here, they are over here. You try to pin them down here, they slide over here. They do not speak the same language as science. It is a different system, a different world, with different rules. You cannot bring them down with science. They either dismiss it, or embrace it by flipping it on its head, or they ignore it."

"But surely they cannot ignore real evidence? Real evidence showing them that their claims are false?"

"'Ah, but what is true?' they say. You tell them they are false, they redefine truth." Dufort took a sip of his coffee.

"But people are not stupid." Michael insisted, leaning forward again. "If I had known what I know now, if I had heard you talk years ago, I would have seen them immediately for what they are."

"Would you? I think not, my friend. You see, the secret weapon of religion is emotion. Scientists, we explain away emotions, chemical reactions in the brain. We do not make them part of our language. We may be passionate about our work, but the language of science is always neutral. The language of religion is never neutral. The religious are the experts in the manipulation of emotions. Fear, guilt, hope, *l'amour*, desire, longing, righteous anger." Dufort slammed his fist on the table making the cups jump in their saucers, and the table to the right look over in surprise.

Michael sat back in his chair. If he had known then, before Celeste died, what he had learned since, would he really have seen it all differently? Or would the temptation of hope still have been too much for him to have resisted? It unsettled him to realise that he did not have an answer to that question.

"So, what are you saying?"

"I am saying religion does not respond to research, to science. All the money in the world will not fund enough research to bring down religion. It has its own framework, its own rules. Its own language."

The silence that fell between them was filled with the clamour of the bistro. The sounds of crockery and cutlery, of laughter, the rain against the awning, the scraping of chairs, the rhythms of indistinguishable conversations of which theirs had been a part.

"Then what do we do?"

"I do not know, Michael." Dufort, he noticed, looked suddenly tired. He looked out of the window at the flooded street, his breath adding to the steam on the glass. "I do not speak this language."

Michael reached forward and put his hand on the old man's arm, which was still slightly damp. He squeezed his wrist, perhaps harder than he had intended.

"Then, Professor Dufort, we must find someone who does."

3

Ravenscroft House was reachable by three means: Land Rover, foot, or air. From the nearest road, it would take twenty minutes to reach the outer gates by car, by foot several hours across the hilly, heathered terrain. By helicopter it took no time at all. The stone mansion sat nestled between the sides of two interlocking hills in the deep crevice a glacier had clawed slowly out of the high ground in a time when ice and not humans had dominated the earth. In the summer, the vast expanses that lay around the estate bloomed a mottled purple as the browned bracken reluctantly gave way to its brighter shades. The house itself, originally built as a hunting lodge for the landed gentry of the sixteenth century was not overly large, but the numerous outhouses and workers' quarters expanded its appearance. Rumour once had it that the property had been gifted to one of the married mistresses of Henry VIII – perhaps as a deal sweetener as part of her seduction, perhaps as compensation for her cuckolded spouse. When Michael Sergeant bought it in the months after his wife's death, it had fallen somewhat into disrepair. He could very easily have purchased any large property anywhere in the country, but he chose this remote spot in Cumbria, high up near the borders of Scotland, precisely because of its isolation.

In many ways the house was far too grand for someone of his standing, he was not of wealth but money. Not even his own money but the vast sums he had inherited from his wife, left to her by her father who had until his death shared Michael's hope that there was hope for his daughter, or at the very least, even if there wasn't that she would be able to spend her final days in comfort.

There was a knock on the door of his study. Cooper pushed it open and stood in the doorway, his hands clasped behind his back.

"The last of your guests has arrived, sir. They are seated in the library."

"Thank you, Cooper." Michael turned from his position at the window, which let in the greying light of the wintry afternoon sky patchworked by pregnant rain clouds. He tipped back the last of the amber liquid in his glass, the Templeton Rye he had imported from the States, which he had developed a taste for on one of his trips to the Midwest with Celeste. She had given a keynote at the opening of a new centre at Purdue University, and he had amused himself on a tour of whiskey distilleries.

He followed Cooper to the spiral stone staircase which led up to the wood panelled corridor, barely lit by a window at the far end. He pushed open the heavy door to his right and stepped into the room.

The library was well lit by tall windows which reached almost all the way up to the high ceilings on one side. All the other walls were lined with countless rows of books. Leather bound volumes, tome upon tome, some of which had been left with the house, others of which Michael had invested in himself. Around the room, arranged in a rough circle were sofas and armchairs, interspersed with small tables. Seated in these were four people, two men and two women. Michael nodded to Cooper who now stood in the doorway behind him. Cooper pulled the door closed.

"Ladies and gentlemen," Michael said, taking a seat in a large leather armchair by the fireplace, "I need your help."

The four guests represented the best minds in the field of religious history. Michael had gathered them from the finest universities across the world. The non-disclosure agreements they had been asked to sign upon arrival were stacked neatly on the desk in the corner of the room. Some of them had come willingly at Michael's invitation, others had come out of curiosity, some had been sceptical, but Cooper had convinced them. Michael had hired him on account of his skills of persuasion and discretion. Where he had acquired his string-pulling skills, Michael did not know, nor did he ask.

"Well… Jesus spent time in the wilderness, not long after his baptism." The woman with silver hair, sat with her legs crossed on the far end of an eggshell-coloured sofa, spoke with an almost solemn tone in response to one of Michael's many questions.

"Yes, the Temptation, I remember." Michael was listening intently. "But what was he doing during that time?"

"Fasting, according to some accounts. Deprivation."

"The Buddha, too, it's said that he lived in the jungle for a time." The middle-aged man with wet looking dirty blonde curls who had taken to walking around the room chimed in. "Moses travelled through the wilderness, too. That's when he encountered the burning bush. And in the forty years the Israelites wandered the desert. But there are conflicting theories about the validity of all of this."

"Leave validity aside for now, I want to know about traditions." Michael walked towards the fireplace which had now burned down to embers. Cooper would be in soon to stoke it.

"According to Biblical traditions, Abraham, Moses, David, and Amos were all shepherds." The older woman uncrossed her legs and crossed them again.

"Muhammad, too. He spent time as a shepherd." The woman with red hair which fell around her shoulders waved her coffee cup in Michael's direction as she said this.

"Perfect, great. So, shepherding, time in the wilderness, fasting. What else? What else do we know about preparation for prophethood?"

"I'd say travel." The elderly man with a long white beard who had been silent most of the evening now spoke.

"Travel?" quizzed the blonde man who had now completed another full circuit of the room. "Muhammad didn't travel."

"Oh, but of course he did, every year. On trade routes from Yemen to Syria. And Moses travelled, Abraham too. Joseph, obviously, was taken from his home to Egypt. The Gospels even claim that Jesus travelled around Palestine, perhaps as far as Egypt during his infancy."

"Why would travel be important?" asked Michael.

"Because travel meant two things: exposure and an audience," replied the elderly man in a voice that spoke of half a century of smoking and dry spirits.

"Exposure to what?"

"Ideas." It was the red-haired woman who spoke before the old man had a chance to answer.

"Exposure... Ideas..." Michael repeated the words slowly, as if with their articulation he was able to examine them from multiple angles. The room was quiet but for the sounds of spoons in coffee cups and the gentle crackling of the dying fire. Noiselessly, Cooper opened the door and took the poker from the rack by the fireplace. Sitting back down in his chair, Michael watched the embers send up angry sparks as they were nudged back to their roaring heat.

The red-headed woman continued. "Tradition claims that Muhammad met Jews and Christians on his travels to Syria. He would have not only witnessed different ways of life but engaged with practitioners of other faiths there."

"I remember hearing that he spoke to a Christian in Syria on one of his trips." Michael had a vague recollection of this in a biography of the Prophet of Islam he had read in his attempt to uncover something that might help him help Celeste, in his attempt to replicate true belief in the desperate hope that this might earn them both salvation from their respective torments.

"Yes, Bahira the monk." She confirmed his recollection. "His wife's cousin was also Christian and he is known to have had conversations with Muhammad, although he passed away not long after revelation began. We have quite a few details of the lead up to Muhammad's prophethood, although a lot of the reports are considered weak by western standards."

"I'd argue his is the most detailed account we have of the process of preparation for prophethood." The elderly gentleman pulled his wiry white beard through his fist as he said this. "We have reports on almost every phase of his life in the lead up to the beginning of his prophecy; his early childhood being raised by a wet nurse in the desert, his working life, his travels, his relationship, with each phase featuring a person who seems to dominate. Some periods are certainly hazy, but in comparison to other historical religious figures – Moses, Jesus – we have an abundance of these reports. Of course, an abundance of information is always suspect to historians. But Islam is the most recent of the major religions, so on some level it makes sense that we have a more detailed picture."

For the first time that evening, Michael felt his frustration with the fragmented picture he seemed to constantly face subside. He leaned forward. "Tell me more."

*

It was two thirty in the morning by the time Michael had extracted all the information he wanted from the minds gathered in his library. He had prodded and poked from every possible angle, he wanted no stone unturned, no aspect left unexamined. It had taken almost twelve hours, but he felt he finally had all the pieces he needed. Almost. One final question remained. "Where does it happen?" The fire in the grate had dwindled back to scarlet embers, the thick logs were blackened and crumbling. Coffee cups and whiskey glasses were scattered across the surfaces. The room was getting cold.

"The revelation?" the woman with red hair asked.

"Yes." Michael leaned forward, his palms on the desk behind which he was now standing. "The first revelation, the culmination of all this preparation." Perhaps he had once been taught this or come across it in his ardent reading of religious texts in his desperation to uncover a cure between the lines or even within them, but they had now become smudged, an endless stream of cureless chanting and stories that so overlapped they had blurred into an oblivion that underlay his hatred.

The woman smiled. "Well, everyone knows Moses went up the mountain, but Muhammad went in it." Outside the window, a tree tapped its branches against the glass.

"In it? Inside the mountain?" Michael's brow was furrowed into deep lines. His pupils reflected the embers in the grate.

"Into the Cave of Hira." The woman swilled the last dregs of cold coffee at the bottom of her cup and raised it to her lips. "And it was there, overlooking Mecca, so tradition has it, that the revelation was received."

Vague visions sifted their way to the surface of Michael's memory as she began to tell the story. A cave, silence, meditation, darkness, isolation, days and nights that stretched and blended into one another. And then, the words. The revelation arriving - an overwhelming sensation, blinding lights, speech that shook him, an embrace so tight it took his breath away.

"And then?"

"And then it was over, and Muhammad ran with the words inside him, trembling, utterly terrified, to his wife, who wrapped him in her embrace. We don't know if he ever went to the cave again. From then on, the revelation found him wherever he happened to be."

"But it began in the cave?" Michael insisted. He had to be sure.

"It did."

4

"So, it's possible?"

"I'd need a team."

"Get a team. Whoever you need. But they will all have to be discreet. Sign the same papers."

"Shouldn't be a problem."

The man standing in front of Michael was short, slightly balding, and had small eyes magnified by large square spectacles. He worked for Ordnance Survey, geospatial specialists and the organisation responsible for national cartography. Michael spun around the map resting on the bonnet of the Land Rover, the hood still warm. The driver who had driven him there still sat invisibly in the front seat.

"It would be much easier to use drones…" The man squinted his exaggerated eyes at the area which Michael had circled, his breath creeping up into the frosty air around them.

"I don't want drones. I want people, and I want pictures, and I want videos. The entire thing taped. Each option documented in full. Sunlight, temperature, humidity. All of it."

A thick red circle delineated the five-mile radius around Ravenscroft, which sat at the centre, a cartographic bullseye, the rippling contour lines charting the hills, crags and peaks that rose around them. Michael had already marked two potential options; caves which could hold a human. But he needed more, it had to be as close a match as possible.

"Cooper will email you the exact specifications. Come up with a list." Michael concertinaed the map back into its small oblong and handed it to the man.

"When do you need it?" he asked, watching Michael open the car door for him.

"You have six months." He shook the man's hand brusquely as he took Michael's cue and clambered into the vehicle. Closing the door behind him, Michael thudded the roof twice with the palm of his hand. The Land Rover drove off down the drive towards the long dirt road that wound its way through the bracken.

Michael watched the vehicle for a while as it shrank smaller and smaller. He was deep in thought. The pale silvery strands of his breath suffused into the frigid air before him. It was quiet. The noise of the engine was no longer audible. The only sounds came from the occasional cawing of the rooks that nested in the trees dotted around the estate.

"Sir?"

Michael was roused from his rumination by Cooper, who was now walking towards him, the gravel crunching beneath his polished Oxford lace ups.

"I have a task for you, Cooper. Let's head inside."

The fire was roaring in his study. Cooper stood by the desk, his hands as usual clasped behind him. He had refused the offer of a drink, as Michael had known he would. He poured a drink for himself and gulped it back, feeling the burn at the back of his throat make its way down into his chest. He poured himself another.

"Take a seat, Cooper."

Cooper drew up a chair to the desk.

"I need a woman."

Anyone else would have at the very least raised an eyebrow to this request, but Cooper had been employed for his tact as well as his discretion.

"A woman, sir," he repeated without the slightest hint of question or curiosity.

"A girl, actually. And she must meet each and every one of these requirements."

Michael handed him a brown cardboard folder of the unmistakable type that important documents are kept in. Cooper looked from Michael to the folder and opened the cover. There were three sheets of paper inside. Cooper scanned them slowly.

"Any questions?"

"None, sir." He closed the folder and stood up. "Will there be anything else, sir?"

"Not yet."

Cooper nodded and left the study. Michael drained the contents of his second glass of Templeton Rye and poured himself a third. This time it didn't burn as much as it stoked the heat that he already felt in his throat and chest. He was tempted to pour a fourth but decided against it. He needed strength not sedation now. He could drink more tonight when he knew he would really need it.

He stood up slowly and made his way to the stone staircase. At the very top of the house was the attic. To most people this meant some sort of crawl space where they would store Christmas lights and winter blankets. When he was very little, Michael's mother had developed a system of storing half his toys in the attic so that every few months she could bring them down and Michael and his brother would be excited about them all over again. She'd take the rest back up in two cardboard boxes and, balancing on a wooden ladder, she'd slide them into the space in the ceiling just outside the bathroom.

The attic Michael walked into now could have housed their entire flat. The wooden stairs leading up to it were old and creaked under his weight. The room, with its sloping, wooden beamed ceilings had not been opened since Michael had first arrived. He was the only one with the key. The air was thick with dust that swirled and danced in the light that came in from the small, cobwebbed window as Michael walked across the wooden floor.

He had not been able to bring himself to get rid of Celeste's things but neither had he been able to go through them. He had given instructions for them to be collected, packed up from the houses they had lived in around the world, and shipped to the estate.

He himself had brought her suitcase from the hospice, the one she had carried with her from Jerusalem to California, back to England. It was this he was looking for. He shuffled the stacks of boxes and moved picture frames, chests, and small wooden crates containing the material components of the life she had curated over the years. The suitcase he found in a corner. It was cream fabric with a tan leather stripe. He'd never opened it. Slowly, he undid the zip and tipped back the top.

Scents are difficult to describe. The English language is particularly deficient when it comes to capturing aromas. How does one begin to describe the scent of a loved one? If Michael had been inclined to attempt such a task, he would have referred to it with sensations – something at once fragile but potent, something that reminded him of early mornings and red wine. But it was not words that came to him in the moment that he was immersed in the scent of his wife which saturated the clothes in the suitcase, it was the feeling of being hit, hard, right beneath his ribcage. It made him want to tear open his chest in grief and call the world to bear witness to the emptiness he felt inside him. It made him want to disappear, to cease all existence, to erase all possible senses of himself for each and every part of him felt pain. It made him want to die.

As he stared at the contents of the case the torment and agony subsided. He felt his pulse return to him, and he was once again aware of his ability to breathe. In a state somewhat akin to a trance, Michael lifted an item from the suitcase. The fabric was cotton, white, with small flowers embroidered around an ornate hem. At first, he thought it was Celeste's night dress, but then he realised it was her prayer scarf. The one she had worn when they had sat together, knelt together in the hospice, the way the imam had taught them. With a clatter, something fell from inside the fabric onto the floor. Her prayer beads. They were also white, made of a translucent stone, looped together on a silk string.

He put the prayer clothes on the floor on top of the beads. Next, he pulled out a pink tunic she had worn in the ashram, and a book of mantras they had been given when they arrived. Michael had thrown his well-thumbed copy away when he had left. In a small canvas bag, he found the sandals she had worn there. He started pulling things out faster, more tunics, head scarves, he found a wig which he tossed on the pile in disgust, prayer books, rosary beads, a small chain with a crucifix he had bought her in Rome, stockings, a long black skirt, a small glass bottle he could only presume contained sacred water of some sort, a prayer mat, a woven meditation mat. He flung these on the pile, clawing at the contents now as he pulled them from their neatly folded places.

Whether he had expected to find something in the case that reminded him of the wife he wished he could only remember, Michael was not sure. He did not find it. The items that surrounded him now, scattered about him like debris, did not remind him of the Celeste he wished to summon. Only her scent was true to her and that was quickly fading. Michael now stared at the empty case, the silky fabric which lined the inside was patterned with a design of small umbrellas. He got slowly to his feet, his knees stinging from having knelt on the wooden floor for so long. He scraped up the fabrics, the mats, the trinkets, the paraphernalia of faith that lay about him and dumped it back in the case. Looking out over the staircase through the hole in the floor, he tossed the bag before him. It landed with a thick thud, sending the dust it had collected up into a cloud.

When he reached the bottom, Michael dragged the suitcase down the stone stairs and into the back yard. He opened the case and tipped out the contents onto the gravel, throwing the empty case on top of them. Next, he went to the garage and took a large can of petrol down from the shelf. The liquid burned his nostrils as he poured it over the heap. He took a book of matches from his pocket. He struck one, and watched it catch light. It burned quickly. Just before the flames caught the tips of his fingers, he flicked the match onto the pile. The fire burst up around it. First blue as it inhaled the petrol fumes, then black from the billow of smoke as the case caught light, and then finally orange as it settled in to feast on its fuel.

Michael stood watching. The sun set. It turned the sky a bloody red which darkened to a purple and then an inky obsidian. He did not move. When the last of the flames had finally died, he turned his back on the smouldering ashes, went into his study, and locked the door.

5

On the fifth of January 1592, in Lahore in what is now known as Pakistan, Shihab al-Din Muhammad Khurram was born. The name Khurram, a word of Persian origin meaning joyous, was chosen for him by his grandfather, Akbar. Not long before his birth, Akbar's first wife Ruqaiya had been told by a soothsayer that the child was destined for greatness. When the baby was six days old, Akbar took the child from his parents and placed him in the care of Ruqaiya, who had no children of her own.

At the age of fourteen, Shihab al-Din was engaged to a young Persian girl by the name of Arjumand. They married five years later. The date for their wedding was chosen by astronomers, carefully calculated to ensure a long and happy marriage. Arjumand bore him fourteen children, seven of whom survived to adulthood.

The soothsayer, it turned out, had been correct in her prediction. Shihab al-Din became one of the richest men in history. Amongst his vast and expansive wealth was the Koh-i-Noor, a one hundred and five carat diamond which now sits in a cross atop Queen Mary's crown. Legend has it that the stone is only worn by the women of the British royal family. It is believed to bring bad luck if worn by any man. The stone was originally installed in the throne of the emperor in the Red Court in the Hall of Private Audiences at the heart of the Mughal empire. This was said to be known as the Peacock Throne for in its ornate gold facades two peacocks were depicted dancing.

The throne was commissioned by the emperor, and in 1635, on an auspicious date upon which the festivals of both Eid and Nowruz fell, the throne was inaugurated.

Shihab al-Din, seven years into his reign as fifth Mughal emperor of India, sat upon it. He reigned under the name of Shah Jahan, Ruler of the World. When his wife, Arjumand, now known as Mumtaz Mahal, died, Shah Jahan mourned deeply. She had been his lover, adviser, friend, and confidant. Over her tomb, he built a monument of his undying love for her. The structure, made of ivory white marble, which sits upon the banks of the river Yamuna, took almost two decades to complete. It is known as the Taj Mahal.

Some one thousand three hundred kilometres away from the banks of the Yamuna River, Hamida Begum walked along the dirt road towards home. It could barely be called a road. It was a trampled path that picked and wound its way between the mounds of rubbish and filth that oozed out of the ramshackle huts and shacks that made up the Kolkata slum. She passed the man who collected plastic bottles, who was filling a large red plastic tub from a tap shared by twelve families, a young girl in loose trousers that had once been bright orange holding the hand of a small boy who was wearing only a grubby vest which was going translucent from the wear of countless tiny bodies. She dodged the wave of brown water being thrown from a doorway. She had long lost the ability to distinguish the sewage from other scents in these streets.

Her grandmother was squatting outside the door of their home swirling tin cups and plates in a bucket that had the words 'Morgan's Cement' written on the side in English. She was dressed in a bright turquoise tunic, pulled up over her knees away from the stains on the street, over maroon trousers with matching turquoise diamonds around the ankles. The clothes were worn but clean. They had standards, her grandmother told her, they may live in a poverty, but they did not have to look like it. The old woman stood up and tossed the long maroon shawl back over her shoulder from where it had fallen. She kissed her granddaughter on the forehead. Hamida helped her carry the tin cups and plates inside.

In the second of the two rooms in the house, Hamida hung up her school blazer. It was dark green. She pulled off her tie and hung that carefully beside it. She took good care of her clothes. The Saints and Saviours Mission of Kolkata were a strange mixture of generous and scrupulous. They had provided the uniforms freely but had exacting standards for their upkeep. She slid her feet out of the shoes, the ends stuffed with scraps of fabric so that they would fit. She folded her blouse and skirt, changed into the cotton *shalwar kameez* she had left on the wooden stool in the corner of the room, and went back outside to join her grandmother who had gone to drain the washing water.

Hamida had talked little since the day her parents died. The angry mobs that had stormed the streets, raiding, looting, burning, murdering, raping, had not seen her hiding in the tiny alleyway between two houses. But she had seen them. It had been enough to steal her speech for two years. She was six when she began talking again. Seven when her grandmother had persuaded the Mission to enrol her in their school. Now, ten years later, she could talk fluently, but seldom chose to. She preferred to listen. And she listened to no one more than her grandmother. In a quiet, melodious voice that reminded Hamida of running water, her grandmother would tell her stories. She would recount tales of her ancestors, painting vivid scenes from the days when the Mughal empire ruled a quarter of the world's population. She would talk to her about the poetry written in the courts of the emperors, of the wars they waged, of the palaces they built. She would remind Hamida that her name itself meant 'praised'.

Hamida's grandmother was a proud woman. Her hair, pulled back into a tight, neatly shaped bun at the nape of her neck was snow white, and contrasted sharply with the dark chestnut brown of her skin. In her youth, she had been beautiful. With age she had acquired grace, along with the lines that sadness and severity had etched around her eyes and mouth. She had been told she looked like her great grandfather. He had been exiled from Delhi in 1857 when British imperial forces had crushed the Indian Rebellion. In a box kept behind a loose brick in the wall of the second room of the house, Hamida's grandmother kept a picture of her great grandfather. It was black and white, etched on a small piece of card that was yellowed and ragged around the edges. Hamida was eight years old before she learned to read the script beneath it.

A copy of an engraving depicting Bahadur Shah II
Zafar Devout sufi, renowned poet,
and the last in the exalted line of Mughal emperors.
May God bestow mercy upon his soul.

Hamida's grandmother had told her the story of her visit to the holy woman the week after her parents had been killed. She had been desperate. She thought perhaps the holy woman might take Hamida as an apprentice, a maid, anything. She did not know how she would support a small child with no male relative, no remaining family at all to help her, living only on a pitiful government pension. She had told Hamida what the wise woman had said. A day would arrive when someone would come for Hamida. Until then, God would take care of them both. Her grandmother had always assumed this had meant marriage. She had dreamed often of greeting the faceless young man destined to be Hamida's groom at her door. Never in her most far-fetched of dreams had she envisioned herself opening the door to two men dressed in grey suits standing at the threshold of her two roomed tin roofed home. They looked startlingly out of place in the brightness and squalor of the slum. The white man with dark brown hair, greying at the temples spoke first. The tall Indian man beside him interpreted. They were looking for her granddaughter.

Hamida's grandmother was yet to tell her this story. She had sent the two men away. In a voice which carried all the dignity of a descendent of Shah Jahan she had told them she was not here, and that the choice was Hamida's to make. They said they would return the next day.

The old woman looked at the girl, sitting on the mat on the floor, the candlelight catching on the thick braid that hung down her back, wisps of hair coming loose at the end of the long, hot day. She was scribbling something with a small pencil in an exercise book on the floor in front of her, her eyes flicking between the lined page and an open textbook by her knee. She looked up at her grandmother and smiled. She would never agree.

When Hamida returned from school the next day, she was surprised to see two men in grey suits waiting outside. She walked past them silently, noticing the dust they had accumulated on their shoes. No one could escape the dust. No matter how rich, how wealthy, dust would claim them as its resting place. Inside, Hamida found her grandmother waiting. She had a small plastic bag in her hand. Hamida furrowed her brow and looked from the bag to her grandmother. The old woman understood the question. She didn't say a word. Hamida understood her answer. She shook her head and went to walk past her into the second room, ready to resume her rituals as though this had never happened. Her grandmother caught her arm. Hamida looked down at the hand on her forearm, and back up at her grandmother's face. The resolve in the old woman's eyes was inescapable. Hamida had never seen her look so determined. It was not until she pulled her granddaughter to her, wrapped her arms around her, and smoothed the long braid that was already beginning to loosen, that her tears finally fell.

As Hamida pulled away, her grandmother pressed a small, yellowed piece of card into her palm.

"Perhaps one day they will build you a palace, my child."

*

In the week preceding Hamida's first departure from her home in Kolkata, Cooper had placed four folders on Michael Sergeant's desk. They had identified four candidates. Four young women. Each of them an orphan, each of them a descendant of a noble but impoverished line. Each of them fit the criteria perfectly.

The test would not be which family was willing to part with their own flesh, they could always find a sum high enough. Blood is easily thinned by a well calculated cheque, Michael believed. The true test would be which woman was willing to come. One had refused to leave her home at all, to the dismay of her relatives. Two had gotten as far as the helicopter before they ran away, presumably back to their families, though the scouts could not be sure. Only one had silently followed the two men in the grey suits. All the way to the Land Rover parked at the edge of the slum. All the way to the airport where they boarded the private jet. All the way across the ocean. All the way up the long winding track that cut its way through the frosted brown bracken. All the way to the door of Ravenscroft House.

6

Michael watched the car pull up at the back of the property. He had given strict instructions for the girl's arrival. She would be greeted by Joy Patience, the woman Michael had employed to be her caretaker. She should ensure the girl's basic needs were met, make sure she acclimatized smoothly. And more importantly, she would report back to Michael daily on the girl's demeanour, behaviour, and any information she imparted. He watched the woman now, with her short grey hair, black cardigan, and sensible shoes, reach for the passenger door.

The girl who stepped out of the vehicle was slightly taller than Miss Patience. From the window on the third floor of the main house, Michael could not make out the girl's features, her face obscured by the hood of the large parka coat one of the scouts must have lent her. She was wearing a dark green pleated plaid skirt that reached below her knees. Her legs were bare, and from what he could make out, she wore no socks inside the black shoes. She was clutching a small plastic bag in both hands. Miss Patience must be talking to her now, Michael could see her breath rise above her in the frigid air. The girl, it seemed, had not said a word. The woman had now put a hand on the girl's shoulder and was leading her towards the old gardener's cottage at the far end of the yard, some three hundred meters from the house. Michael withdrew from the window. The Land Rover pulled away.

Miss Patience unlocked the door of the cottage and pushed it open. "This is where you'll be staying for now, Hamida," she said with a warm smile. She spoke slowly and clearly as instructed. The girl looked tired and cold. Miss Patience realised that she was not just holding the bag against her to protect its contents, but also for extra warmth. "I'll turn the heaters up for you."

As the woman fiddled with the dials on the radiator in the hallway, Hamida looked around. The narrow hallway, lined with a long jute rug, led to a small kitchen to the left, with a sink, an old oak table, and an assortment of mugs hanging from a series of hooks beneath the cupboard. To the right of the hallway was a sitting room, with a cream sofa and a low table, and an empty fireplace.

"You won't need to worry about a fire, all the radiators are working just fine," Miss Patience reassured her.

The rooms, by most standards, were sparsely furnished, though these two rooms alone contained more items than Hamida's grandmother had ever possessed. What they were lacking was not objects but colour. Even in the slums, the walls of their breezeblock houses had been painted. Greens, blues, oranges. Even the whites of home seemed colourful. Here, it was as though colour had fled, perhaps from the cold.

"You must be hungry."

Hamida had wanted to nod. She was desperately hungry. The last thing she had eaten was at school almost a day ago. They had offered her food on the plane, and she had only managed to sip the water, which seemed far too cold. But it was impolite to take food if it had only been offered once. She stood still.

Miss Patience went back into the kitchen, pulled a chair away from the table, and beckoned for Hamida to sit. From a thermos on the side, she poured a bowl of thick tomato soup. She reached into the bread bin on the counter and cut two large slices of brown bread. She set these on a tray with a spoon and a glass of water and placed it in front of Hamida.

The girl's eyes lit up, but still she did not move. She looked up at Miss Patience. "Eat," she said, gesturing to the food. Hamida would normally have waited for at least a third insistence, but she was far too famished to complete the formalities. She tore off a piece of the bread and dunked it in the soup, burning her tongue slightly as she gulped it down. She tore off more bread and repeated the process, too hungry to care that the flavour also seemed to have fled this strange place. When the bread was finished, she lifted the bowl to her lips and drank the remaining liquid. The spoon remained untouched on the tray. Cooper had informed Miss Patience that the girl may need some instruction on daily etiquette, which saved the woman from any shock she may have otherwise experienced.

Hamida placed the bowl back on the tray and drank the water. This was too cold too, she noticed. But she was full, and there was finally some warmth in her body.

"Thank you sincerely, madam."

"Oh, you're very welcome, Hamida," replied Miss Patience, smiling at the girl's rather antiquated turn of phrase, glad to hear her speak. "Let me show you upstairs."

Hamida followed her up the small staircase. On the second floor was a bedroom and a bathroom.

"You'll wash in here." Miss Patience turned to Hamida and pointed to the bathroom. She made lathering motions against her arm. "I'll show you how it works." Carefully, she demonstrated to Hamida the taps for the bath and how to turn the lever so that the shower worked. She pointed to the towels neatly stacked on a shelf over the sink.

"This is the toilet." She lifted the lid. "The lavatory," she said, seeing the confusion on the girl's face. She made a sitting motion. The girl nodded and looked embarrassed. "Use this afterwards." Miss Patience pulled the chain.

The woman had presumed Hamida's embarrassment to be at the realisation of the use of the toilet bowl. She did not realise Hamida's expressions stemmed from the fact that this woman was assuming she had never seen a Western toilet before. The Missionary had frowned upon traditional Indian toilets, and traditional Indians for the most part.

"This is your bedroom. Why don't you put your things away?"

Though these concepts were foreign to Hamida she was familiar with the words: sitting room, bedroom, kitchen. She'd read them in books at the missionary school, seen pictures in language textbooks. Diagrams of houses with labels pointing to different parts of buildings that the tiny two room structure she had called home could have fit into three times over. The only reason they had two rooms at home was so the interior wall supported the corrugated ceiling. That they happened to sleep in one room and cook in another was determined only by the fact that the back room had less exposure to the street. There was no such thing as a bathroom, but a communal tap and a wooden shack with a hole in the floor under which a large pit was dug. In her worst imaginings of Hamida's living arrangements, Miss Patience would never have come close to such a sanitation set-up.

The bedroom housed a medium-sized bed, blanketed in crisp white linens, a chest of drawers, a tall wooden wardrobe, a bedside table, and a small stool in the corner. Everything again was either wooden or a variation of white. The only colour in the room came from a pile of clothes folded on the end of the bed. A dark blue pair of dungarees, a brown jumper, black socks, and hanging from the bedpost, a khaki coat.

"There is underwear in here," said Miss Patience, pulling open a drawer. "You can put your things away and get ready to shower. I'll leave you to it. I'll be downstairs if you need anything."

Hamida nodded. "Thank you sincerely, madam," she repeated. Her voice had a clipped and formal tone, and to Miss Patience sounded somewhat like bells ringing.

"You can call me Miss Patience, dear."

"Thank you sincerely, Miss Patience," she repeated. The woman smiled and helped the girl out of the oversized parka she was still wearing. She looked warmer now, she noticed. There was a faint pink tinge apparent beneath the skin of her cheeks. She was a handsome girl, Miss Patience realised, now that she was less withdrawn from the shock and the cold. Her dark eyebrows and thick lashed eyes stood out against the deep tones of her skin. She was not what Miss Patience had imagined she would be, although her imaginations of anything beyond Cumbria were usually ill-informed. Her complexion was striking, tawny hues mixed with an undertone of rose. Her nose was aquiline and cut a line down her face that continued into the pronounced cupid's bow of her upper lip. Her mouth was not full, but distinctive, as though drawn deliberately to be noticed. Some people's facial features were easily forgotten. Hamida's were not.

"I'll make us some tea." Miss Patience smiled again and went downstairs to turn on the stove.

For the first time since she had left her grandmother, her home, the crowds of Kolkata, Hamida was alone. Without the presence of another human being, she was suddenly overwhelmed by the silence. By the feeling of absence. The absence of sound, the absence of colour, the absence of smells, the absence of heat.

Joy Patience waited half an hour before going back upstairs. She hadn't heard the shower turn on so presumed Hamida was still in her bedroom. She pushed open the bedroom door. The girl's clothes, she noticed, were folded neatly and placed on the stool in the corner of the room. Her shoes had been placed beneath it. They had been well cared for, but they were old and the deep cracks in leather were stained grey by the accumulation of persistent dust. Hamida was not in the bedroom. Miss Patience knocked on the bathroom door.

"Do you need help, dear?" she called. She could not make out a reply. She turned the handle and pushed the door open.

Hamida was sitting crouched in the bath. She had a thin sheet of white fabric wrapped around her. Both taps were running in the bath, the steam billowing from the stream from the hot faucet. The girl was cupping the water in her hands, trying to mix the hot and the cold before pouring it quickly over herself.

She jumped when she saw Miss Patience. She looked mortified to see the woman standing next to the tub. She shook off the startled expression, as though catching herself. "My apologies, sincere apologies," she

66

repeated, standing up, her furrowed brow still marking out a deep groove above the bridge of her nose.

"Don't apologise, dear. Here, let me help you," Miss Patience reassured her with a compassionate smile.

Hamida stood rigid, her back straight, clutching the now damp translucent fabric around her, her thick wavy hair, jet black, half wet streaming down her back. She was shivering. Her skin was covered in goosebumps, on her slender forearms, from which a fuzz of fine hairs stood on end, her wide full hips around which the wet material now clung. She seemed taller now that she was not drowned in the oversized coat she had been lent. Her neck was long, her shoulders were not broad but angular, and droplets of water had collected above her collar bone. Her fingers were long and delicate, her feet too, the ligaments taught as she clenched her toes against the cold. She had the palms of a Mughal princess, her grandmother had told her, the fingers of a calligrapher, like her great-great-grandfather. Her hands were shaped to carve words and to carry a nation, she had said. Hamida had always smiled and kissed her grandmother's hands whenever she had said this. Empresses did not carry pails of water to wash in the street.

Miss Patience showed her again how to use the shower. "You don't need to wear this. No one will see you," she said pointing to the white cloth. The girl looked at her with an unreadable expression. Miss Patience did not insist.

By the time she had finished, the sky outside was dark. Rather than the clothes that had been laid out for her, Miss Patience reached into another drawer and pulled out some checked pyjamas. They were soft and fleecy, but she was worried now they would not be warm enough, so she took out two extra blankets from the bottom of the wardrobe and laid them over the bed.

"You must be tired," she said. The girl, her cheeks now a vibrant pink from the hot water and the heat in the room, was standing in the doorway, her back still straight, her feet slightly apart. Even swathed in towels, her wet hair straggled over her shoulders, she had a strange and intense dignity about her. Even in her exhaustion, this sense of solemnity did not leave her. It somewhat disconcerted the otherwise immovable Miss Patience. Hamida nodded. Miss Patience pulled back the covers. "You sleep. I'll come and find you in the morning."

She beckoned Hamida to lie under the blankets. Uneasily, the girl climbed into the bed. Miss Patience pulled up the covers over her.

"Good night, dear." She switched off the small light and made her way downstairs. Hamida heard the lock click in the front door. And then the silence returned.

In the darkness, Hamida slid out an arm from under the covers and reached to the bedside table. Her fingers felt for what she was looking for. She clasped the small cold stones in her hand and drew the prayer beads back under the covers with her. In the darkness, the silence, the absence, she slid each bead back along its thread. She fell asleep before she reached twenty-nine.

7

Nine and a half thousand kilometres away, in a small shack, with green breezeblock walls and a corrugated tin roof, Hamida's grandmother stirred in her sleep. She was on a train she had ridden with her father when she was twelve years old. The carriage was rocking from side to side. She rested her arm on the ledge of the open window and lent her chin on it, watching the vibrant green fields pass by. The strong breeze swept back the wisps of white hair that had escaped her bun. The rhythm of the wheels on the train tracks sounded like a chant, but she could not quite make out the words. In her dream, it lulled her to sleep.

The train came to a slow stop. Hamida's grandmother was roused by the sudden stillness. The train had arrived at a garden, a garden unlike any she had ever seen. Its vast expanse of luscious foliage was divided into four spaces, separated by streams flowing along marble beds, each emanating from a fountain in the centre. There were said to be four rivers in Paradise, she remembered. She walked slowly along the path beside the marble stream towards the source. As she neared the fountain, she realised the rhythm from the train had not stopped, though still she could not make out the words. It was not a sound, she realised, but motion, though she was not sure what it was now that was moving.

As she approached, she began to make out shapes surrounding the fountain. At first, she had thought it was water, but as she walked closer, she realised they were birds. Bright blue birds, circling the fountain, some flying, others on the ground, their cascading tails trailing behind them. They were peacocks.

Her grandmother once told her that King Solomon had a fleet of trading ships, and every three years they would bring back gold, ivory, and brilliant blue birds with plumes of jewels. Only the wealth and riches of King Solomon surpassed that of her ancestors, her grandmother had told her. She watched them, circling the fountain. Had she counted them, she would have found them to be twenty-nine.

Hamida's grandmother now noticed that there was someone sitting on the edge of the fountain, gazing into the water. The figure, a woman, was wearing a long white gown of intricate brocade. She put her hand out to touch her and as she did so, the woman turned her head. She had dark brows, an aquiline nose, and a mouth that seemed drawn deliberately. As she touched her granddaughter's arm, she realised that the rhythm that still had not left her was coming from Hamida.

8

It was not that Joy Patience had never wanted children, it had just never occurred to her to engage in a lifestyle conducive to having them. And it was not until it was too late that she started to wonder whether she had missed something. She had worked for thirty years as head housekeeper on an orthopaedic ward in a small hospital in Cumbria. The orderliness and diligence with which she structured her own thoughts permeated her working life, and she immersed herself in honing her skills to ensure that the patients, those whom misfortune had visited, felt cared for if not cured.

Her dedication to her work, however, was not reciprocated. As is the case with outdated hospital equipment, a new model was installed, and Joy was thanked for her years of service with a card, a bunch of flowers, and an offer of early retirement. In the absence of others' family members to care for, she became painfully aware of the lack of her own. There are two remedies for persistent uncomfortable thoughts: confronting them, or distracting oneself from them. Joy had never been one for confrontation.

It came as an intense relief, therefore, when at eight fifteen on a frosty Monday morning two weeks prior, she answered her phone to a man who introduced himself as Mr Cooper. He asked if she might be interested in a job interview for the position of au pair. She most certainly was interested, she had told him. The requirements of the role, he explained, were extraordinary, in the most literal sense of the term. She would be employed to take care of a young woman who would be arriving from abroad. It would be her responsibility to tend to her needs, and ensure she acclimated to her new home. She may need to assist her in developing her language and instruct her where necessary. Under no circumstances should she be exposed to or discuss religious practises or beliefs of any kind.

The French word *au pair* means 'on equal terms'. Neither Joy Patience nor Hamida Begum had met Michael Sergeant, nor did they know exactly why the other was there. In this sense, they were therefore very much on equal terms. They were as much a mystery to each other as they were a source of odd fascination.

Hamida watched the woman washing up the breakfast things in the small kitchen sink. She was wearing a grey skirt this morning, the same black cardigan, and her hair in its perpetual grey bob. It was her fourth morning in the cottage on the Ravenscroft Estate, and the jet lag was beginning to wear off. She still had not developed a taste for what passed as 'tea' in her new home. Like everything else she had been fed here, it resembled the landscape; bare, dull, and bereft of any heat. Nothing made her lips tingle, enkindled her taste buds, or warmed her throat in the way she was used to food doing. Even the simple foods her grandmother cooked with the sparse ingredients she had, were vibrant, their colours and scents enlivened those who ate them, the vivid greens of the coriander leaves, soft and delicate to the touch, that clung to fingertips, the yellows and oranges of the lentils, the bright reds of the chillies that spat and sizzled, protesting against the heat of the oil which competed with their own, the tea that was infused with layers of flavour, cracked cardamom pods, the tiny seed pellets escaping, the embracing aromas of cinnamon and spiky star anise. Hamida took a sip of the flat milky tea before her. Its flavours were entirely foreign, but it heated her from the inside and so she drank without complaint.

Miss Patience dried her hands on the tea towel hanging from the handle of a drawer. The warm water had soothed some of the aches she'd felt in her stiffening joints. She was watching Hamida's reflection discreetly in the window over the sink. The girl had finally begun to warm to her. She'd noted this in her report. Hamida had not been anything other than polite since her arrival, but she had been withdrawn, not suspicious as much as uneasy. Miss Patience couldn't blame her. She imagined she would have been far more terrified to have been taken from her home and installed in a foreign country, where the language may be somewhat familiar but the customs were completely alien.

The girl was sharp, this much she could tell. She had adapted to the subtleties quickly, this she reported too. She didn't speak much still. She only ever responded to questions, she never initiated conversation. But she listened intently, Miss Patience noticed. She didn't have the distracted or dismissive look some people had when she talked, as if only humouring her thoughts and opinions; as if to say, what could this middle-aged woman possibly have to say that hasn't been said already? As if waiting for her to finish so that they might resume whatever it was they were doing before her interruption. Hamida listened, as though absorbing not just the words she said but all the ones Miss Patience unknowingly censored, the multiple synonyms she might have otherwise used, looking for completion to unfinished sentences.

Perhaps she hoped she'd find an answer to the mystery of her presence here. She knew she had a benefactor, who had paid for her to be brought from India, and that they had selected her. This much she divulged to Miss Patience in response to her questioning. This much Miss Patience wrote in her report. She also wrote that the girl's

English was good, fluent although somewhat dated, as though she had been taught during the Victorian era. She wrote that she liked to read, this she had told Miss Patience. And that other than her scant appetite, she reported that the girl seemed healthy. The sadness she did not include in her daily report. The strange feeling that the girl seemed to fill the room with her emotion. And that at night, when Miss Patience closed the door, she seemed to take this sadness with her, like a shawl that she wore that permeated something deep inside her with a melancholy she could not shake. Even had she been able to find the words to put this in a formal report, she was sure the custodian would not be interested in such an impalpable detail. Besides, it was easily explainable as homesickness. That was what she would say if she were asked for more details. Homesickness. Though why she herself should be feeling an intense longing for something missing that she brought into the darkness of her own bedroom, Miss Patience could not explain.

But she could perhaps do something about it. She had asked permission from Mr Cooper to take Hamida on an outing. The girl needed human connection, she must have come from a big family, she thought. She misses people. Mr Cooper consulted with his employer. Permission was granted, but they would have to be driven there and back by a personal driver. Joy had no issue with this, in fact she would be glad not to have to drive the bumpy track in her small Ford Fiesta.

She turned to Hamida. "Finish your tea, dear, and grab your coat. I think the car is outside. I can't wait for you to meet my sister and her family."

Hamida smiled and nodded. Miss Patience had been relieved to see the excitement in the girl's face when she had told her of her plan that morning. She had asked Mr Cooper also for permission to bring the girl some prettier clothes. The items that had been left in the cottage were somewhat dull. She had brought the girl a cornflower blue jumper that she had bought for the staff Christmas party that she had never attended after her retirement. It looked beautiful on her. Hamida had stroked it and thanked her again and again.

They bundled into the car together, Miss Patience in the front next to the driver, and Hamida in the back, and drove slowly along the frosted track to the main road.

"Do you feel okay, Hamida dear?"

Hamida nodded, although she did not turn her face from the window. She seemed eager to absorb every sight that passed them by, what would otherwise have been considered the mundanity of suburbia was as captivating to foreign eyes as the streets of Kolkata would have been to Miss Patience. It made Miss Patience wonder what it must look like through a stranger's eyes – which parts of her ordinary were extraordinary to Hamida? She rubbed the knuckle of her little finger which was starting to ache again.

Gloria was overjoyed to see her sister. She had invited her daughter too, with her grandchildren, three young girls, aged six, five and three to meet the visitor. Joy had a soft spot in particular for the youngest, Eve, a child with unruly blonde curls who always walked on her tiptoes and lived life largely inside her own head.

It always lifted Miss Patience's spirits to see her grandnieces. Her sister had made a big spread for lunch, and although Hamida did not eat a great deal, the colours and sounds that children always seem inevitably surrounded by appeared to have lent the girl some appetite. She was particularly fond of the fruit cake, and accepted a second piece, which Miss Patience was pleased to see, though made no comment on. After lunch, they sat in the cosy living room on plump chintz armchairs, chatting. Miss Patience had told her sister to act as though Hamida was a part of the family, not to treat her as a guest, or ask her too many questions. Gloria, who shared her sister's easy-going and generous temperament, did just that. Miss Patience made a mental note to mention that the girl seemed at ease in the setting in her report. She would not mention that Gloria's two cats, who usually hid with the presence of new visitors in the house, had immediately twirled themselves between Hamida's legs, and were now both curled up in her lap, fast asleep, gently purring.

When Gloria's daughter put her children to bed that night in their grandmother's guest bedroom, she asked them if they had liked the special visitor.

"She was very pretty. I liked her hair," said the eldest.

The middle child nodded, sleepily. "She was very quiet."

"I like her singing," murmured the little one.

"Her singing? She wasn't singing, sweetheart."

"I heard her. I did."

Her mother smiled at her youngest daughter's imagination. "Do you want to sing me her song?"

The little girl nodded and started humming through her nose. It was not a tune her mother had heard before, but then children were capable of surprising creativity.

"I can't do it like her." The little girl shook her head and pulled up her blankets.

"That's ok, sweetheart. Maybe she can teach you."

*

Hamida sat in the back seat of the Land Rover. It was dark outside but Miss Patience could still make out her face in the mirror. She had her eyes closed.

"Did you have a nice time, dear?" She turned her head away from the road towards Hamida so she would hear her question over the whirring of the engine and the tyres on the road.

Hamida opened her eyes and smiled broadly. "I did, I enjoyed it immensely, Miss Patience. Your family are truly wonderful."

Miss Patience did not see the deer jump out into the middle of the road into the beams of the headlights. Nor did the driver, until just too late. He pulled down hard on the steering wheel and slammed on the breaks. The car span in circles on the icy road, coming to a screeching halt on the grassy verge.

The three of them sat breathing heavily in shock, before the driver, collecting himself, unbuckled his seatbelt, and opened the door. "Stay here," he told them both.

Miss Patience looked back at Hamida, shaking herself out of the shock and realising with terror that the girl was in the back and might be hurt. "Are you alright, dear? Are you okay?"

The girl's eyes were closed again. Not tight this time, but almost as though she were asleep. She was breathing steadily and deeply. Miss Patience reached a hand back to touch her.

"I'm okay, Miss Patience. I am entirely fine." She did not open her eyes.

"Oh, thank goodness. Oh, but that poor creature! We must have hit it."

The driver had walked cautiously over to the animal lying in the road. It seemed motionless. But just as the driver was about to reach down to inspect it, the creature jolted its legs. With a swift movement, it sprang to its feet, and bounded back into the pitch black of the woods beyond the verge.

"I was sure I'd killed it," the driver said through the window, shaking his head. He seemed shaken but relieved. He circled the vehicle once, running his hand along the bumper. He circled it again and then climbed back in.

"Everything ok?" asked Miss Patience.

"You know, I could have sworn we hit it. I hit one once and the bonnet of my jeep was destroyed." He tried the engine, the Land Rover started up. "Well, I'll be..." He shook his head again. "Everyone in here ok?" He angled the mirror at Hamida in the back.

"Yes, thank you, sir," she replied. Had Miss Patience looked back again she would have noticed that the girl's eyes were now open, and that she looked utterly exhausted.

Back in the cottage, Miss Patience helped Hamida up the stairs and into bed. She fell asleep before her head hit the pillow.

Miss Patience sat down at the kitchen table to write her report:

*Accident on the road returning from outing. Deer
jumped into the road. No one hurt, no damage
to vehicle.*

She thought she heard a sound from upstairs and she
paused to see whether or not it was Hamida. Only the
low clicking of the radiator responded to her intense
listening. She was unlikely to be awake, the girl had
been exhausted. She was probably worn out from the
visit, plus shock can do that to you. There it was again,
she realised. The sound she thought she had heard had
returned. A thrumming and a sharp rustle. Miss Patience
stood up to try and ascertain the source of the sound.
It seemed to be coming from the window. Slowly, she
walked over to the sink.

"Oh, it's you again." It was a bumblebee. She had taken
one outside in a glass covered with a piece of paper
only this morning. Its wings were whirring, knocking
gently against the window in an attempt to reach the
tantalizing open space beyond. It was cold outside, it
would surely freeze to death, but it might die in here,
too. Better to allow it to choose, Miss Patience thought.
She opened the window a crack, feeling the sharp
breeze steal in as though trying to flee the cold itself.
The bumblebee hovered momentarily at the window's
edge, then to her surprise, it settled on the wooden
frame. It walked in a circle twice, and then nestled
itself in the join between the edges of the frame. Miss
Patience closed the window gently and sat back in the
kitchen chair.

That accident had really been a close one. They could
easily have been very hurt. Miss Patience wrapped
her hands around her mug of tea to warm her joints.
What a close call, she thought to herself. She was
surprised how remarkably calm she felt. She should

79

feel shaken, emotional. Perhaps it was the shock, she thought, gathering up the papers. She stepped outside the cottage into the cold night air. An owl hooted. The sadness, she noticed, that she usually carried home with her, wasn't there tonight. What was it she was feeling? Miss Patience tried to identify it. It wasn't happiness, that wasn't it. What she was feeling didn't seem to be an emotion at all, though it wasn't the numbness that usually came with shock, either. If she had had to describe it, she might have called it a quiet, and yet that implied an absence of sound. This was not an absence, but a fullness. Miss Patience shook her head, pulled her woollen coat around her, and headed into the cold.

At the end of the first week of her employment, Mr Cooper had requested a meeting with Miss Patience. She sat in his small office on a moss green chair. The walls were a lighter shade of the same colour. A wooden clock sat on the mantelpiece, ticking quietly, its face almost surveying the room as the hands cast away second after second into an ever-expanding past. It's said by the age of forty, a person will have crossed paths with at least one individual from every category of character type. Having worked for three decades in a hospital, Miss Patience was certain she had met every type of person there was to meet, but in the last week of her life, she was no longer so sure. Mr Cooper, for one, seemed on the surface to fit the category of civilianised military man. His stiff posture, fastidiousness, clipped and polished articulation reminded her of many of the patients she had seen in the orthopaedic ward, although he was perhaps a decade or two away from any infirmity.

And yet, there was a certain unsettling softness to him. The way he moved was calculated but fluid. His conversation, too, could at any moment take an unexpected turn. He was direct without his interlocutor realising it. Charming and personable without ever disclosing the slightest bit of information about himself. When she left his office, Miss Patience realised that she could not for the life of her recall the colour of Mr Cooper's eyes.

"You've been most helpful, Miss Patience. Mr Sergeant is happy for you to continue to conduct your employment in the manner in which you've engaged." Mr Cooper stood up to indicate their meeting was now over. "If there's anything else…" he had started to say, when Miss

Patience, now standing too, suddenly remembered her request.

"Oh, actually, there is one thing." She rummaged in the large leather handbag she had hauled up over her shoulder. "Hamida told me she loves to read, and I brought a few books with me. Things I'd read as a child. I wondered if it would be okay for me to give her these?"

She pulled out a pile of books from the depths of her bag. Mr Cooper frowned ever so slightly. He spread the books out on his desk, one by one, and then arranged them into two piles.

"These I will run past Mr Sergeant," he said, pointing to the smaller pile. "These, I'm afraid," he pointed to the larger stack, "won't be appropriate."

"Oh…" Miss Patience fanned the books out and read the titles. "C.S. Lewis? He's harmless, surely? I'm sure she'd love these." There was a tone of disappointment in her voice.

Mr Cooper shook his head. "Might I remind you, Miss Patience, that Mr Sergeant has a strict policy against any religious influences in Miss Begum's surroundings. I trust you will ensure that this policy is adhered to in the fullest sense at all times."

"Yes, of course, Mr Cooper." She slid the books slowly back into her handbag and shook the man's proffered hand. Now that she thought of it, she vaguely remembered one of her teachers mentioning the religious symbolism in *The Lion, The Witch and the Wardrobe*. She couldn't imagine how that might be a harmful influence, or why her employer would have such a stance against religion that he would write it into a contract. But each to their own, she thought. So long as they were not hurting anyone, she was content to save others from unnecessary scrutiny.

On her way to the cottage, Miss Patience scanned the events of the past week in her mind and tried to remember whether she had inadvertently shared anything of a religious nature. Hers was a quiet and unexamined faith. If asked, she might have said she believed in God, but she never considered herself a religious person. She had been raised to be good and didn't consider this to be a trait attached to any particular spiritual path. She collected various approaches to existence that she found comforting and nurtured them in her own life in the way someone might plant and tend a wildflower garden. It bloomed and withered of its own accord, depending on the season. Occasionally, Miss Patience might feel the need to draw upon her flora of faith, when a patient had died, or in the rare undistracted moments when she became aware of her loneliness. Otherwise, she was quite content to be good.

"Hamida?" Miss Patience called as she unlocked the front door. The girl emerged from the sitting room. "I brought you something." She pulled out a turquoise satin-like shirt from her handbag. "This should fit you. Try it on?"

The girl stood holding the fabric, staring at it. The nascent cheer that Miss Patience had observed and carefully attempted to coax out of the girl seemed to have suddenly vanished. A sudden sadness had washed over her, stealing away her smile like a wave reclaiming a shell from the beach into its dark depths.

"What's wrong, dear?"

"It was the favourite colour of my grandmother." The girl sighed deeply. "I don't know if she is okay."

"Oh, Hamida." Miss Patience put her arm around the girl, introducing a layer of contact that until then Hamida's demeanour had not permitted. As she squeezed the girl's upper arm, she felt a slight tingling in her fingers. Static from her jumper, she thought. She had just taken off her coat. "You must miss her terribly."

The girl nodded, her eyes were welling with tears. She wiped them away with the back of her sleeve. Miss Patience, well versed in the stoicism of dealing with the pain of others, held Hamida whilst the well of emotion spilled over. It was not healthy to dam the flow, she had found, it would only find another outlet. And besides, the poor child had not yet had anyone to bear witness to her suffering. The girl inhaled deeply, her face still buried in Miss Patience's shoulder. The wave slowly passed.

"You know," she said, taking Hamida by the arms, feeling the tingling once again, "I find the best way not to miss someone is to keep busy." She led her into the kitchen and started unpacking her handbag.

"I will hazard a guess that you've never made apple pie before."

"I have not."

"You're going to love it."

The kitchen was soon filled with the sharp scent of stewing apples, and the aromas of cinnamon that always reminded Miss Patience of log fires. They rolled out the pastry, and she showed Hamida how to lay a lattice lid over the softening fruit. As they worked, Miss Patience talked. She talked about her childhood, stories of her mother, younger sisters. She told Hamida about her work, how she had always been told she was good at helping people. She found herself sharing stories she didn't think she'd ever told anyone before. Her family shared many of her memories, so there had never been a need to relive them in such detail, and her friends had always talked about the lives of other people, their husbands, their children. When they talked about themselves, they shared updates like a community newsletter. Now she thought of it, Miss Patience had gone through life never having shared her hopes or dreams with anyone. But there was something about the way Hamida, this young woman from half a world away, listened that encouraged Miss Patience now to talk, freely and fully, about herself.

Hamida would watch her intently as she spoke, as though observing her was a vital part of the process of listening. Every now and then she would ask her a question, picking up on a small detail that Miss Patience herself had never pondered.

"I don't understand. They did not ask you to leave the hospital?"

"Well, no... I suppose they didn't, not directly."

"So, why did you leave, Miss Patience?"

Joy paused. The girl was right. She had never been asked directly to leave, and yet she had done so, even though she hadn't wanted to, even though she'd wanted desperately to stay and had been heartbroken to say goodbye. She wanted to tell Hamida that that was a very difficult question to answer. But the answer was simple.

"I left… because I was no longer wanted. It's very hard to exist in a space where you are not valued. Where something about you is no longer welcome. In my case, it was my age. Women my age, we don't necessarily become invisible, but we do become overlooked. Our opinions are not important anymore. We are not different, we are not new. We are easily silenced, and for the most part too polite, or scared, to make a noise. And even when we do, we are easily ignored. Things are changing now, but for most of my generation it's almost too late. I was expected to realise that it was my time to go. That I was no longer of value. And… I did."

Miss Patience picked up a plate from the rack and dried it with the tea towel in her hands.

"You have great value to me, Miss Patience." Hamida was looking intently at her. "Immense value."

Miss Patience smiled and squeezed the girl's arm. The tingling, subtle yet palpable, was there again. "My goodness," she said, looking at the clock, "the pie must be ready!"

*

By the fifth week of her employment, Miss Patience had taught Hamida to make apple pie, crumble, soups, stews, and casseroles. She'd learned early on that the girl was vegetarian when she brought home chicken to make a Sunday lunch. She'd asked if her whole family didn't eat meat. Just her, the girl had replied. Just her.

With the growth in the girl's appetite, her capacity for laughter had also blossomed. She was still relatively quiet, but her questions and interjections were more frequent, and far less hesitant. Miss Patience was surprised by the extent of her fluency. Only occasionally did she gently correct an error or offer Hamida a way to rephrase some of her more archaic turns of speech. She had shown her around the estate, to all the areas previously cleared with Mr Cooper. She'd shown her flowers growing in the garden, and taught her the names and how to arrange them in a vase on the kitchen table. She'd pointed out birds and insects, the owls nesting in one of the barns, the hedgehogs that came to drink the milk they left in saucers outside the cottage door, the bees that were active in surprising numbers for this time of year in the garden. She had taken Hamida to the supermarket too in the closest village and Hamida had shown her spices and taught her which ones to add to which dishes to coax more flavour from the ingredients. Miss Patience, who had a low threshold for any heat, had needed several glasses of water and a handkerchief to stop her eyes streaming when she'd tried Hamida's stew, but she did enjoy the earthy flavours of the turmeric and cumin that she had now taken to adding to her own cooking. They had visited Gloria again and made Lego houses with her grandchildren and Hamida had taught them how to count to ten in the Urdu her grandmother had taught her. The two elder children had run around the house repeating the numbers, mixing all the consonants, until they had formed their own language which, of course, stuck far more thoroughly than the real thing. The youngest child followed them, humming a song which no one had ever heard before, and which she fell asleep still murmuring under her breath.

It was true that Joy had not worked with a patient for longer than a month at a time, but she had mastered the art of maintaining emotional distance from those in her care. It was not healthy to become attached to those who would inevitably leave, neither for the patient, nor the one in whose care they were entrusted. It lent itself to too much heartache. And yet she found herself, against her own better judgement, inordinately fond of Hamida Begum. The simplest of activities, folding laundry, or reading in the small sitting room, brought her a fulfilment she had not experienced even on the most enjoyable days of her career. She wondered if perhaps she had reached an age where she had learned to be content with simple pleasures, and yet she knew that this was not a resignatory contentment, a silent agreement to appreciate whatever scraps of purpose life cast her way. She looked forward to her hours spent with this young woman, who had, despite the gulf in age and cultures, become her companion. She left the cottage later and later, finding excuses to stay and talk to Hamida, who was not only happy to listen but who encouraged her to talk. It was a rare gift in a person, the ability not just to hear, but to pay the kind of attention that took energy and effort. What Miss Patience gave to Hamida by way of care, Hamida repaid in genuine conversation.

"You look well, Joy."

"Oh, thank you, Dr. Pierce. You know, I feel well."

Miss Patience had taken Tuesday morning off to visit her doctor to renew her prescription.

"Do you mind if I have a look at your hands? We can start with the right." The young doctor put out her hand to examine Miss Patience's. "Bend your fingers for me."

"You know, it's the funniest thing. I haven't had the usual aches and pains at all. Not for at least a month."

The doctor was examining her other hand now. "Bend these fingers for me as well."

"It's really quite strange. This time of the year is usually the worst, especially at night. Goodness me, last year the pain kept me up for hours."

The doctor swivelled round on her chair and typed some notes on the computer. She turned around again to examine Miss Patience's right hand a second time. She turned it over in her palms, running her gloved fingers along the papery skin of Miss Patience's.

"Have you been doing anything differently? Taking any other medication?"

"No, nothing at all."

"It's really quite remarkable," said Dr. Pierce, taking off her glasses. "I've never seen such a drastic improvement in a case of acute arthritis before. It was the little finger on your right hand that was particularly bad, wasn't it?"

"Yes, and the left had started seizing up too, just like my mother's."

"Wiggle them again for me, Joy."

Miss Patience flexed the fingers of both hands before Dr. Pierce.

"Well, whatever it is you are or aren't doing, Joy, keep it up. It's clearly working wonders!"

The next day was Hamida's eighteenth birthday. It was quite by chance that Miss Patience had asked the week before when Hamida had been born. Hamida had not been sure when her official birthdate had been, but she remembered the date her grandmother had put on her school registration certificates.

"Oh, but that's only eight days away!" Miss Patience had exclaimed.

The celebration had taken careful planning. Miss Patience and her sister, with the help of Gloria's daughter, had looked up recipes from India. They had searched the supermarket for the ingredients, lentils, okra, fresh ginger, coriander seeds and cinnamon sticks, facilitated somewhat by Miss Patience's newfound knowledge of spices, and following the recipes carefully, stickying the pages with wet fingers and various pastes, they had prepared what they at least hoped might remind Hamida of home.

The elation Miss Patience felt at Hamida's surprise was quite overwhelming. It is one thing to be the recipient of pure kindness, it is another to witness someone receive it. Miss Patience's reward was thus twofold, the gratification she had felt at pouring her heart and soul into the celebration of eighteen years of life which she had had the pleasure of being part of, and the delight at seeing the amazement on Hamida's face when she came into the room, and Gloria uncovered the girl's eyes. Somewhere, in a crevice of her subconscious, she wondered if this was what it was like to have a child of her own.

Hamida had refused her gifts at first. She'd shaken her head and Miss Patience was almost afraid she could not be persuaded. But the girl's insistence was eroded when Gloria's grandchildren came forward with their gift. Their mother had let them wrap it themselves, and when Hamida had managed to pick her way through the layers of tape and paper, she lifted the small rectangular object.

"Open it, open it!" the two eldest children pleaded, beaming, barely able to contain their excitement at what they knew she'd find inside.

Hamida prised open the lid of the rectangular box. As she lifted it back, dainty notes chimed from the small mechanism hidden beneath the velvet inlay.

"Do you like it? Do you like it?" the youngest one asked, pulling on Hamida's hand.

"It is... so beautiful." Hamida ran her finger around the edge of the music box. "Thank you all sincerely." She bent down to kiss each child on the head. They huddled around her legs, embracing her knees and hips as high up as they could reach. She knelt down to child height and wrapped them up in her arms.

"Now for the cake!" announced Gloria's daughter, as she turned off the sitting room lights. Hamida turned to the door, through which Miss Patience was now walking, holding aloft a large cake alight with eighteen candles. The room broke out into song.

Hamida's face was lit a strawberry pink in the glow of the candles.

"You have to close your eyes and make a wish," whispered the eldest of the three children.

"And then blow out the candles!" said the second, barely containing her excitement at the prospect of wishes and cake.

Hamida closed her eyes. The youngest child, by instinct, joined her in her moment of silence, her eyes tightly shut, making her own private request of the place where all things came from. Hamida opened her eyes and smiled at the little girl beside her, still deep in concentration. She blew her wish over the cake like the holy women would blow their prayers over the sick and dying, sending the words away to do the bidding of those who uttered them. She left a candle for the little girl, who puffed out her cheeks ceremoniously and blew out the final flame.

It was late when they arrived back at the cottage. Miss Patience had told Hamida to go upstairs and put on her pyjamas whilst she heated some milk for the hot chocolate. She smiled to herself as she reached for the cinnamon to add to the milk. It is a strange thing that happy thoughts are often the precipitant to sad ones, as though opening the door to one emotion is an invitation for any of those lurking beneath to emerge. In the moment Miss Patient reflected on the implausible happiness she had experienced, a rush of sadness pervaded her thoughts. She had only a week left of her employment. Though she had paid little thought to the fact that her contract had been for a period of just under six weeks when she had signed it, she now felt a desperation to avoid the inevitable, looming end. It was the struggle of a rider pulling at the reins of a horse set furiously on its own destination. Miss Patience stirred the simmering milk and added the cocoa powder determinedly. She set two mugs of the rich steaming drink down on the table and called Hamida to come and join her.

There was no answer from upstairs. "Hamida? The hot chocolate is ready." Perhaps she was already asleep. Miss Patience made her way up the narrow wooden staircase.

The door to Hamida's bedroom was slightly ajar. The light was on inside although the room seemed to be lit strangely. She noticed the top of the girl's head; she was sitting at the foot of the bed, on the floor. "Hamida?" Miss Patience repeated. The girl did not move.

Miss Patience walked around to the foot of the bed. The girl was sitting in her pyjamas, cross-legged. She looked pale. She was cradling something in her palm.

"Hamida, what…?"

As though suddenly aware of her presence, Hamida looked up. Her face was framed by her hair, which seemed wet. Strands were stuck across her forehead. She was breathing deeply. As their eyes met, Joy felt a sudden unsteadiness, as though gravity had faltered momentarily; it was not dissimilar to the sensation of part of one's body catching up with the rest when an elevator begins to move, except Miss Patience was not sure it was a part of her body that had been dislocated and reconnected.

Hamida looked down again at her palm. Miss Patience's gaze followed hers. There was a small black object in the centre. Miss Patience bent down, the thing was moving, throbbing, in strange waves.

"Oh Hamida, it's a leech! Where did you…? Where did it come from…?"

The girl opened her mouth, perhaps to explain, perhaps to convey that she had no explanation, but before she could offer either utterance, Miss Patience had swiped a tissue from the box by the bed and made to grab the creature.

"No, please, Miss Patience. Don't hurt it." The girl wrapped her palm around the animal.

"But they're dangerous, Hamida." Miss Patience's repulsion had not left her.

"But it's alive," the girl replied, looking up again at Miss Patience and meeting her gaze. Miss Patience once again felt the unnerving jolt.

She stood watching the girl as she opened her palm again. "Your chest, Hamida. Did you hurt yourself?"

The girl looked down at the three open buttons at the top of her pyjama shirt. Beneath them, just over the top of her left breast, there seemed to be a red scratch. Hamida looked at it for a long time, and then did up the buttons with her free hand.

"I'd like to put it outside."

Miss Patience did not feel like she could object. The girl had said this with a determination she had not heard from her before. She got a flashlight, their coats, wellington boots, and headed outside.

They returned in silence. Hamida seemed tired. Miss Patience was not sure what she was feeling. It was somewhere between revulsion, terror, and a shuddering sense of guilt. How had the girl been hurt in her care?

What on earth would her employer say if he found out? She decided, as she helped Hamida out of her coat, that she would not mention this in her report. She had one week left.

She pulled the covers back on the bed. Hamida climbed in. "Thank you for my first birthday, Miss Patience." She murmured the words as if using the last of her energy to impart her gratitude. "It was truly magnificent."

Miss Patience looked down at the girl, her hair spread over the pillow. Her thick lashes interlocking, her lips slightly parted, breathing steadily. She was already asleep. Only a week left. Miss Patience felt the sadness return.

She turned to leave the room and noticed the lamp had fallen off the bedside table onto the floor. Perhaps she had knocked it off when she had entered the room. She couldn't remember. She set it back on the table and noticed the little music box. Hamida had set it by her bed. It was open, though the music was no longer playing. Inside, the girl had placed a string of pearl white beads. Miss Patience quietly closed the lid, and pulled the door shut behind her.

11

Michael's silhouette was dark against the weak light of the grey afternoon outside. The fields stretching out beyond the tall windows of his office were gaining colour. Like most things in this remote part of the country, the change was happening slowly. Perhaps it was this fact that gave Michael's instructions their urgency.

"When does he arrive?" Michael asked, still with his back to Cooper.

"Beginning of April, he informed me, sir."

"I want a date. Second of April at the latest."

"I'll get back to him and ensure he makes the arrangements."

"I'll be meeting him before he meets the girl. So, make sure he comes here as soon as he lands. You've made all the reservations?"

"Yes, sir."

"Good."

Cooper understood this as his cue to leave. Michael stood looking out over the undulating landscape. If he were just to flick a single match into the bracken, just the weakest of flames, the whole area would catch light. He saw it, the fire, spreading like an oil spill rimmed with a blazing orange hem. Just one match into the bracken, and he'd reduce it all to blackened ashes.

*

"You must be Hamida." The woman stuck out her hand. Hamida shook it, noticing the skin felt rough and dry.

The woman's hands were sturdy, her fingers almost root-like. The woman clasped her hand firmly, engulfing Hamida's long fingers, and shook her arm up and down as though working a water pump.

"I'm Charlotte," she beamed. She had the type of smile that seemed to take up at least half of her face, pushing up her reddened cheeks and causing her eyes to disappear into two lashed crescents. Her hair was light brown, though streaks of blonde ran through it, bleached by exposure to the sun over the years. Her eyes were brown as were her eyebrows, which looked like they had been drawn on with the sweep of a calligraphy pen.

It was cold outside. Hamida was not yet warm in her waxed jacket, jeans, and boots. She'd been instructed to dress warmly, though she had felt this was an obvious request. She had wrapped the woollen scarf that Miss Patience had left for her as a parting gift around her neck and shoved her hands back now into her pockets. She was not sure how Charlotte could possibly be warm in the short corduroy skirt she was wearing over woollen tights. Perhaps people here had thicker skin. Her hands certainly suggested they might.

"Pleasure to meet you," she said, raising her mouth over the rim of her scarf.

"You'll warm up once we start walking. I'll fill you in on the way." Charlotte smiled at the girl with a look of good-humoured pity. Hamida concentrated hard to catch every word she was saying. The way she spoke was different to Miss Patience and Cooper, who had both sounded far more similar to the teachers in the Mission, although their speech was less – Hamida thought of the correct word – creative. This woman seemed to stretch words in strange ways. Her intonation rose and fell in unfamiliar waves, much like the hilly landscape around them.

Charlotte led Hamida over to a rusty jeep that seemed like it had seen far better days. Hamida pulled the stiff handle of the passenger's door and climbed up into the seat. The floor was covered in dried mud, straw, and bits of orange twine. She heard a shuffling in the back and turned around to see a dog lying with its head on its paws, looking up at her. The only dogs Hamida had ever encountered were the dust-coloured creatures that roamed around the edges of the slums, fighting over scraps, with brown muzzles and ears that stood out at strange angles, and whom they were told as children to steer clear from for a bite from any one of them could mean death. They might have been dangerous creatures, but Hamida hated it still when children from the area would throw stones at the animals to drive them away. She had taken to picking out the meat from her school meals and saving it for the dogs, whose ribs showed vividly through their mangy coats.

This dog seemed almost entirely unrelated to such animals. It was a beautiful creature. Its long coat was black and white, its ears folded over its head. Its eyes did not have the savage look of hunger that she had seen in many a man and beast. These were inquisitive, doleful. The dog moved its head to one side as though to see the girl from a different angle.

Charlotte climbed into the jeep. "Say hello, Jasper. He's ever so friendly. Give him a pat."

Hamida reached out her hand cautiously to stroke the dog's head. Its hair was thick and Hamida was surprised at how soft it felt. The dog closed its eyes. Hamida scratched it behind the ears.

"He likes you! Look at that. You're a good boy, aren't you, Jasper?" She reached her hand back and scratched Jasper behind his other ear and smiled at Hamida.

The engine took some coaxing to cooperate when she turned the key. Charlotte spoke to it much the same way as she'd spoken to Jasper. They headed off across the yard towards the field beyond the gate at the back along a bumpy track. The uneven ground tossed them gently from side to side as the wind buffeted the side of the car. Charlotte drove with one hand on the steering wheel as if the bumps and battering were no bother at all.

They arrived at a large metal gate set into a stone wall that came up to Hamida's chest. Charlotte parked the jeep and swung herself out, landing with the hollow thud of her wellington boots.

"We gotta feed these sheep. There's not a huge amount of grass in the winter so we gotta keep 'em topped up."

"Where are they?" Hamida asked.

"Over the top of the hill. It's too steep to get the jeep up so we do it ourselves."

Hamida, straining to understand the melody of this woman's speech, wanted to be sure she had heard correctly.

"Over the hill?"

"That's right," Charlotte said, with a chuckle.

She walked around to the boot of the vehicle and pulled out two large rectangular bales. There were four in total. The strands of hay were compacted and bound with orange twine. Charlotte grabbed the twine and hauled the bales out onto the ground.

"One for me and one for you, chook." Grabbing the bale she swung her arms over her shoulder, so the straw was resting on her back. Hamida copied her. Charlotte held open the metal gate and closed it with a clang behind them. She gave out a high shrill whistle and Jasper came bounding up next to them.

She stood for a moment, with her back to the hill, looking out over the swathes of the Ravenscroft Estate. "It's beautiful, inn 'it?"

Hamida nodded. Not in all her life had she seen such a sea of unpopulated space.

Charlotte took a deep breath, swiped the straggling hairs from her forehead, and turned to the hill. "Right, off we go."

The trek up the hill was difficult. Waves of mud had slid glacially down the face of the hill and hardened over the decades of interchanging seasons so the route up to the top had to be picked out carefully. Badgers, Charlotte explained, dug out their sets too in this area, so they had to be careful not to put their foot in the deep holes hidden by the grass and thistles.

"Cooper says I'm to try and show you traditional shepherding. We tend to do things slightly differently nowadays, we don't spend as much time with the sheep as they used to back in the day. Only at lambing and shearing time. You're lucky you're here now, they're due to lamb soon."

Hamida noticed Charlotte seemed to be talking less to her than voicing her thoughts aloud, so she chose not to interrupt the flow and save her breath for the climb.

"He's a strange one, that Coop. Never met him before, just heard about him from Davison, he's the farm manager. Military man, I think he was, Coop. Sandringham, possibly. Never met his boss though. Can't even remember his name now. What was it? Have you met him? Must be rich to buy up all this. Jasper, here boy."

Charlotte was concentrating now on Jasper. Hamida shifted the bale on her back and planted her boot on the next ridge of hardened earth. The twine was digging into her fingers and her boots were rubbing her ankles, her socks had slowly slipped down, exposing the skin to the inside of the rubber. She concentrated on the sound of her breathing to try and distract herself from the discomfort.

"You doing alright back there?" Charlotte had climbed up ahead of Hamida.

"I'm fine," she called back.

"We're almost there, chook."

Hamida made an effort to nod. She was sweating now from the exertion, the scarf over her mouth was damp with condensation from her breath. The tip of her nose and tops of her cheeks were cold from the wind. With a final heave, she made it to the top.

The summit of the hill was flatter than she had expected, it rolled out at a gentler slope into a large field before her. There was a wide iron water trough over at the far end near the stone wall which had joined them from the bottom of the hill. Charlotte deposited her hay bale heavily not far from the trough. Hamida did the same. She was out of breath.

Charlotte grinned. "You'll get used to it. Why don't you stay here and I'll go and get the other two? Jasper'll keep you company. Stay, Jasper. Good boy." Jasper looked up at Charlotte and then sat back on his hind legs.

Hamida lent against the stone wall next to the trough and looked out over the field. The sheep were dotted around it, clustering in small groups here and there, grazing. For a place with so much life, it was eerily quiet. Every now and then a sheep might bleat, and a crow overhead might caw, but other than that, the only sounds were the wind against the grass, which whispered quietly, as if trying to impart some secret Hamida ought to know.

She watched the sheep. They moved slowly, almost unintentionally, as if letting only their next mouthful guide them. Their coats were thick, not white so much as a dirty cream. Some of their stomachs extended sideways, making them appear almost oval shaped from behind. These must be the ones with lambs, Hamida thought. She wondered if they knew what was to happen to them soon, how offspring, utterly dependent on them, would emerge from inside them, and use brand new lungs for the first time, make their first audible sounds. The world would be seen with yet another new set of eyes.

Her sweat was beginning to cool on her back now, and it made her shiver. Jasper was lying down with his head on his paws, watching the sheep intently. Hamida crouched down next to him and stroked his head.

The sheep were marked with different coloured dots, spray painted on their coats; red and yellow. Each of them, she noticed, had a small tag on their ear. Two sheep lumbered over to the water trough. Hamida remained still, her hand on Jasper's head. They paid no attention to her at all. Their eyes, she noticed, were a honey brown, and she was surprised to see that the pupils were slit horizontally across them.

She could see Charlotte emerge over the crest of the hill with another bale. Some of the sheep had congregated at the edge. One of them, surprised suddenly by Charlotte's presence behind them, bolted, causing the rest of them to startle and run off across the field, their hooves pummelling the hard ground. Hamida could feel faint vibrations in the earth from their movement all the way from the far end of the field.

"One more to go!" Charlotte sang cheerfully as she dropped the bale next to the other two and headed back the way she'd come.

Hamida offered to help but Charlotte waved her away with a smile. "I'll tell you what you can do. You can tell me if you spot any lame ones. Any that are walking funny."

"I can do that." Hamida was pleased to be able to contribute. She looked out over the field again. All the sheep she could see seemed to be walking without hindrance. She decided to make her way around the wall to get a closer look at some in the distance. Jasper trotted along next to her.

Hamida listened to the quiet. She was not a stranger to spending time with her own thoughts, but she was not used to the absence of people. For the past six weeks most of her waking hours had been spent with Miss Patience, and most of them had been indoors in one form or another. The effect of being in such a vast open space was new to Hamida. And being alone in this expanse, she noticed, had a curious effect on her. It was as though the confines of her own being had expanded, had been allowed to somehow loosen, as if the limits of her body were no longer dictated by the presence of other people, as if they were settling into a new shape. She was not sure yet what this looked like.

For some inexplicable reason, this made her think of her mother. Hamida had been told she looked like her mother, but she had never seen a picture of her. Their home had been burned by the mobs and if her parents had ever had a photograph, its ashes had long been scraped away.

She wondered how her life might have been different with a mother. It was not that she longed for her presence, nor even that she missed it, she had been very young when they had been killed. But she did wonder. On some days, her attention remained in the realms of curiosity, what might it have looked like to come home from school to greet her, would she have had any siblings, what would her voice have sounded like? On other days, these questions gave way to anger, like the sides of a gash split by a seismic tremor falling into the ravine that this quake had opened up. It would rise from the pit of her stomach, like bile. A loathing so severe it would almost make her sick. She wondered what she would say if she ever met the men who had taken her mother from her in the name of religious righteousness. Her grandmother had never told her exactly how her parents had been killed. Some part of her wanted to know. Wanted an image so visceral it would eclipse the deluge of scenes she could only imagine, like the pain of a sharp blade that might distract her from the pain of her own internal suffering in those moments. She despised those men and their hatred. And she despised the men from her own communities who had raided the Hindu dwellings two weeks before. And the Hindu gangs who had attacked the Muslim woman in the street a few weeks before that. She abhorred them and the way they talked about revenge as if honour could ever depend on something so despicable as hurting the innocent and ignorant. She wondered what she'd say if she ever met them. What words would possibly crack the fossilised shells of their own god-enforced egos? How could the rancid cataracts of their self-righteousness ever be scraped from their eyes?

She hadn't noticed how far she had walked. She could see Charlotte in the distance heading over to the water trough. She made to turn around, to head back to the shepherdess but found herself rooted to the spot. Something was wrong. Jasper had sensed it too. He was slightly crouched, his hind legs poised, and his front legs slightly bent. His ears were rigid and upright. Hamida listened. Outside of her own thoughts now, the sounds of her environment became clearer, as if she had emerged from underwater. There was an agitated rustling, the sound of a struggle. It seemed to be coming from behind the shrubbery growing against the wall ahead of her. As she neared, she caught sight of the animal's face, its eyes wide. It froze as it saw her, every muscle of its body tense with fear. The sheep's leg was trapped under some stones which had fallen from the wall. Its hoof was obscured by the flint-like stones lying at odd angles on top of it. Hamida noticed traces of blood on its leg, and scratches in the earth where it had tried pawing the ground to free itself. The sheep bleated and struggled again.

Hamida, slowly and ever so cautiously as if walking across ice, made her way towards the animal. She spoke to it gently. The sheep, its gaze riveted on her approaching figure, seemed to soften its pose. She put out her hand and touched its woollen fleece. It was spongey, ever so slightly oily; it was not the sensation she had expected but the surprise did not distract her from her susurrations. She reached its hind quarters where the rocks had fallen.

Jasper, who had followed her, was still crouched some six feet behind her. "Get Charlotte, Jasper. Get Charlotte." The dog stared at her. Then suddenly bounded off in the direction of the water trough, its tongue lolling from its open mouth.

Hamida started to remove the jagged stones, one by one, careful not to startle the animal with any sudden movements. She piled them up next to the wall. The animal's leg seemed badly broken, and the skin was cut and bloodied from the initial wound and its subsequent struggle to free itself. Hamida removed the last stone. Sensing its freedom, the sheep scrabbled to its legs. Realising it was wounded, it raised its broken hoof slightly off the ground. It stayed where it was. Hamida reached her hand out again, this time stroking the short black fur on its face. She could hear it breathing. She turned to see Charlotte approaching with Jasper from across the field.

"Oh my, you have got yourself in a mess, you silly creature." Charlotte walked around to the back of the animal to check the damage.

"It was the wall. The stones must have fallen. I took them off."

"You did an amazing job, Hamida. Natural shepherd instincts you got there. Well done, you!" Charlotte beamed at her over her shoulder, still crouched down by the creature's leg.

"We'll have to get the vet up for this one. Good job you found her. A couple more days and she'd have starved to death. Couldn't see her at all from across the field. We'll have to get this shrubbery cut back. Don't want the same thing happening again."

The sheep was getting agitated now. Hamida stroked its muzzle again instinctively, and the animal stopped, sinking into a calm stupor. Charlotte looked from Hamida to the sheep.

"You're quite the natural," she said. "Have you looked after animals before?"

Hamida shook her head.

*

Hamida had never slept so deeply as she did that night. Perhaps it had been exhaustion, perhaps it had been the lungfuls of open air she had inhaled, perhaps it had been the sensation of limitlessness. Whatever it was that sent her to the innermost fathoms of unconsciousness, Hamida had the sensation of being buried deep under the earth, blanketed beneath civilisations, so far beneath the present and the past of the planet that she was no longer a part of it. The weight that pressed down on her was strangely soothing. It was almost an embrace. Engulfed, enveloped, deep within whatever the expanse was that contained her, she felt a pulse, a rhythm, an ebb and a flow, that permeated her. When she awoke in her bed, alone in the cottage, before the light of dawn had leaked over the horizon, she was not sure she had been on earth at all. In the soft darkness of her room, she reached for her string of beads and lay her head back on her pillow.

Sheep were remarkably like children, Hamida thought. She had spent two weeks now accompanying Charlotte and Jasper up onto the hill where the animals were grazing. They needed regular feeding, occasional steering, aid when they were hurt, but otherwise their instincts guided them. They needed a watchful eye but little interference. They reminded her of the children in the playground in the missionary school at lunchtimes. She remembered sitting on the bench next to the wire fence around the dusty tarmac watching the little groups of children immersed in their games, eating their lunch from whatever their parents had found to constitute lunchboxes. From afar, they all looked so similar in their faded emerald green uniforms, passed down from year to year, from siblings or relatives, scrubbed to the rigorous standards of the staff. And yet, close observation revealed subtleties which attention transformed into individuals. Black hair was never just black hair. It was wavy or straight, thick or thin, combed through with oil or brittle and dry. Skin was never just brown, it was smooth or pockmarked, tinged with flushes of red or grey which spoke to the health of whatever lay beneath it.

So, it was with the sheep. They were different shapes and sizes, their faces different colours, their eyes different shades, their ears different lengths. Hamida spent long hours watching for patterns. Did the playground patterns of friendship emerge in the flock? Did each sheep have places they preferred to eat? Did any of them sit on the side as she had, watching?

In the beginning, the girls from her class had asked her to play when she'd been in the lower years. She'd joined them, intrigued to see what it was they did in their corner of the playground. She'd engage in their games with interest for a while, but would slowly withdraw to the side-lines, immersed instead in observation until the bell would ring and the children would stampede to their lines in front of the school buildings, their games abandoned. They soon stopped asking her. When she was older, and games had become a thing to be scorned by the upper years, she noticed the girls would talk amongst themselves, braid each other's hair, compare narratives of their lives and experiences that seemed to follow familiar patterns. They'd smile at Hamida, who always smiled back, but her silence did not elicit invitations to participate in their swapping of stories. She retreated instead to the steps beside the schoolhouse, where she would sit and read, distracted only occasionally by the schoolyard scuffles that would break out, soon to be broken up by the teacher on duty.

"We are concerned about your granddaughter," the headmistress had explained. She remembered her grandmother sitting on a wooden chair in front of the headmistress's desk, piled high with papers, in a classroom that had been converted into her office. Hamida had been instructed to sit on a chair adjacent to the desk, its back against the wall. She remembered pointing her toes to see if she could touch the floor from her seat.

"The other children in her class have complained about her," the headmistress was saying. "They've told their teacher that she plays with insects, and that she makes strange noises."

"What noises?"

"Humming. They've asked her to stop this strange behaviour, but she doesn't listen, and if she continues to disturb the other children, we will have to ask her to leave."

She had meant this as a threat. It was a successful tactic with parents; issuing ultimatums, the warning of withdrawal of schooling if rules were not abided by, if conditions were not met. The availability of education was so scarce that most parents would do anything to keep their children in school. Hamida had remembered her grandmother's face. Still as stone. Her neck poised, the tendons taught. Her next words she spoke very slowly.

"When my granddaughter was born, her mother saw a vision of a white palace, and an empire of words, unlike anything ever described in the history of humankind. This child has lost her mother and her father. She has endured that which would break grown men. She is not strange, she is special. And I suggest you find a swift way to address these students' complaints in a manner that does not affect her education."

She rose from the chair. She was not a tall woman, but that day, Hamida looked upon her grandmother, towering over the desk and the headmistress looking up at her from her chair, and felt she was a giant. She took Hamida's hand and walked her home. The next day, Hamida was transferred to the class above, and the complaints were never repeated.

12

"What do you do in the evenings, Hamida? You must get really lonely all by yourself in that cottage." Charlotte was driving the jeep across the bumpy track to the field where the sheep were about to be transferred now that many of them had given birth to their lambs. She wanted to check the fencing to make sure it was secure. "You know, you should join us tonight. It's Friday. You need to let your hair down a bit. Come to the pub. I'm going with some friends from the farm. It'll be a laugh. It's a bit of a walk but you'll be alright, it's not getting dark so late anymore, now the clocks have gone forward."

She pulled up at the gate and reached over to the glove compartment in front of Hamida. The lid clunked down on her knees. Charlotte pulled out an old envelope and rummaged around for a pen. She pulled the lid off with her teeth and smoothed the loose wisps of her hair back down from around her forehead. Pressing against the steering wheel, she scribbled some directions and a rough map. "I can drop you off in the jeep afterwards so you don't have to walk back in the dark. We'll be there around half five."

Hamida scanned the map as Charlotte explained the scribbles. She was excited at the prospect of new people, of hearing them talk, of seeing them laugh. She enjoyed the quiet of the outdoors, and the landscape of the farm she realised was far from monotonous. But she felt the urge for change, a break in the pattern. And she liked Charlotte; there was a simple warmth to her, a sensibility that was deep in its capacity for care but not complexity. Charlotte spoke of things as they were. She was not entangled in the often messy threads of other people's lives, as far as Hamida could tell.

Charlotte dropped her off at the cottage that afternoon and explained the directions again. With a cheery wave, she climbed back in the jeep, Jasper jumping in behind her, and honked her horn as she drove off.

Hamida unlocked the cottage door and went inside. She pulled off the jeans with their muddied knees, browned from kneeling in the dirt securing fence posts, and washed her hands, scraping out the dirt from beneath her nails. She went to the chest of drawers and pulled out the cornflower blue jumper that Miss Patience had given her and laid it on the bed.

At four, she left the house, locking the door behind her. She pulled the map from her pocket and headed in the direction of the shortcut across the farm Charlotte had shown her. The air, which had been warm not a few hours before, was starting to chill. Hamida trudged across the field. She noticed how dramatically different the sunshine made things look. It gave them a tinge that did something to her mood. Perhaps it reminded her of home. There the sunshine had been a constant. Reliable and predictable. Lending its intensity to the vividness with which everything, even the dust, was perceived. Here, Hamida had been sure that the grey would last forever. She had been moved almost to tears when she had opened the curtains a few weeks ago to find that somehow the sun had found its way back to this corner of the earth, as though it had been sick and was finally beginning to recover, and the bandages of clouds that had enshrouded it could finally be peeled away. She had stood in the gentle beams that poured through the window, soaking them up with her skin. Today, even the late afternoon sun still lent its brightness to the intensifying green of the grass.

Hamida could see the barn Charlotte had told her about in the distance. It didn't seem to be getting much closer. She was getting tired. She'd make it to the barn and sit for a few minutes, she thought. She trudged on. By the time she had reached the yard in front of the open structure of the barn, the sun was beginning to set. Hamida made her way over to the bales of straw inside. She'd sit for a moment. Just a moment.

She looked back out over the field across which she'd walked. The sun was teetering just on the edge of the horizon, masked by a few strips of cotton-like clouds. The entire sky in front of her was dyed a deep, rich pink which bled into a vibrant orange the further she turned her gaze. Not even beggars, those whom the entirety of humanity had turned their backs on, were deprived of sunsets. The palette of the firmaments displayed its masterpieces each and every dawn and dusk without fail to whomever chose to look up. Hamida watched the colours slowly change and lent her back against the bale of straw behind her.

*

"Hamida… Hamida…?" Her shoulders were being shaken, the voice which had seemed to be coming from far away now rang in her ears.

"Bloody hell, chook. You didn't half give me a fright. I've been looking for you all morning."

Charlotte's face was pale. The pink flush of her cheeks noticeably absent. "Are you alright?"

Hamida was still dazed. One side of her face felt strange. She put her hand up to it and realised it was ridged with the imprint of the straw she'd been lying on. The light in the barn was a yellowy white.

"I'm fine. I… I think I fell asleep."

Charlotte laughed in relief, some colour returning to her cheeks. "I thought maybe you'd changed your mind, so I went to the cottage this morning, but you weren't there. I didn't dare ask old Coop, so I jumped in the jeep and headed out in the direction I'd told you. I was so worried you'd fallen in a ditch or something." She laughed again. "Jeepers, you gave me such a fright." She shook her head and let out her tension with a sigh that seemed to emanate from her stomach. "Here," she reached into her pocket and pulled out a thermos flask. "Drink some tea. We've got to see to the last of the lambs today."

They drove back over the field the way Hamida had walked the evening before. The field seemed surprisingly small in comparison this morning. They arrived at the farm buildings the other side of the Ravenscroft estate. Jasper stayed in the jeep. Charlotte led Hamida inside the large wooden building that was filled with metal pens. Most were empty but about six were still full.

"These two are struggling somewhat." Charlotte pointed to two ewes in the furthest pens, lying on the ground in the straw. The vet, whom Hamida recognised from when she had come to dress the leg of the wounded sheep she had rescued, was inspecting the stomach of one of the animals.

"Not long to go now," she said to Charlotte.

"They're having triplets, these two. They might need a bit of help, so you and I are on standby."

Hamida nodded. Most of the sheep had given birth on their own in the field, and Charlotte had tended to the ones that had been brought down to the barn herself until now, leaving Hamida to watch the flock.

Hamida had never seen anything being born before. She had certainly heard the sounds of birth from the mouths of neighbouring women. The sharp cries, and low, extended moans that rang out in the tightly packed streets; the shrill sounds of a child's first screams, its greeting to life, or the silence, followed by the wails with which death was met.

'Not long' turned out to be several hours. When it finally happened, birth itself was not what Hamida had expected at all. It was quick, slippery, bloodied, and unsightly. And yet, breath-taking. Hamida knelt down next to Charlotte as the lambs were squeezed into a world of air, of cold, of noise, and separation. They rubbed the small, wet creatures, soaked in the fluids of life with straw before placing them in front of the ewes. Six small lives were due. Five arrived. The last lamb slid into the world still. The vet rubbed the tiny creature's chest, trying to coax out of it the life that had been promised. It did not move. Hamida watched, willing the lamb with all her might to breathe. The vet wrapped its body in hay and took it out of the pen.

Charlotte put an arm around Hamida. "It happens, chook. They don't all make it."

Hamida nodded. They sat in silence, watching the ewe nuzzle her two surviving babies. "Can I bury it?" she asked quietly.

Charlotte helped Hamida dig the small grave behind the cottage. They buried the lamb together, wrapped in a hessian sack. Hamida knelt down and compacted the dirt over the grave with her hands. Before she left, Charlotte gave the girl a tight hug, feeling a strange tingle in her fingers. Hamida went inside and washed the mud from her hands. That night, she dreamt of her mother.

13

It took forty days for Humayun to convince Hamida Banu Begum to marry him. Their nuptials took place on a day selected by his father, the Emperor, himself a keen astronomer. Over the next fifteen years, Hamida travelled with her husband across treacherous terrain from Sindh to Umerkot, from Jun to shrines across Persia, the land of her ancestors, from Ardabil to Sabzawar, and from Kandahar to Kabul.

Hamida Banu Begum had eyes of deep ochre, jet black hair that fell around her shoulders in ringlets, and lips that stood out starkly from her almond skin. Her son, Emperor Akbar, transported her palanquin himself across the river between Lahore and Agra. When she died in 1604, Akbar removed every hair from his head and his face in mourning and proclaimed his mother's posthumous title. She would be known as Maryam Makani, the One Who Dwells with the Madonna.

When she was born, centuries later, in the slums of Kolkata, Hamida's grandmother raised the small child before her in the palms of her hands. Then, drawing her close to her chest, she whispered, in words no one but Hamida heard:

"Welcome to the world, my Maryam Makani."

*

"Michael, what is this game you are playing? I sent you my nephew for consultation, not for some ridiculous romance scheme! C'est ridicule!"

"Dufort, if I may…" Michael held the phone away from his ear whilst Dufort continued his obstreperous bilingual tirade. When he had calmed down, Michael brought the phone back to his ear.

"If I may explain, Dufort, you have been misinformed. What I am conducting here is a project which I believe would be of great interest to you. If you would be so kind as to visit me at Ravenscroft Estate, I shall explain the matter in full. Cooper can make the necessary arrangements."

Silence met him from the other end of the line, broken by a deep sigh of resignation. "Alright, Michael, I shall come."

Dufort had arrived at Ravenscroft Estate in his long trench coat, creased beyond the point of salvaging. He towered over Cooper, himself a tall man, who had met the Land Rover at the front entrance to the house. He was sitting now in the library with coffee, an empty tumbler of whiskey at his elbow, and the stub of a cigarette smouldering between his fingers.

Michael was standing at the edge of the fireplace, leaning against the mantelpiece.

"So, this… bond is an essential part of this experiment?"

"Vital."

"The travel I understand, travel is exhausting, it wears one down to the truest version of themselves."

"And, of course, it cultivates the mind. New images, new experiences. But these reasons are beside the point, Dufort. If we are to be true to the model, the girl travels. Muhammad travelled, the girl travels. Marriage is archaic and there are too many legal implications, but Muhammad married, so the girl must at least fall in love."

Dufort still did not seem convinced. "But if she knows she must fall in love for the sake of an experiment, it will not be authentic. It will be mere acting."

"Oh, my dear friend, Hamida Begum is not aware she is to fall for your nephew. She does not have the slightest clue."

"Then, how do you justify this? Surely, this is coercion, duplicity, deceit."

"Maurice has been instructed to be very convincing in his proposition. She will believe he truly desires her."

"What if she refuses?"

"Then his contract will be voided, and the remainder of his payment will not be transferred."

"That is certainly one form of incentive..." Dufort seemed now enthralled and repulsed by the idea in equal measure. He stared into his drink, deep in thought, and then looked up at Michael and shook his head.

"Michael, *mon ami*, if you'll permit me to be honest, do you not see how this looks? A subtle, no, not even subtle form of exploitation, colonialism. European colonialism at its worst. Think of what you will be accused of. In essence, the trafficking a young girl from an impoverished background and her enslavement. Does she even know what she is here for? Have you even spoken to her?"

The sneer on Michael's face was sharp. In a moment, he shifted from persuasion to attack. "I am surprised at your lack of forward thinking, Dufort," he said, slowly and deliberately. "How do you propose we defeat an enemy who considers child marriage, the decapitation of infidels, and the stoning of women to be their divine right? You want to keep publishing papers condemning them? What have you achieved exactly with your methods?"

Dufort was silent. Michael continued to stare at him, his posture softened, though his features did not.

"As you once said, Dufort, religion deals in emotions. Let us not deal in emotions. Maurice himself is actually quite eager to learn of the end results of this experiment. I have spoken to him at length about this. Might I remind you, Dufort, this was, after all, inspired by you. If they will not listen to reason, then we must speak their language."

Dufort stubbed out his cigarette in the ashtray next to him. Michael walked to the assortment of decanters on the table, removed the stopper from the whiskey and refilled the glass next to Dufort.

"Are we speaking the same language, Dufort?"

The professor looked up at the man through his watery grey eyes, his eyebrows pulled into the centre of his brow, in what he knew was the moment he could either surrender himself to the defeat he had avoided admitting for the last two decades of his life, or embrace what seemed on the surface to be utter lunacy. With a silent but definitive nod, he stepped over the threshold of rationality into Michael Sergeant's laboratory. He tipped back his whiskey in a single gulp.

*

Dufort's empty whiskey glass was still perched on the arm of the chair in the corner of Michael's office. The room was quiet now, but for the echoes of their conversation. Michael stood by the window, having watched the car drive Dufort down the long and winding track. His head rang with the multitude of words he might also have shared. How he had wanted it to be him, how he had wanted to put himself through the very experiment he had engineered, but how he knew this was impossible. Everything about him disqualified him. How it had to be someone on the inside, the edges of the inside. How it had to be a woman. How it had to be Hamida Begum.

*

Estelle had given birth five weeks before the date her child was supposed to arrive. The pain had started in the shower. Her husband, Dufort's brother, had done his best to help her into the nearest clothes he could find as he shouted desperate instructions to the emergency operator. They did not make it to the hospital. Maurice arrived at a roundabout in the back of the ambulance. He remained in an incubator for two weeks longer than his mother's patience lasted. Unable to see or hold her child, she suffered a breakdown from which it took her four months to recover. As the doctors had forewarned her, Maurice had been a strange child. He struggled with his balance and grew slowly. But by the time they were able to test for any serious underlying issues, they discovered that the child was entirely healthy.

Michael had arranged for Maurice to arrive by helicopter. Cooper was waiting at the edge of the helipad. Hamida was waiting in the foyer outside his office. She looked down at the shoes that had been delivered at the cottage the day before, along with two suitcases of clothes. They were brown leather, perforated with small holes in patterns that reminded her of henna designs she had seen on the palms of the girls in her class. They rubbed slightly around her ankles.

*

This was the perfect distraction. Maurice had spent almost two years oscillating between the library and the laboratory. Most of that time he had spent with his head in his hands or talking to his peers and professors about anything other than his own doctoral research in the hope that inspiration would strike him unexpectedly. Neurotheology was a nascent field with room for experimentation. The books had not been written, the tests had not been done. In theory, it was the perfect area for someone to establish their name, to immerse themselves in their own research without the constraints of precedence, established arguments, and professors that dominated the academic airspace. Perhaps it was this freedom that was so paralysing. Maurice needed an angle, the golden thread that would tie the various strands of his studies together. Thus far, he was clutching at straws. And his funding was running out.

He'd agreed to Michael's proposal almost before he had finished describing the experiment. Maurice did not believe in divine intervention, but if he had, this is how he might have described it.

"Just a hundred and twenty days?"

"Yes, three sets of forty days, after which your contract will be completed, and you will receive the remainder of your payment."

That was a little over a semester. He could very easily suspend his studies for that duration and use the money he desperately needed to complete his research upon his return. Time away was precisely what he needed. And not just time away from the university. Travel. All expenses paid. And in the company of a young woman, what more could he ask for?

There was the issue of the relationship. That made him somewhat uncomfortable.

"She absolutely has to fall in love with me?"

"It's non-negotiable. See it as a personal challenge."

Michael clearly knew what he was doing. In presenting it as a challenge, he had addressed something in Maurice that bristled at the thought of failure and saw Michael's answer as a suggestion that he may struggle in the seduction of a young woman. He had never had any trouble with women before. Why should he have any problem with this one? And besides, it was only for a matter of months, and what was it really but a series of chemical processes in the brain? And it was all in the name of science.

Maurice walked into the foyer behind Cooper, looking up at the high ceiling of the building. "Remember, you have three objectives." Cooper had sounded like an army general, Maurice thought to himself. "Educate, seduce, immerse."

"Educate, seduce, immerse. I got it."

Hamida had stood up when they entered. She caught Maurice quite by surprise. He had imagined a small, timid young woman from Cooper's descriptions. She was taller than he had expected. Not quite his five foot eleven, but only a couple of inches shorter. And her dark hair fell about her shoulders like a mane. She blinked slowly. The vermilion of her lips was somewhere between brown and pink and they stood out starkly against her skin.

"Miss Begum, this is Maurice Dufort."

Hearing his name reminded Maurice of his manners, which had been momentarily suspended along with all other sense of himself. He put out his hand. Hamida shook it firmly. He felt something inside him turn over, as if an organ in him had been upside down and had now righted its way up. He cleared his throat in a dismissal of these sensations.

"*Enchanté.*"

She looked at him quizzically.

"Nice to meet you."

"It is a pleasure to meet you, Maurice."

The organ inside him flipped upside down again. He withdrew his hand.

"Shall we get going? I've transferred your cases to the Land Rover, Mr Dufort. Miss Begum, I will put yours in there too."

Michael's private jet was stationed at Newcastle airport, some sixty miles from Ravenscroft Estate. Maurice had sat in the front next to the driver, Hamida behind him. She was looking out of the window. He was surprised at how nervous he suddenly felt. He had given no thought to a strategy of seduction. It had been so easy with women in the past, he met them in the bar, in the cafeteria, lecture halls, common rooms, corridors, parties. Conversation flowed naturally from the environment. Here, the environment was alien, and he was not approaching her from the other side of a room but the other side of an ocean. What should he say to her? What was appropriate to ask? Was her English good enough to sustain conversation? Cooper had said she was fluent, but she had barely said a word. She was confident of herself, but her composure did not inspire any confidence in him. He was thinking too much. He looked at her in the rear-view mirror discreetly. Was she beautiful? He wasn't sure. She challenged the image of beauty that he had not even realised he had cultivated through the choice of women he interacted with. What was she? She was... what was the word? Arresting? He was thinking too much. He would talk to her on the plane.

The flight from Newcastle to New York took nine hours. Maurice sat opposite Hamida, a small table between them. He had collected himself and his thoughts and methodically mapped out a series of questions to ask. This was a social experiment, so he would approach it like one. This was how he functioned best, with a plan.

By the time they had arrived in New York he had asked her where in India she was from, about her family, her education, and how she had found her stay in England so far. He had been surprised to find himself sharing far more information about his own life than he had planned. It was not her questions that prompted his responses so much as a strange desire to share details of his life. He told himself this was a sensible way of ensuring she felt comfortable talking about herself. But now that the conversation had finished, and she was asleep in front of him, her head against the window, he felt strangely exposed.

She had taken off her brown tailored jacket and folded it on the chair next to her. Her shoes she'd slipped off almost as soon as they sat down. To Maurice's surprise, she'd also taken off the black socks she was wearing, folded them up neatly and placed them inside the shoes. He stared at the strange young woman in front of him. The black turtleneck that she'd pulled up was covering the tip of her chin, her jeans grazed her ankles.

She was sitting with one leg tucked underneath her, the toes of her other foot resting on the floor. Her chest rose and fell in a gentle rhythm.

He'd keep the conversation focused on her from now on. He turned his thoughts to New York and the plans he had made for when they arrived.

14

The taxi had pulled up at the St Regis. Maurice had tried his best not to look impressed. He did not like the feeling of being seen to be out of place, and something in him liked the idea that Hamida might presume this was his usual standard of living. All the same, the red carpeted steps and gold handrails leading up to the revolving doors were already miles away from life as a PhD student on a shoestring budget. He did not like to be inawed by luxury, he would have preferred to have dismissed it, not even noticed it, but being excluded from something always afforded it an appeal.

His shoes squeaked on the marble floors as he entered the foyer. He looked up from the highly polished stone bumping into the doorman, almost knocking him over. Steadying the man in the grey uniform, Maurice tried to help him regain his balance.

"I'm so sorry, sir," the man was saying, straightening his hat.

"No, no, it was entirely my fault." Maurice checked the man was okay and turned to Hamida, smiling sheepishly. She smiled back at him. She seemed far more composed and at ease, although he assumed she'd never seen anything of the likes of the fresco ceilings, painted to mimic a Mediterranean summer sky, with an enormous chandelier, dripping crystal, hanging like ripe fruit from its centre.

Two concierges led them to their rooms. Maurice nodded to Hamida as she was let into hers a little way down the corridor from his, telling her he'd come and knock for her. The electronic lock clicked at the tap of the key card. Maurice thanked the young man and tipped him generously, allowing himself now to truly experience the mixture of awe and exhilaration he'd been attempting to restrain ever since they had arrived.

The walls in the first room were carved wood, painted an ivory white, with large rectangles of patterned red wallpaper, of the type only found in the wealthiest or tawdriest of homes. The curtains, a deeper shade of the same red and bordered with golden Greek patterns, were tied back with thick twisted silk cords, and swept from ceiling to floor. From the ornately edged ceiling hung a smaller but equally beautiful chandelier. There were sofas and armchairs arranged around the room, scattered with cushions of various shades of beige and carnelian. The bedroom shared the colour scheme and had its own chandelier. The vast expanse of the bed was blanketed in the crispest white sheet Maurice had ever seen, so smooth he felt almost hesitant to sit on it.

He walked into the bathroom, made mostly of a mottled grey marble. He contemplated taking a shower, but he was far too hungry, and knew that if he did, he would want to go straight to sleep. He settled for washing his face and the back of his neck, burying his face in the soft white towels. He looked in the mirror. He wanted a shave too, he'd been travelling for a long time and it was starting to show. He ran his hands through hair, attempting feebly to tidy the untameable loose brown curls.

He knew he needed to check on Hamida. There was something about seeing a person sleep which engenders a strange sense of protectiveness. Perhaps it is the vulnerability inherent in the act of sleeping, or perhaps it is the trust implicit in the ability to fall asleep in the presence of another person. Maurice himself was not sure why he felt the urge to check on her, but he was reluctant to leave her alone for too long.

He knocked gently on her door. There was no answer. He knocked again and waited. Perhaps she was in the bathroom. He knocked a third time, harder so that the sound would travel further into the room. He called her name. He was about to panic when he heard the click on the other side and the door opened.

"Are you ok, Hamida?"

"Oh yes, I'm fine," she smiled. He noticed her room was decorated in shades of green. He examined her face to try to ascertain why she hadn't answered. She looked surprisingly well rested. He felt it was rude at this stage to ask; she may simply have not heard him.

"Are you hungry?"

*

The first thing he wanted was a hotdog. It was almost blasphemous for a Frenchman to crave such a gastronomical horror, he knew, but there was something about the commonness, almost vulgarity of processed meat, slathered in everything he could order – the relish, mustard, cheese, the juice and sauce smeared around your mouth, the resistance of the hotdog skin with the first bite, that slight pop as teeth broke through it into the flavoured pink pulp – that was irresistible. There was no polite way to eat a hot dog. This, it occurred to him, was precisely what he needed to break the ice. Food eaten with fingers.

The diner was small, and their food came in plastic baskets lined with paper, the fries, like crispy, greasy flowers, blossoming from the tin cup they were served in. After the plane journey and the hotel check in, the unctuous smell of sizzling meat that made one feel hungry and full at the same time soothed him. He was no stranger to refined food, he'd made a point of celebrating birthdays and any other celebration always at a restaurant, either in Paris or London. But refined food required a certain type of appetite. Fine food was not eaten quickly, and it did not leave you feeling full. It was an experience of art, he'd always thought, that engaged all of the senses. This food was to be eaten. Really eaten. And he was hungry.

He was halfway through his hot dog when he realised Hamida was watching him. It reassured him at first that he'd been so engaged in his food, that he'd immersed himself in the experience of eating to such a degree, that he'd blocked out everything else; this was exactly what he needed. But then he'd felt guilty. This must be so entirely alien to her.

"You've never had a hot dog before?"

Hamida gave him a quizzical look. Maurice laughed with a realisation of just how bizarre this dish must sound to someone who had never eaten one.

"It's a meat sausage in bread." He pointed at the various components of the hot dog as if explaining a piece of art on a gallery wall.

She let him finish his explanation. "I can't eat animals." She shook her head slowly.

"Oh, you're a vegetarian?" He seemed almost disappointed. "Well… here, these are fries. They're made of potato, and you dip them in the sauces."

He dunked them in the bright red ketchup he'd squirted in his basket, and then the mayonnaise.

"Both?"

"No, no. You can choose. Do you like creamy or tangy?"

"Both," she smiled.

Maurice laughed again. He squirted the sauces next to her food and picked up the laminated menu again propped up against the salt and pepper.

"I know what you'd like." He ordered her a large portion of deep-fried mozzarella sticks. "They're almost as good as a hot dog," he said with a wink. He waited for them to arrive before diving back into his bun. Hamida examined the fried cheese portions. "You can dunk those, too."

She stuck the hot battered mozzarella deep into the ketchup.

"And you should try the milkshake, it's vanilla flavoured." He picked up his own cup and drew a big gulp through the straw.

Hamida copied him. It was cold, creamy, and sweet, and reminded her of a type of ice cream she'd tried once at school. She could feel the coolness travel through her throat and chest as she gulped it down.

"You know I came to a place like this a few years ago, and I've craved it ever since." Maurice looked around at the diner, with its squeaky pleather, shiny metal, and garish yellow and red signage. "It's funny what you fall in love with."

He finished Hamida's hot dog too, sucking up the last of his milkshake with a hollow slurping sound, shaking his cardboard cup just to make sure he really had reached the bottom. He ordered another round of fries and mozzarella sticks and a large coke as he told her about his last trip to America. And when she asked, without him even realising that she had, he told her how he'd travelled to almost every continent, and how he'd moved to London for his studies. She must have been as hungry as he was, because she kept up with his pace, albeit in a far tidier fashion.

Maurice paid for the food with the credit card Cooper had arranged for him, reminded with a smile of the glorious words Cooper had shared: "No limit."

They were headed now to the American Museum of Natural History on the other side of Central Park. Maurice was excited. He had loved science ever since he was young. His parents had showered him, their only child, with illustrated encyclopaedias, figurines of every animal they could think of, chemistry sets, and magnifying glasses. He'd spent hours in the park looking for bugs and scooping up frogspawn in glass jars, watching them hatch. As he'd grown, his interest in biology had deepened to the molecular level until he'd finally settled on the field of neuroscience for his master's, but he could not resist the childhood pull of seeing science in all its tangible forms as far back as human history could stretch encased behind glass. He pulled his phone from his pocket to check the tickets, and the careful list of exhibits he had picked out and run past Cooper when he had planned their itinerary.

"Oh, that reminds me, I need your mobile number."

Hamida looked at him and furrowed her brow. "I don't have a mobile." She seemed surprised Maurice did not know this.

"You don't? Did you leave it in the hotel?"

"No, I've never had one." She had seen Miss Patience use one to call her sister, and Charlotte had one with a cracked screen which she used to call the vet. But she had never been given one herself. And besides, she had no one to call.

"Hmmm…. Well, in that case we'd better not lose each other." Maurice laughed, but he looked slightly worried.

"I won't get lost." Hamida shook her head and turned to look out of the taxi window at the buildings whizzing by.

She'd never experienced a place with so little sky. The buildings, as if clawing at the clouds, like ferns competing for sunlight, seemed almost to cave in above them. The smooth undulations, waves, irregular angles of nature had been replaced by a rigid geometry of straight lines and harsh edges. Hamida was no stranger to noise. There had never been any respite from the sounds of the harshness and rawness of life in the slum. The clanging of pots, the high-pitched drones of scooters, the cries of tradesmen, the clamouring of children, but here the sound was different. It was a rumble, a mixture of engines, the arguing of car horns competing again construction, drills, clanging, smashing, and a never-ending stream of highly charged speech, the melange of urgent utterances, indistinguishable voices, thousands of somethings that merged into a conglomerate of nothingness. Hamida closed her eyes.

She remembered the look on her grandmother's face before she had left; in the moment she had tried to walk past her, to walk out of a story that involved anyone other than the two of them. The look of resolution on the face of a woman who had seen enough hardship and tragedy for many more lifetimes than her own. A woman who kneaded dough on a flat stone between her feet whilst telling her stories of her ancestors who had once ruled an entire empire. That look was the reason she was now sitting in the back of a car, next to a strange young man from France, a country she had only read about in battered history books, driving through New York, a land that only existed in the laughable dreams of her classmates who talked of fleeing to the fantasy they had heard about only via hearsay and the occasional snippets of news they heard old men discuss over newspapers and cigarettes. It was why she had endured the cold that made her want to cry, the quiet that had seemed to echo in her ears, the emptiness of the landscape, the overwhelming manifestations of otherness, and the blisters on her ankles from the shoes she'd been given. She did not know what conversation had taken place between her grandmother and the two men who had arrived at their door with dust clinging to their shoes. But she trusted her grandmother, she would never have sent her somewhere for any other reason than her own wellbeing. She could not entertain any other idea. Hamida was not a person of portions. If she was to trust, she would trust fully. Not without consideration or caution, but without parsimoniousness. Wherever she was, she was here because her grandmother had agreed. To think otherwise was to suspect her grandmother of either negligence or ignorance, neither of which she knew her to possess.

She opened her eyes and turned her head to look at Maurice. He was looking out of his passenger window. His head was a mess of loose dark brown curls which fell just over the collar of his navy coat. He was friendly, that had been obvious. A little awkward and unsure of how to interact with her, but she was not unused to this response.

She had two measures of people. The way they talked about their childhoods and the way they interacted with other living things. Miss Patience had talked about her childhood with a gentle warmth, as if reading a poem. Charlotte had cared for every animal as if it were her own family. Until they had stepped out of the hotel, Hamida had not been sure about Maurice. But as they waited for a taxi, he had noticed a piece of rubble from a nearby building site on the pavement. Everyone else had simply walked over or around it. But she watched him kick it to the side of the building. She hadn't asked for an explanation, but when he did it again with a piece of glass on the floor outside the deli, she'd realised what he was doing. She had not decided whether or not she liked him, it was a foreign thought for her entirely to contemplate liking a man, but she knew she could trust him.

*

They would approach the museum methodically. Maurice knew he could very easily fall into the temptation of distraction, following signs that sounded interesting and missing other sections simply because they'd been signposted elsewhere. There were five floors in total, and they had hours. Never before had he had such freedom and liberty to indulge in looking, reading, immersing. He had to remind himself that the purpose of the trip was not to cater to his own interests alone, but to educate. He'd focus on seduction later. He needed to figure out a separate plan for that objective. He would show Hamida everything. They would start at the top and make their way down, he thought. They'd begin with dinosaurs and end with the Origins of Man. They took the elevator to the top floor.

There was something awe-inspiring about meandering through the skeletons of these huge beasts, which were old enough to have fallen out of legends even.

Had their bones not been unearthed, they may have never been remembered. He looked around at Hamida to examine the expression on her face. He had been looking forward to seeing her response. She was standing at the threshold of the hall, her eyes wide, her mouth slightly open, craning up through the ribcage of the Barosaurus, rearing up on the bare bones of its hind legs, its mouth open wide, silent echoes of all the possible cries it might have made ringing around the hall. He nudged her, breaking her trance.

"One hundred and fifty million years old. Give or take."

Hamida did not take her eyes off the shiny brown bones. Finally lowering her head, she walked towards the sign beneath the monstrous skeleton and read the information intently. She walked to the case next to it and peered through the glass, reading each and every label. Maurice walked along next to her, floods of boyhood memories now returning to him; figurines, pages of illustrated dinosaur facts, videos of excavators carefully brushing off the dust from the remains of these giant reptilian beasts. He did not need to share his enthusiasm, though it overflowed from him. Hamida seemed to have her own; a pointed, careful, concentrated intensity of interest. She absorbed everything. Occasionally, he would spot something particularly important and call her over – the eggs, the feathered reptiles, the fossils – and explain how in the map of the Jurassic age, this was a landmark.

Next, they made their way down around the third floor: the amphibians, birds, primates, stuffed, glazed, and preserved in replicas of their habitats. On the first floor, Hamida turned in a slow circle looking up at the model of the blue whale, its back arched against the ceiling, its tail poised to propel it further through the sea it would have swum in. It was a strange sensation to see life-size models of the animals she had only ever seen diagrams of, never bigger than her palm. She was struck by her size; how miniscule her existence was in terms of both time and space.

"We are so small," she whispered to Maurice, who looked back up at the whale. Unexpectedly, in that instant, he saw the thing not as a model, a three-dimensional image, but something that existed somewhere, something breathing, its heart beating.

"Let's go and meet Lucy," Maurice said, pulling himself away from his uncomfortable smallness to an exhibit on the other side of the floor.

*

In 1974, Dr. Donald Johanson, a professor of palaeoanthropology, had been excavating in the deserts of Ethiopia with his graduate student Tom Gray, listening to the Beatles new hit song, when they unearthed a piece of bone. They later identified this as an ulna bone, located in the elbow of humans. The nerve of this bone, when hit, sends a tingling feeling up one's arm. Exploring further, they uncovered a collection of several hundred fossilized bone fragments. Piecing these together, they announced that they had discovered the remains of the earliest known human ancestor. They named her 'Lucy' after the song they had been listening to, 'Lucy in the Sky with Diamonds'. In the Amharic language of Ethiopia, she is known as Dinkinesh. In English, this means 'You are marvellous'. She is, according to the most accurate estimates, over three million years old.

"Put's a nail in the coffin of the old Adam and Eve story. How people can still believe that fairy tale beats me."

Maurice laughed, looking at the model of Lucy, covered in a thin coat of brown fur, walking on two feet, her mouth open as if in conversation with the male hominin immortalized in wax with his arm around her.

"It's just a metaphor," said Hamida quietly, looking at the figures, her head tilted to one side.

15

Time outside the museum had slipped by and when they emerged from the mouth of the building, they were surprised to see that dusk had settled into the city. Cars zoomed past chasing the beams of light before them, and people paced along the pavement, heads down, their faces illuminated by the blue light from their phones. Hamida was deep in thought. It was as though she had been given a stack of disorganised papers, each with fragments of information, and she was trying to arrange them in some sort of orderly fashion in amongst the pieces she had already filed away. Bones, feathers, colours, ceilings, donations of the vastest sums of money, animals older than humans, stones older than animals, manuscripts, the collision of atoms, and the beginnings and end of life and all its manifestations.

"You're limping. Are you alright?" Maurice put his hand on Hamida's shoulder, making her jump. Something about her reaction startled him. "I'm sorry, I didn't mean to… Is your foot okay?"

"It hurts a little."

"Here, sit down and let me take a look. Do you mind…?"

Hamida had sat down and Maurice, his hands hovering over her laces, was asking permission to remove her shoes. Hamida nodded. Now that her attention had been drawn to the pain it was quite acute. A needle-like gnawing under her ankle and above her heel.

"*Aie, c'est mauvais*. That looks painful." Maurice was grimacing. "You poor thing, you should have said something."

The skin around her ankles had rubbed raw, and a flap had come away at the back; the blood had congealed around the wound.

Maurice was looking around him now. "I have an idea. Stay here, please don't go anywhere. I will be back very soon. Please, don't move." He ran quickly down the steps to the museum, turning back to Hamida at the bottom, raising a finger to remind her of his promise to be quick.

For the first time, Hamida watched people walking. Until that point, she had registered the presence of crowds, of the unfamiliar lilts and twangs of speech that filled the air, but she had not yet truly focused on the sources of these sounds. Obtaining her bearings, she'd found, was first achieved by focussing on the place, then the people.

A family walked past, a father, mother, and a small child, a girl, wearing a pink tiara and thick pink framed spectacles. She was pulling on her mother's arm, scuffing her feet as though using them to add weight to her petitions for them to stop walking. A woman whose whole body seemed to turn with every step passed her accompanied by a man with his head shaved except for a strip of pink hair down the middle with a large black earring stretching his earlobe. Two more women walked past with long straight hair hanging like a silken sheet down their backs, one was wearing boots and shorts, the other was wearing leather trousers and a coat that seemed to be made of animal fur. Their heels clacked in time with their steps, and they seemed to bounce as they strode. There were singular walkers too, mostly dressed in suits of various shades of sensible colours. A constant trickle of groups was spilling out of the doors behind her. Hamida turned her attention to them now.

It was still light enough to make out colour as well as form.

"Where did you last see it?" Someone was talking behind her.

"I had it before we came in the museum, I'm sure." A man's voice now.

"It must be in your bag."

Hamida suddenly realised why the voices had struck her as odd. They were speaking Urdu. It had been months now since she had heard someone speak the language of her home. It sounded intensely foreign and familiar all at the same time. She tried to remember the last words she had heard in Urdu. Had they been her own? Her grandmother's? Who had spoken last? When would she hear it again? Would she be resigned to snatching sentences from overheard conversations? A breeze blew the dusk chill inside of her. She pulled her jacket around her. This was nothing compared to the cold of Cumbria, but her loneliness somehow made her shiver. She looked again at the slow tributary of people trickling down the steps. A woman with a tight fuzz of black hair pulled back away from her face, blossoming from the folds of a colourful ribbon, was walking down the steps holding a young child in her arms. The child in turn was cradling a toy dinosaur, babbling to the soft creature, and making it talk back in the deepest roars its small throat could muster. The child caught Hamida watching and beamed. Did it really matter what language she was surrounded by? Children knew exactly what they meant. Even when all they were doing was crying, they were still communicating. And the adults around them, if they paid enough attention, could often make sense of their streams of sounds eventually.

Hamida closed her eyes and listened. In the hum and burble of noise around her, she started to pick out streams. English, Urdu, Bengali, Hindi, languages with which she was familiar, and languages she'd never heard before, some sounded like the chiming of clocks, others like the strumming of stringed instruments, others like fingers running over smooth fabric, others like the cawing of birds.

"Hamida?"

She opened her eyes. Maurice was kneeling in front of her with an armful of small boxes, his face tightened in an earnest worry. "Are you alright?"

She noticed that he pronounced her name without the 'h' and his 'r's grated in his throat.

"What language do you dream in, Maurice?" she asked him.

Maurice was out of breath. He made an attempt to steady his breathing as he tried to balance his attention between Hamida and her question. Her words had given him the sensation that he'd slipped whilst walking along a wall. He knew he needed to keep walking and stop himself falling at the same time.

He'd been taken somewhere strange last night. He tried to remember how long it had been since he slept, and what time it would be now in London. He abandoned the arithmetic and concentrated instead on opening the boxes and tubes he'd bought from the nearest pharmacy, which had turned out to be further away than he'd anticipated.

"What language do I dream in?" He repeated the question to buy himself time as he contemplated his answer. Something in him was resisting the revisit to the

144

place he gone to in his sleep. Now that he thought about it, coaxing his brain beyond its discomfort, it was less of a place than a state. Somewhere, some state beyond himself. He had always been present in his dreams, as a character or at the very least as an observer. If the dream had not been about him, he was least watching it unfold. But in this dream, there was no 'he', no part of him was present. There was just… something else. The closest he could come to a description had been a colour. A magnificent peacock blue. He'd woken in stages, each a shallower depth of the state he'd experienced, until finally he was himself again, and he was awake. And the colour had faded.

He shook his head. 'I'm not sure, Hamida. I can't remember."

He ripped open a packet of antiseptic wipes. She took it from him and gently wiped the blood stains from her foot, trying not to wince. Maurice felt terrible. How could he not have noticed that she had been suffering this entire time? He must have been so absorbed in showing her the exhibits that he'd not paid attention to anything other than the responses on her face.

He opened a tube of cream. She took this too, as he placed the bloodied wipe into the bag. "This will help it heal quickly, and make sure it doesn't get infected." She winced again as she dabbed on the cream. Maurice felt another pang of guilt.

"Allow me?"

He had opened a packet of soft gauze adhesive pads. He raised her foot on his knee and gently applied the bandage. The coolness of the cream, now that the sting had gone, was soothing.

"And… the final thing." Maurice made an effort to smile to reassure her. He lifted an orange bag from the step beside him.

"Trainers!"

He pulled a box from the bag and unwrapped the tissue paper inside, titling the box so Hamida could see. Inside were a pair of trainers, light grey with purple and green embellishments and thick spongy soles.

"I hope they fit…" He bared his teeth in a mixture of hope and worry.

Hamida slid her foot into the shoe.

"Like Cinderella," Maurice laughed. Hamida did not know what he meant, she was bracing herself for the pain. There was only a slight tingle at the back of her ankle.

"Oh!" she exclaimed. They felt soft, almost pillowy.

Maurice took her hand and helped her to her feet. "How do they feel?"

"Wonderful!"

"Phew!" He laughed with relief. "We'll walk slowly. And if you feel any pain at all, even a little bit, you must tell me. Promise?"

"I shall," Hamida replied solemnly.

They walked together down the steps and hailed a cab back to the hotel.

16

Hamida lay on the edge of the bed, almost bigger than the entire room she had slept in with her grandmother. She flipped over the feathered pillow in the hope that the coolness might divert her attention from the endless flood of thoughts.

She clasped the beads, which had now absorbed her heat, in her hand. She raised them to her cheek. She wanted to be home. As intense as her discomfort was with the squalor, the benignness of the everyday, the focus on survival, the monotony of the mundane, the constant encroachment on the dignity of those around her, she was also uneasy with this: the wealth, the extravagance, the luxury, the opulence. No bed in the world could seduce one to sleep if what they lay on the pillow with was their own discomfort.

And it was not the contrast between the glaring wealth of the city they'd travelled through and her home, but between the skyline and the streets. The beggars here, so many of them, who shuffled along the sidewalks in shoes that had never fit them, clothes that had absorbed years of sweat and despair, rooting around in rubbish, their gnarled hands held out for money they knew no one would spare. The contrast between the flashing lights and the dimness in their eyes, the full bellies of tourists and the hollowness of their cheeks. Each of them muttering to themselves in the ubiquitous language of poverty with which she was all too familiar.

She was tired to the point of exasperation. Perhaps that was why questions she was sure she had already answered swam insistently to the surface of her consciousness. Why was she here? Why had her grandmother agreed? It was true that everyone she'd ever met was desperate to leave, but she had never expressed such a desire. She had wanted to be where her grandmother was. To go to school and to read, to spend time with herself and the only other person in the world who understood her, who nurtured her mind. She would work, when she'd finished school, but she'd continue to learn through words, text, ink on paper, and avoid the exhaustion of other people; their thoughts, their motives, their uncertainties, their questions, their noise.

But did she really want to go back? She was learning. Perhaps not always through words, but with her eyes, her hands, her ears. She'd learned about other lives, not by reading about them, but by living them, feeling them, tasting them, hearing them, the quiet and the noise. Perhaps that was why she could not sleep. Part of her knew she could not go back. Did not want to… She longed to see her grandmother, to sit and hear her stories, and to share her own. To talk to her like she had never talked before. But she knew that now she had contrast she could never be content. Perhaps she was mourning. Perhaps that explained the hand clutching something inside her chest. This did not happen to anyone, this opportunity, to be taken from one extreme of life to another. She should be happy, and she was, and yet some part of her wanted to stop the men who had come and taken her away, to pull on the arm of the self who had followed them. Perhaps the clutching in her chest was not grief, but an attempt by something inside of her to pull these disparate parts of her together.

As she turned over, Hamida realised that her own hand was clasped tightly around the beads, so hard that they had left indentations in her palm. She uncurled her fingers. The beads slid along the string with a gentle click.

In a room a few doors down the corridor, Maurice was sitting on the edge of his bed, flicking through the channels on a large screen. Nothing appealed to him.

There are times when a person hears something so unexpected that it is easier not to react at all than to sift through the multitude of possible reactions for the appropriate one. What had Hamida meant by 'metaphor' as they stood before the Lucy exhibit? Whose metaphor? What was his response to such a comment? He could have laughed, but that would have seemed cruel and dismissive. He did not want to dismiss what she had said, but what would he have replied? He played various answers over in his head until his frustration with his own inarticulateness got the better of him.

He shook his head. And what was that tingling he had felt when he touched her arm in the museum, almost an electric shock, the same tingling when he held her foot to apply the bandage? Static. It must be. And yet, he knew it felt different. He'd try again tomorrow. Do an experiment. Touch someone else and then touch her. And then touch someone else again. He'd repeat it multiple times. Just to prove to himself there was nothing there. Nothing there at all.

He flicked through more channels. That wasn't the only thing that was gnawing at him. How was he supposed to seduce her? And why the hell was he supposed to? He knew why. Michael had explained it very clearly, and he'd understood it so clearly then, but now that he was here, with her, it felt deceptive. Almost cruel. And she was eighteen, fifteen years younger than him. Perhaps that's what was gnawing at him. That he liked her, despite that. That he felt a rush of something when she smiled, that maybe that's what the tingling was when he touched her, that it wasn't static at all. That he couldn't sleep because she was three doors down the hall and that he knew he'd see her tomorrow, and he liked that thought. He jabbed at the off button on the remote control and decided to run a bath.

*

Maurice and Hamida shuffled along the row of seats to their allocated spaces. Maurice slid his coat off his shoulders and tossed it over the back of his chair. He grinned at Hamida. She smiled back at him, one side of her mouth rising higher than the other. He plonked himself down in the seat. They'd arrived in Houston only that morning and had grabbed snacks from a convenience store on their way from the hotel, wolfing down the sandwiches and drinks in the taxi. Maurice felt the grumblings of indigestion from the spongey white bread start behind his solar plexus, but he was far too excited to pay the acidic activity too much attention. Hamida looked out at the screen before them. It started at the bottom of the theatre floor and swooped up over all the seats in a gigantic concave arch. Everywhere they looked they felt they could see screen. She cast her gaze around her. People were filing in and filling the seats around them.

"Is this a cinema?" She'd seen signs for them all over New York.

"Sort of, it's more like a simulator. They have this great system, the Digistar 6," Maurice turned his ticket over reading the name, "it basically makes you feel like you are in space. It's the best in the world." He grinned again.

Hamida turned her attention back to the screen. The huge domed building they had walked into, Maurice told her, was a planetarium. This one, he had explained, was used to teach astronauts working for NASA.

"NASA?"

"Oh, yes, the National Space… something." He pulled out his phone and searched for the acronym. "National Aeronautics and Space Administration. They're the ones who put a man on the moon. You've never heard of it?"

She shook her head. He was often seduced by her sharpness into forgetting the surprising limits of her knowledge in so many areas.

"You'll see in the video." He pointed to the screen.

The lights in the theatre now dimmed and a hush fell over the audience, replaced by an anticipatory silence, heavy with held breaths. Hamida realised she was holding her own.

With a sudden flash of light and colour the screen exploded into a flood of stars and galaxies. Hamida gasped. Maurice looked at her. He was doing it again, checking for her appreciation. He decided not to care, for the moment at least. He squeezed her arm and turned his eyes back to the screen. For the next hour, Hamida was alone, surrounded only by the firmaments. If she put her hand out, she felt, she could touch them. Things beyond sight, things humans could only see with instruments. Sounds translated into images, light in colours humans could not see, things so miniscule they were invisible but only because they were so far away. She'd never known scientists could listen for stars. The atmosphere around us, the voice from behind the screen told them, is filled with waves from outer space. Places mankind could not trace. Everything had a noise. A sound. An energy. Waves. Frequencies.

"So much for the seven heavens," Maurice leaned over and whispered in her ear. Hamida did not hear him. She was entranced. The voice died, and the lights of the screen dimmed, but she sat rooted to her chair. Sounds, noise, waves. Spaces that were not empty at all but filled with movement. Noise, frequencies, movement. Everything had an energy.

Maurice had stood up and put on his coat, but Hamida hadn't notice. Waves, movement, frequencies. Energy humans did not have the instruments to measure. She felt like she was suspended in a web of thoughts, criss-crossing, overlapping, each of them vibrating. The more she twisted, trying to make sense of them, the more entangled she found herself. If she sat still, she might be able to put her finger on the nexus of them all.

"Hamida, we have to go." Maurice had put his hand on her shoulder but quickly withdrew it, as though he'd hurt himself. He was holding his wrist looking at his palm.

"I'm sorry," she said, picking up her jacket. "Are you alright?"

"Yes, I'm fine, just got an electric shock, I think. It's nothing."

*

After the dark of the theatre, the sun outside was almost painful. It took a few seconds for them to adjust to the vibrancy of the roses in the garden around the building.

Hamida was looking down at her feet as she walked, watching her trainers emerge and disappear in turn from beneath her body. The more she concentrated on walking, the harder it became. She slipped in between her steps and the web of thoughts which had not yet left her.

"I can't wait for you to see where we're going next. You're going to love this."

In truth, Maurice was not sure whether or not Hamida would love it. It was one thing to see dead specimens of animals, quite another to expose someone to live ones. He had once taken a girlfriend to a similar exhibit in London, only to have her run from the room screaming, flapping her arms against her hair. Hamida, he suspected, would not have the same response.

"Butterflies!"

Maurice spun round at the doors to the Butterfly Centre, flinging his arms open to convey and hopefully transfer his excitement.

Hamida's eyes opened wide. "Butterflies? They live in there?" she asked.

"Hundreds of them!"

"Oh..." She followed him through the glass doors, through the hanging flaps of heavy plastic into the warm air of the butterfly sanctuary.

Maurice turned around to look at Hamida again. Her gaze was cast upwards towards the domed glass ceiling, framed with thick tropical creepers and towering branches. Her mouth was slightly open, she seemed utterly captivated. This was becoming an addiction, his desire to see her amazed. To show her something no one else in the world had, to be the first to offer her an experience, to see her eyes light up and know the neurons of her mind were firing in ways they never had before.

As she stood, her chin titled upwards, a black and bright blue butterfly fluttered down like an autumn leaf and landed on her shoulder. She turned her head to look at it. The streak of colour across it was iridescent, catching the light as its wings moved ever so slightly up and down, as if in time with its breath.

"You have one on your hair too!" Maurice pointed. On the braid hanging over her shoulder a black and white butterfly had landed. The intricate patterns on its wings looked like lace.

"Turn around, there's some on your back."

Hamida turned slowly.

"There's three!"

Hamida looked up. In the air around them, butterflies were bobbing their delicate wings, skipping around the leaves and other visitors, all making their way towards her.

A woman in khaki was also making her way towards them.

"Oh my!" The woman's cheeks were a friendly rosy red. "I've never seen that many on anyone before." Hamida liked her voice. Her words came out slowly, vowels elongated in unexpected places; she seemed to bounce on certain syllables. "Are you wearing any perfume?"

Hamida went to shake her head but was afraid of scaring the fragile creatures. "No, I'm not," she said.

"Well, they must just really like you!" The woman laughed with the same intonation as her speech. "If you walk carefully, they'll fly away, you won't hurt them."

Hamida took a step forward. A few of them fluttered away. By the time they'd wandered along the leafy paths winding their way along the floor of the centre all but the bright blue butterfly on her shoulder had danced their way off through the air.

The Blue Morpho, they read on the information boards dotted around the sanctuary, was in fact not blue at all. The colour came from tiny ridges on its wings which reflected sunlight back at a new wavelength which made it appear blue.

Hamida looked down at the creature on her shoulder. "You're not what you seem, are you?"

Hamida had seemed almost sad to leave the sanctuary. The wistful expression that had passed across her face when the woman in uniform by the doors to the sanctuary had scooped the last butterfly from her shoulder had not left her. Maurice had an idea. He led her through the museum to the gift shop.

"Have a look around," he told her. "I'll be back."

She wandered slowly around the low aisles of the store, looking at pencils topped with rubber dinosaurs, wallets with various animal prints, pieces of amber containing ants and flies, key rings made of sharks' teeth. Her soft trainers squeaked slightly on the highly polished wooden floors. She came to the space-themed section. In amongst the notebooks and planet-shaped erasers, she found a stack of silk scarves, dyed with the purples, pinks, and blues of the galaxies that had flown past them on the lens-like screen. For the first time, she wished she had money. She wanted to buy one for her grandmother. She ran her hand over the slippery cool fabric. She imagined her grandmother unwrapping it, looking up at her, and lifting it over her neck, flicking one end with an expert movement of the wrist over her shoulder where it would float down her back. She'd hug her granddaughter, and then tell her of the silks and satins the emperors wore, and how Hamida would have fit right in at court.

"They would have made you Empress at first glance," she'd tell her with a knowing nod. Hamida would smile and kiss her grandmother's forehead, and then cut up onions for their supper.

"Ready?" Maurice was at her side. He noticed the scarf in her hands. "Did you want to buy that? We can buy it. You know, I'd give you your own card, but Cooper gave me strict instructions." He looked woeful, "I did ask."

Hamida shook her head and placed the scarf back on the shelf. Even if she could buy it, even if she could wrap it up and post it, she did not know if it would ever arrive.

"Are you ready to go?" Maurice asked. "I've found the perfect place for dinner."

*

Govinda's was twenty minutes away by taxi. "It's hot dog free!" Maurice told her in the cab. Hamida laughed. It had only been two days since she had allowed herself to accept that she liked Maurice. The initial foreignness of the feeling, she'd realised, was because the concept was so alien to her, not because it was forbidden. Her grandmother had never uttered a word about spending time in male company, and indeed spoke at length with men in the area who often came to her for counsel in times of neighbourhood disputes. But men and women did not mix or mingle if they could help it, and along the streets, the touch of a man was never friendly. She herself had never been touched in stalls or in narrow

156

alleyways, but she'd heard girls in her class whisper to each other about unwelcome caresses, squeezes, and gropes. She had seen the stray eyes of men that sought out women's flesh while their wives were looking the other way, not just in Kolkata, but here on the other side of the world too. There were, of course, exceptions; men whose heads bowed as she passed, their eyes cast downwards; men who reminded her of the stories her grandmother shared about her ancestors. Maurice's eyes did not avoid her, but they had never slithered or snatched at her either. He had been respectful, eager but not insistent, and more importantly kind. Nothing was more captivating to her than kindness.

The restaurant was large and brightly lit. The octagonal domes in the ceilings lent the otherwise fast-food feel of the place an almost temple-like air. Wooden chairs and square tables were scattered around the room, which was filled with the chatter and tinkling of customers and their cutlery.

"I thought you might like a taste of home," Maurice said, beaming as they made their way to the counter at the back of the restaurant.

Lined up in deep silver trays, was a long row of colourful food. Hamida was hit by the smells of cumin, turmeric, ginger, and the prickly aroma of hot spices.

Maurice handed her a plate from the stack. "You have to help me, tell me what's good," he said.

Hamida turned her head from the food to look at him. Something somewhere in her wanted unexpectedly to touch his arm. She walked along the counter and examined the food. She was surprised to see such ordinary dishes being sold here, on the other side of the world, to people who had probably only ever seen

India on a screen. The curious feeling of foreignness and familiarity crept around her chest, encouraging her to engage with it, but she was too hungry.

Maurice needed rice, of course. She tipped a spoonful of the loose white grains scattered with coriander leaves carefully onto his plate. *Saag paneer* was her favourite dish, spinach cooked so it was almost creamy, mixed with pieces of white cheese.

"Do you like eggplant?" She hesitated, realising she was piling things onto his plate without asking him.

"I want whatever you like."

Eggplant it was. Grilled, minced, and mixed with onions and garlic, tomatoes, and spices. Next, *bhindi masala*, okra sauteed in a sauce flavoured with ginger and garam masala. She spooned a generous portion onto Maurice's plate and her own. By the time they reached the end of the row, their plates were piled with an assortment of yellows, oranges, browns, greens, and reds that made their mouths water.

Maurice took a spoonful of *daal*, red lentils cooked almost into a yellow soup, pungent with onions and cumin, and tasted.

"Oh wow. This is so good! Did you eat this at home?"

Hamida nodded. She felt a pang deep in her chest. She swallowed, ripping off a piece of flatbread.

They ate, Maurice's eyes watering, mixing lentils with tomatoey red sauces, pieces of okra with yoghurt, scooping up sauces with bread, and spooning down saturated piles of beautifully cooked white rice. When their plates were clean, Maurice went back for seconds. Hamida followed him, this time watching as he spooned heaps of the dishes he had enjoyed the most onto his plate. Hamida took a bowl from the stack next to the plates and ladled out two helpings of *khir*. She placed the bowl next to Maurice when they sat down at the table.

"For when you're finished," she said.

The dish resembled rice pudding but was slightly wetter, flavoured with saffron and cardamom, topped with shaved pistachios. *Khir* had not been a staple of Hamida's diet but on special occasions, her grandmother would soak the grains and boil them in milk with the cardamom pods and saffron that she'd ground in a pestle and mortar. The smell was more than comforting, it was the scent of a joyous safety, the aroma of happiness, and a home she never thought she'd leave. Hamida scraped her spoon around the bowl, carefully collecting the final traces.

17

It was half past three. Only the hunting animals were awake. Michael leaned his elbows on his desk, clicking through the files on his computer. It had been two weeks since the girl had left, and he had four measly reports from Maurice. He scrolled through the list of credit card purchases. Hotel, food, clothes, items at the museums, taxis, nothing that hinted at any cause for concern. The absence of information had been irksome, but Maurice's questions had crossed the line.

"What do you mean, 'Do they have to go to Japan?'"

Cooper had shifted on his feet. "He's asking if they can visit galleries in the States instead. He's identified several more museums and exhibits back in New York and some in Pennsylvania."

"Oh, he has, has he? Who the fuck asked him to identify more museums?" A shower of spit burst from Michael's mouth as he spat out the words. He snatched a glass from his desk and sloshed in the whiskey. He gulped it back. Swallowing seemed to help calm him. He breathed heavily through his nose.

"This is a very delicate stage of the experiment. Perhaps it's my fault, I should have explained more clearly. Travel needs to be extensive, from one end of the world to the other, from one civilisation to another. It is the Yemen to Syria journey, and it has to be done properly."

"Yes, sir." Cooper nodded, though whether or not he understood was not clear.

"Tell him I'll have someone meet them in Japan."

Arrogant little French bastard, Michael fumed, thinking he knew better. Or maybe Maurice was just lazy. Michael wasn't sure which was worse. He closed the reports and lowered the screen of the laptop. Then, changing his mind, opened it again and checked the reply he had received that morning. Dominic would meet them at the airport in Japan, that way Michael could confirm their arrival and could cross check Maurice's reports.

Michael exhaled deeply. His eyes itched. He rubbed them with his forefingers. Pushing his chair back, he started his slow pace around the room, twisting the ring on his left index finger, slipping it up and down the knuckle. It had left a ridge where his hands had changed shape around it, a band of a lighter shade of skin.

He ran through the stages of the experiment in his mind like a mantra. Structure was reassuring, a plan was soothing, the prospect of results was the one thing, the only thing, that kept his mind from giving up on itself, from surrendering to the aching loss he kept barely at bay.

When he was awake, he could control his thoughts, he was master of his mind. When he slept, when he could sleep, he was at the mercy of his memories. And he did not want to remember. He wanted to act. He had learned where the quicksand was, the areas of thought that would let him drown even before he was aware he was sinking, those unstable states where struggling only sucked you in deeper. He would stick to his map, and he would not think about sleep.

*

If America had been meant as an immersion in natural sciences, Japan, Maurice now realised, was an immersion in technology. It occurred to him when they stepped

162

off the plane, that this may have been what Hamida felt when she stepped off the plane in England or in America – into a world so foreign. He felt immediately stranded. Languages, customs, cultures, procedures, even food, everything was different. The strokes of the Japanese characters on every signpost, pamphlet, train station, mocked him for his illiteracy. Even the air felt different, though he could not put his finger on why. His ineptitude made him feel more protective of Hamida, and at the same time utterly useless. He was grateful for Dominic's presence, although the knowledge that they were to be chaperoned had initially perturbed him.

They made an odd trio. In New York, even Houston, they may have blended in, or at least not have been so conspicuous. But Dominic, at over six feet tall, with hair the colour of copper tied at the nape of his neck into a thick ponytail, seemed to exaggerate their own foreignness here and mark them out immediately as tourists. Perhaps this was an advantage. Maurice remembered arriving in the UK as a student and struggling with the assumptions that he was a native, being scorned and quietly derided for making errors of etiquette. At least now any faux pas they may commit inadvertently would be overlooked, if not forgiven, on account of their obvious ignorance.

Japanese, Dominic had explained, on their way out of the Miraikan – literally translated as 'Future Museum', housing exhibits on cutting edge science and innovation – was actually made up of three alphabets. Two had forty-six letters each. Every letter had a different sound. The third consisted of characters and wasn't really an alphabet at all but collections of symbols, each of which represented a word. Children learned these by heart. Maurice was fascinated, he had always felt Japanese was difficult but had had no idea how it was constructed.

What must that have meant for the brain, he thought now. So much of how people think is based on the language tools available to them. He knew when he was angry, he resorted to French, that he counted in French often too, but when he wanted to write an article, he automatically fell into English. He remembered Hamida's question. He still did not know what language he dreamt in. He made a mental note to incorporate a section on language in his thesis.

Was it language that led to such differences in culture, or differences in culture that bred such a different understanding of sounds and words? He looked over at Hamida walking beside him, her face illuminated by the jungle of electronic signs that towered over them from both sides of the street, stretching as far as the eye could see.

It suddenly struck him, the reason why Michael had sent them here. It wasn't the museums, although they were clearly designed to make a point, to convey information, to educate. It was the difference. America had been different, certainly miles away from the Cumbria and sheep that Hamida had described. But this was as different as one could possibly get from anything she had already experienced. He thought back to Michael's explanation of his experiment. There was no God here. At least not in the traditional sense. Shintoism and Buddhism, where they were practised and adhered to, did not ascribe to a central, pivotal divine component. Had Hamida ever experienced such a way of seeing the world? Certainly not on this scale, he imagined. He wondered what she was making of all of this, but the busy streets of Tokyo were not the place to ask.

Dominic was taking them to a ramen restaurant he was fond of. He'd been vague about what exactly it was he did in Japan, but he knew his way around and could speak the language fluently, so they had little option but to trust him. They both had to walk quickly to keep up with his strides, though there was no chance of losing him. He ducked into a small alleyway leading off the main road, then turned right, left, and right again down increasingly small streets.

The word 'restaurant' had been misleading. The shop was no bigger than a convenience store, the windows at the front plastered in posters advertising who knew what to who knew whom. Dominic pushed open the door and gave a small bow. The inside was smaller than the shop had looked from the outside, perhaps because almost half of it was taken up by stoves, lined with bubbling pots and pans. The back wall was lined with more cooking ware, sharp knives, and utensils Maurice had never seen. The smell engulfed them, mixtures of broths and pickles, freshly chopped vegetables and herbs. They sat down at the bench overlooking the stoves. The steam heated their cheeks and made their eyebrows damp.

"Meat, fish or veg?" Dominic asked them.

"Vegetables, please," Hamida replied.

Maurice nodded. "I'll have the same."

Hamida looked at him quizzically, then turned her attention back to Dominic who was reeling off versions of the strange sounds that had surrounded them all day.

He had been a great help in the museum. Although most of the information boards had English translations, occasionally there were signs and descriptions that didn't, and he'd willingly obliged Hamida's requests for interpretations.

She was surprised at how freely she'd made these requests. A month ago, something in her would have been reluctant to ask. It was one thing to ask questions about someone's life, this was rarely a burden, and so often people valued the invitation to fill in the gaps of their past and present which they could not portray all at once. But asking for help was different; it was a request, it required someone to give, not just to share. And yet slowly, she had overcome this hesitance. Perhaps it had been the pain she'd suffered in the museum all the way back in New York when she'd ignored the rubbing on her ankles until they had bled. Perhaps it was Maurice's constant insistence that she ask for anything she needed, and his delight on the occasions when she did.

Her ease now at asking him for things seemed to have trickled over into her other interactions. In Houston, she had asked for directions, asked for more towels in the hotel, asked for them to stop when she felt tired, or eat when she felt hungry. Maurice sat next to her now on the high stools, leaning on the bench. His arm was touching hers, she could feel the slight movements he was making as he peered over the counter into the pots. She leaned ever so slightly against him and looked around. The interior of the shop was made of wood with small white lanterns encasing the light bulbs above them. The walls, what was visible of them, were a soft cream. The chatter in here was quieter, and the neutral tones of the wood were almost calming in contrast to the chaos of colour outside. The museum had been overwhelming. So much of what she'd seen had been metal. Robots with metal bones and veins, trains suspended by magnets. What was not metal seemed to be made of glass or plastic. The lines here seemed to be straighter even than the stone and concrete of New York, the lights were brighter, the screens bigger.

Hamida breathed in the warm scented air around them. Three bowls were placed in front of them, with two wooden sticks and a ceramic spoon, shaped almost like a swan. Inside the bowl, in a crystal-clear brown broth swam swarms of noodles, sliced vegetables, squares of creamy white tofu, and a boiled egg split down the middle, its bright orange yolk seeping into the soup. It smelled unlike anything Hamida had ever eaten.

Dominic was showing her how to use the chopsticks. It was not dissimilar to using a pencil, except that there were two of them. She soon caught the hang of it. They had not realised how hungry they had been. In the act of immersing herself into the food, which seemed so at odds with the world they had just come from, Hamida relaxed. She no longer felt Maurice's arm against her own, the feeling of his foreignness faded into familiarity. She felt warm, in a way she had not done in a long time. The clutching feeling she had not realised she had been carrying all this time in her chest, suddenly released itself, as if realising it had no need to be there. Why should she be tense? Reserved? Maurice was not just kind, but gentle. She had noticed his constant glances, his search for her responses, her reactions. And this was all part of an arrangement. With her signature, her grandmother had provided her with permission; the permission she may have needed weeks ago, but which she knew now even her grandmother would want her to seek from within herself. If there was no reason why, then why did she, and if there was no reason not to, then why didn't she? She turned this phrase over in her mind, repeating it, watching imaginary beads fall along an imaginary string.

168

18

It was cherry blossom season. They'd come to Japan at the perfect time, Dominic told them. They should see them before they left. He could not join them, but he'd arranged for a driver to pick them up at their hotel and take them.

The paths of the park were carpeted in what looked like pink snow. Hamida and Maurice had avoided the main crowds and found a walkway around the edge that most of the tourists had avoided. The canopy of pink petals above them let in the warm spring light in small pools. An occasional breeze would send flurries raining down around them. Their hair and shoulders were soon covered.

"What time is our flight tomorrow?"

"Ten."

Hamida nodded. "And we're going to London?"

"That's right."

Hamida seemed immersed in the strange sensation that beauty often brings with it. A sense of displacement. A desire not to disturb something which they seemed only to have strayed into. She asked her questions only to keep from losing her sense of self completely, as though she needed to tether herself to the earth for fear that she may disappear. It was why, when Maurice had reached for her hand, she had been grateful. It was keeping her grounded. At the same time, the warmth of his palm added to the sense of otherworldliness that swirled around and inside her.

The unsettled feeling she often felt in the city, surrounded by human civilization, she was not experiencing here. The entrance to the Maruyama Park was through the Yasaka shrine, dedicated to Susanoo, the god of sea and storms, love and marriage. This was the first reference to a deity Hamida had seen or heard in Japan, although they had been here for two weeks. Dominic had explained to her that most Japanese were Shintos or Buddhists, and that although they had religious figures, they had no central deity, and most did not believe in a god at all.

"At all?" Hamida had asked.

"Nope."

Of all the foreignness she had experienced, this was the most alien, and yet in some sense strangely familiar. Her grandmother had never mentioned God in words. The images she had been surrounded by, she realised, had all belonged to strangers. She knew that people believed in different gods; Hindus, Muslims, the Christians of the Mission. She knew they fought over their claims to the truth about this power. And she hated so many of the things people did in the name of something she had only ever been sure wanted them to be kind. She had known of the divine in absence, in her grandmother's description of the long line of feminine faith bearers, who not once had been ascribed a religion, and yet whom, in her grandmother's eyes, had been women of unshakeable conviction.

Maurice squeezed her hand. They had reached the entrance to the park again and the crowds had suddenly swarmed around them. He put his arm around her and guided her out of the gates towards the car that was waiting for them.

170

They spent the rest of the day in the restaurant of the hotel, balancing sushi rolls between the tips of their chopsticks, picking up slivers of pickled ginger, asking each other questions about their childhoods. It seemed apt, in a place where they knew no one, to delve deep into the personal.

"I was bullied as a kid," Maurice was looking down at his plate, drawing patterns in the drops of soy sauce that had slipped from his sushi. "I was smaller than everyone else, I wore glasses, and my skin was darker than all the other kids. My mother jokes I must have North African ancestry, from my father's side, she always insists. They would call me names and take my lunch. My mother would make these small pastries for me to take with me to school, and every day I watched as one by one these boys would take them out and drop them into the toilet. They wouldn't even flush it, they would just be floating there. And I'd go hungry. I never told my parents about it. You know, it's cruel for a child to be made to feel so alone. I'd actually try and talk to God. I thought he could be my friend. I'd imagine conversations, and him taking revenge on all those boys who picked on me. And then, when I got older, I realised I never got any answers, and the boys were never punished, and the whole thing had been an embarrassing attempt to cover up my own loneliness."

He scribbled out the pattern he'd drawn in the brown liquid.

"I'm so sorry," Hamida said. She put her hand out to touch his wrist.

"Oh, no, it's all stupid. I grew up quickly. Made friends in the next school." He seemed embarrassed at what he'd shared. "I'm going to use the bathroom, I'll be right back."

Hamida looked around the restaurant, its huge windows overlooking the crowded city of Tokyo. Most of the tables were empty now. It was almost ten o'clock, but a few guests lingered, sipping glasses of various liquids, picking at remnants in bowls and on plates. She noticed a couple sitting across the room. They seemed deep in conversation, an exchange being conveyed not just in words, which Hamida could not hear, but movements; hands, eyes, the corners of mouths, shifts of feet and hips. The man put his hand out to stroke the woman's hair. She took his hand and wrapped her fingers around it, joining them across the table.

She could see Maurice emerge from the corridor across the room, he ran his hand through his unruly waves. He smiled as he caught her eye.

They headed slowly up to their rooms. Hamida had just unlocked the door when Maurice turned to her suddenly. "I have something for you. Let me find it and I'll bring it to you."

She had washed her hands and face in the sink when Maurice knocked. She opened the door, wider than she had expected. He seemed hesitant to come in until she stood back, indicating for him to enter. Her invitation gave him courage.

"Close your eyes," he told her. She closed her eyes and held her breath. She heard a rustling sound, and then felt something cold around her neck. His hands were moving her braid from her back. She felt her skin and something deep inside her tingle.

"There!" he said. "Open them!" He stood before her, with the same intense look of anticipation as he waited for her response, examining every slight movement of her eyes and lips for an indication.

She felt the small object hanging around her neck. Touching it first with her fingers, she then raised it up so she could see it. It was a small chain, and from it hung a pendant. It was made of silver, black and the brightest of blues, fashioned in the shape of a butterfly.

19

They were four hours into their flight. Hamida's head rested on Maurice's shoulder. He could tell by the rise and fall of her chest that she was sleeping.

He wanted to stay as still as possible so he wouldn't disturb her. He closed his eyes, trying to sleep, but all he could see were the scenes - darkened, shadowy - memories and traces of sensations from the night before. It pulled breath from him from the deepest parts of his lungs, it made him quiver as waves like wind across fields of long grass passed over him, and heat emanated from areas in him he did not know.

He hadn't asked Hamida what made her knock on his door in the dead of night. He'd been sure, when she closed the door behind him after she'd thanked him for the necklace, that he'd sleep alone. Though a part in him had ached to touch her for weeks now, he'd had no expectations, she'd given him no indication that she would permit it. And then, there she had stood at the door to his hotel room in her dressing gown, the soft light from the hallway illuminating her silhouette; her presence there not the successful culmination of a plot he had been paid to orchestrate, but which he could only guess was a result of something they had both experienced, and which she, not he, had the courage to first claim. He did not know, and perhaps he never would, that her decision to knock on his door came moments after she had been awakened not merely by desire but a conviction. By a dream in which she knew their bond had been sealed in words clearer than ink.

*

She had been standing in the Diwan-i-Khas, the Hall of Private Audiences. The vast ceilings, ornate with intricate patterns stretched out above her, supported by powerful pillars, carved with symmetrical vines and inlaid with marble tiles. The air smelled of tuberose and night blooming cestrum. The palace was silent but for the low pulse of the heartbeats of the twenty-eight figures, arranged in two arms stretching out from the throne. Before it, stood Hamida Begum.

The woman on the throne wore a headdress of rich ochre, adorned with the feathers of two peacocks. Inlaid into the gold upon it were rubies. On her brow rested the Koh-i-Noor. The woman wore a garment of red satin, around her shoulders was wrapped a shawl of jet-black silk, embroidered with the emblems of two empires. Her feet, bare but for the delicate gold chains encircling her ankles, rested on the throne steps upon which two of the women sat. When she turned her head, the room quivered. Of the House of Borjigin by birth and the House of Timurid by marriage, she was the Queen Consort of the Ferghana Valley, direct descendent of Genghis Khan. She was known as Qutlugh Nigar Khanum, and from her womb was born the first Emperor of the Mughal Dynasty.

The woman to her right rose to her feet. She was dressed in blue, the colour of the poppies that grow in the Himalayas, embroidered with the thinnest of red threads. On her head sat a turban, dyed the richest shades of sunsets, from which arched the feather of a peacock and from which her dark hair cascaded in tight curls across her shoulders. At her waist hung a sword, sheathed in gold and vermillion.

From something in the air, she drew a parchment. From within her chest, she drew a quill. With sweeps of her long, slender fingers she wrote words in the language of sound and silence. Words which sealed two souls.

She carried the parchment to Hamida. Hamida caught her reflection in the paper. A cluster of teardrop pearls, suspended on a golden chain, hung across her brow. The long gown she was wearing was intricately brocaded and was made of silk of the purest white.

Hamida knew what was written on the parchment, she had written it herself. Each and every woman there had written it. She looked to the figure on the throne who nodded without the slightest of movements.

She felt a hand on her arm. It was her grandmother. From within the folds of her turquoise robes, her grandmother drew a golden seal. She pressed it to the parchment, signing her name beneath the chain of women who stood around the throne.

Qutlugh Nigar Khanum

Maham Begum

Hamida Banu Begum

Maryam uz-Zamani

Taj Bibi Bilqis Maham

Arjumand Banu Begum

Nawab Bai

Dilras Banu Begum

Nizam Bai

Anup Begum

Sahiba Nizwan Begum

Fakr un-Nissa Begum

Raziat un-Nissa Begum

Inayat Banu Begum

Nur un-Nissa

Qudsiyat al-Alqab Hazrat Begum

Qudsiya Begum

Gauhar Afruz Banu Begum

Anup Bai

Zinat Mahal

Rushqimi Begum

Sadat Begum

Qudsiya Begum

Lela Banu Begum

Zeenat Mahal

Nawab Shah Zamani Begum

The woman to the right of the Empress of Empresses now stood up. She walked towards her, her feet silent on the marble. She smiled at Hamida and kissed her forehead. She too signed her name. Hamida did not need to read it to know it was her mother's.

The woman in blue now removed her ring, she took Hamida's hand in her own and placed it on her finger. Hamida pressed it to the parchment. In an ink of the brightest blue, the ring left its seal, an orb encircled by twenty-eight lobes each reaching out to an infinity. Within it was a name.

Her own.

20

There are two possible states in which one may awaken in the dead of night. One is with a sense of tranquillity, a calmness that comes with the knowledge that the whole world is asleep and that one can be alone with their thoughts. The other is in the grip of a profound existential dread, wracked with an innominate anxiety that reaches out into the darkness for a face, a terror that comes with the knowledge that the whole world is asleep and one is utterly alone with their thoughts.

When Michael's sense of panic finally found its form, he headed to his office and picked up his phone. It took three rings for Cooper to answer, and half an hour before Michael's request was fulfilled. He would have to wait a day, but it could be arranged before the girl got to London.

Michael, who had been pacing in his habitual circle around his office, now sat down heavily in his chair and reached for the decanter. He opened his drawer, took out the little white pot of pills Cooper had given him, and dropped them into the bin.

*

When she arrived, the tall slender woman with red hair and translucent skin eyed Michael with an air of suspicious apprehension. What could possibly have been so urgent that it required the immediate attention of a professor of Islamic History? She adjusted her navy-blue skirt over her knees as she sat down in the chair opposite Michael's desk. She had agreed to the second summons, as she had seen it, on one condition; that she know to what use the information she provided was being put. She was not a slot machine into which someone simply placed money and withdrew historical accounts, nor was she so shallow as to be flattered by the attention of a renowned billionaire, nor anyone for that matter.

In exchange for such information, as well as a fee not to be sniffed at, she would impart to Michael in intricate detail the period of Muhammad's life after he married Khadijah, and before he claimed to have received revelation. He wanted to know everything possible, their friends, her interests, his habits. She should leave no detail unshared.

Michael made copious notes as she spoke. Page after page he scribbled. When she had finished and sipped the coffee which had gone cold resting on her knee, Michael sat back and flipped through the points he had written. He circled some, put stars by others, then turned to a fresh sheet and scribbled some more.

The woman watched him through curious narrowed eyes. Other than the scratching of the pen on paper and the hollow ticking of the grandfather clock, the place was eerily silent. She coughed uncomfortably. Michael seemed not to hear it and carried on writing. She felt as though she were invigilating an exam, except it was she who had been rigorously questioned. She noticed the dark circles under his eyes, and the half empty decanters in the corner. It was a beautiful May afternoon, she could see through the window behind him. She wondered whether her doctoral student had finished marking the assignments back home.

Michael finally looked up from his page, and sat back in his chair, rolling the pen between his fingers.

"Am I right in thinking, then, that Muhammad spent those early years with his wife in the company of two types of people? The…" he looked down at his paper to check the pronunciation of the word, "*kahinat*, poetesses, priestesses, oracles, and soothsayers; and the religious learned, with whom she regularly conversed, such as her cousin?"

"That would be correct. Both groups were considered friends of Khadijah. Though to make it more complicated, some of the priestesses were not polytheists, but had converted to Judaism and were well versed in the scriptures. Fatimah bint Murr is a good example. She converted to Judaism but remained an oracle. She actually had wanted to marry the Prophet's father since, according to some traditions, she recognised something sacred in him." She had made brief mention of this already, but in her hardwired resistance to oversimplification, she thought it wise to repeat the overlap between the two categories Michael had derived. Michael was nodding pensively. Her eyes narrowed again as if trying to read into his silence. The insistence with which this information had been elicited did not seem to match the significance of its content, at least not as far as she could see.

"So, would you agree that he is being exposed during this period to both scriptural content and poetic form?" Michael asked this slowly.

"I would, to a degree. The oracles spoke in a form of rhythmic rhymed utterances, and we certainly know that Khadijah had conversations with her cousin about matters of religion and theology and appears to have even corresponded with Christian figures outside of Mecca during this period."

"Bahira the Monk?"

"Yes. You know, if you were to ask me, he's the grand conspirator in all of this, as uncomfortable as I am with the idea of conspiracies." She laughed. "Bahira asked Khadijah to marry Muhammad after having met him as a young man and recognising what he saw as the signs of prophethood in him, and he was most probably a disgruntled Arian Christian living in a time when his brand of Christianity was becoming extinct. It's the perfect alignment of factors. The irony is whatever it was he had in mind for Muhammad was completely eclipsed by what actually took place."

Michael furrowed his brow. Perhaps she had distracted him from his point, she thought.

"And this took place over a period of fifteen years, before Muhammad began his prophetic career at the age of forty?"

"That's right."

Michael closed his notebook with a click. He stood up and held out his hand. The woman, surprised, remained seated.

"Mr Sergeant, you're forgetting our agreement. What is all this for?"

Michael paused, placing the lid on his fountain pen. "Cooper will oblige you with the details of our project here. I'm afraid I have a very pressing matter to attend to. You've been most helpful."

Before the woman could object, Cooper, who had been thoroughly coached on Michael's expected response, had opened the door and was standing outside. Michael had already picked up the phone.

*

Hamida stood in the kitchen by the stove leaning against the countertop, feeling the coolness of the tiles against the soles of her feet. She was staring out of the tall window, divided into small rectangular panes of glass, over the leafy treetops which lined the edge of the park. It was the first time she had been alone during the day in at least four months. The feeling was somewhat alien to her now. Maurice's absence, having been whisked away at the airport on their arrival in London by a driver Cooper had sent, had unsettled her somewhat. It was one thing to enjoy being alone, it was another to have solitude imposed upon you.

The stove hissed as the milk in the small pan boiled over onto the ring. The sound drew her abruptly from her ruminations. She spooned in the tea leaves she had found in the cupboard, allowing the mixture now to simmer along with the spices she had already added. She watched the ripples on top of the milk, tinged with cinnamon, star anise, and cloves. It darkened to a luxurious creamy brown. She strained the leaves and spices as she poured the tea into a cup and turned off the heat.

She sipped the drink slowly, sitting at the table, looking out of the window. From the sitting room she could see the busy street below, people scurrying by at varying speeds. It seemed that everywhere in the world, people were in a hurry. A hurry to leave home, a hurry to return, a hurry to arrive and depart from every place in between. They looked like moving points on a map. She saw her own point, firmly fixed in an apartment on the ninth floor of a tall building, somewhere in London. She thought about her grandmother's point, somewhere firmly fixed in an overcrowded street in the depths of Kolkata.

She did not yet know what London sounded like, she had slept most of the way from the airport to the apartment. The woman who greeted her had tapped on the window to rouse her when they arrived. She'd shown her around the rooms, tastefully furnished, with a king size bed in the main bedroom, sofas and armchairs scattered about the living room and a piano in the corner, and the kitchen, fully stocked, and had told her that Maurice would be back the next evening; he'd been called away on urgent business.

Food would be delivered at lunch time and supper time, the woman had said cheerfully, and she left a card with her number in case there was anything Hamida needed. She should, under no circumstances except an emergency, leave the apartment.

Hamida had decided what she would do to distract from the questions she did not know who to ask. Their suitcases were stacked neatly in the bedroom. Although the woman had told her there were clothes in the wardrobe for them both, Hamida felt a deep need for the familiar.

She placed her first suitcase on her bed and pulled the zip. It purred as its teeth were unlocked. She lifted the lid. One by one, she took out the items. They were all neatly folded as she had placed them there when they had left Tokyo, but she folded them again and stacked them into piles. Shirts, sweaters, trousers, socks, underwear. They may, in their majority, have been picked for her, but she had worn them, and they had soaked up something of her, and something of the memories she had formed in them, thus she considered them hers. Next, she pulled open the drawers and carefully placed each item inside. The cornflower blue sweater, the turquoise shirt, the music box, and the thin white sheet she saved until last. She placed these together in a small drawer by themselves. On top, she placed a small, tattered piece of card.

Now she pulled Maurice's suitcase onto the bed. She ran her hands across its dark blue fabric surfaces and felt the leather tab attached to the zip between her thumb and forefinger. She pulled it gently around the case and slowly tipped back the lid. Inside, his clothes were roughly folded, tightly packed, so they almost poured forth when she opened it. She pulled out a sweater, burgundy red, the one he had been wearing the day she had met him in Cumbria. She raised the light woollen fabric to her face. In the moment she inhaled his scent, she was taken back to the embrace he had held her in just a day before.

She was surprised by the pain it caused her. The pain of missing her grandmother had been deep and aching, emanating from the pit of her stomach. This was a sharp and pointed pang that seemed to radiate out across her chest. She brushed the tears that stung the corners of her eyes away with the back of her hand, and folded the sweater carefully, placing it on the bed. She pulled out a shirt, raised it to her face, breathed in the scents of cedarwood and citrus that seemed to emanate from the fabric, and folded this too, placing it in a new pile.

The folding settled the pain somewhat. And in its place arrived thought. Through words other than language, she became aware that it was not grief at Maurice's absence which she was experiencing, but something else. If it had been grief, it should have resembled the ache she had for her grandmother. This was something different. She pulled out a pair of jeans, folded them in half, and half again, and placed them on the pile. This was not something she had experienced before. This was uncertainty. She knew, she realised, that Maurice would return. What she did not know was when he would leave again. Miss Patience had left, pressing her gift into Hamida's hands, as her eyes had welled. Charlotte had embraced her tightly and Jasper had wound himself around her legs with soulful eyes. But neither of them had she permitted within the borders of herself, neither of them had she allowed in. Maurice she had taken inside, and at any minute, he could be withdrawn. For the first time, in words beyond language, Hamida gave voice to a fear.

21

Maurice drummed his fingers on the armrest beneath the car window, paying no attention to the flashes of red and amber lights speeding past. He was tired and anxious to see Hamida. He craved the calm that he had not realised she imbued him with until he had been separated from her. Cooper had grilled him for what seemed hours on the details of their trip in a small glass office in a nondescript building somewhere in Canary Wharf. After his first warning, Maurice had submitted the daily reports promptly each night by email, but Cooper seemed to want the details delivered verbally too.

When Cooper had thanked him, Maurice had stood as if to leave, before being informed that there were some more people he needed to meet. This next stage of the experiment was very delicate, Cooper told him. The people they had gathered were experts in their field, meticulously selected and it was important that Maurice give the impression that these were his friends, Cooper explained as he led him to a larger glass walled room with steel and dark grey fabric chairs, clearly not designed to be sat on for the amount of time he was to spend in there.

The folder on his lap now contained the names, pictures, and details of each of the people he had met, four in total. A strange collection of people, specialists in what seemed an eclectic assortment of subjects and skills. They had been friendly, and he was sure he'd have no trouble spending time with them. What he was worried about, were he to permit himself to think about it, was maintaining a facade in front of Hamida. She was sharp, she noticed things that he himself overlooked. And though her interactions gave the impression that people only ever brushed past her, she caught things about them that seemed to have no obvious indication. The only reassurance he could draw upon was that the feelings Hamida drew from him were undeniably genuine, that they were not the result of an experiment he was now increasingly participating in out of a desire not to be separated from her.

Cooper had made it very clear she should not suspect that they were not his friends for the sake of the experiment because she needed to trust them. But Maurice was not worried about disrupting the experiment, nor whether or not Hamida trusted these people, but whether or not she would trust him, were his act to slip.

"You'll continue to bond with her, of course, during all of this," Cooper had instructed him, as he stood next to him in the elevator they took down to the carpark on the ground floor.

Maurice had not responded. He had watched the numbers flash on the small screen above the door, a countdown of distance. Something in him felt sick. The mention of bonding as part of a business contract felt distasteful now, like talk of replacing original artworks in a gallery with replicas since no one would be able to tell either way. If he had really developed feelings for this woman, the likes of whom he had never imagined meeting, was he still a fraud? He had a metallic taste in his mouth.

What would she be thinking, left all alone, would she have doubted him by now? Would she have suspected? The very night after sleeping in his bed, he disappears, leaving her to spend the night alone, that was enough to plant the seeds of suspicion under the most normal of circumstances. What had they told her? How had they explained his absence? Had they said anything to her at all? He was thinking too much. He had no answers to these questions, and no one to ask.

He scratched at the leather of the armrest, as though to distract himself from the pain he felt emanate across his chest, sharp and pointed. The navigation system said they had half an hour until their arrival, and it was already eleven thirty. Knowing London traffic, he knew they might not arrive until one. He was not sure whether he wished he were alone, sitting on a seat on the underground, saturated with the sweat and smells of a thousand commuters, or whether the presence of more strangers might make him scream. They stopped at a red light. Maurice breathed deeply and ground his teeth. He had ground his teeth as a child in his sleep. The dentist told his mother he must be having nightmares. The people crossing the road in front of them seemed to be walking through water. Laughing, joking, staring at their phones, all as if in slow motion. Maurice stared at the red light and tried to suspend his thoughts. They'd given his cohort a session on mindfulness during his master's. Allow yourself to focus on external sights, sounds and sensations. He scratched the leather again, stared at the light, and resisted the urge to scream.

When, after what had seemed a lifetime, he opened the door of the apartment of the ninth floor, he found Hamida asleep on the couch. Her cheek rested on the back of her hand, her feet were pressed together against the velvet coverings. The butterfly pendant had fallen out of her shirt and was resting against her arm. She was curled up tightly. She must have gotten cold. Maurice reached for the blanket on the back of the armchair across the room, and gently placed it over her. As he lowered it around her shoulders, Hamida stirred. She opened her eyes and smiled. For the first time since arriving in London, Maurice felt calm.

"Who is it?"

"It's Olivia and Alex!"

Maurice looked behind him at the clock on the wall, it was half past twelve. He sighed and unlocked the lock, this was the second time they'd arrived when he and Hamida had been sleeping.

They exchanged high pitched, perhaps overly exuberant greetings, and awkward hugs, arms flung around the instrument cases and backpacks, and stooped to take off their shoes, a ritual Hamida had introduced.

She emerged at the living room door. She had pulled on a loose top and a pair of slacks. Her hair tumbled around her, sleep still lingering in the outer corners of her eyes. Olivia kissed her on the cheek and Alex, who was unpacking his case, waved from the other side of the living room.

"I'll put the kettle on," called Maurice as he headed to the kitchen.

"Oh, I'm gasping for a cuppa!" said Olivia, tossing her long blonde hair over her shoulder and collapsing on the couch. Alex sank into the sofa next to her, leaning his slim frame against her side. Hamida had at first thought they were siblings, with their matching fair complexions and similar shades of strawberry blonde hair. Alex's was cropped short, and he wore an earring in one ear, and sat now with one leg over Olivia's lap, fiddling on his phone.

"We just came from a gig," Olivia was explaining. "We meant to come earlier but Alex got into a raging fight with Jim, and then Jim stormed out, and Alex wanted to go after him, but I managed to persuade him not to chase after him again. It's always the same bloody pattern. Jim acts up and Alex has to go and fix things. If it were me, I'd have dumped him years ago. He's ridiculously high maintenance." Alex thumped her on the shoulder.

"Who's Jim?" asked Hamida, who was now perched on the side of an armchair, one bare foot dangling in the air.

"The love of my life, and the pain in my arse," Alex swept his arm forth as though delivering a line on stage.

"His boyfriend," Olivia volunteered.

Hamida nodded. She could hear the kettle whistling on the stove and looked towards the kitchen where Maurice was standing watching her. He caught her eye, and a wave of heat washed over him. He loved catching her in moments alone, moments when she was not aware of him, observing her from afar; just before she woke up next to him, deep in thought while brushing her teeth, wandering around an aisle in the supermarket when he'd gone to pick up something they'd forgotten. It was as though in those moments he was looking at her in a mirror.

He poured the tea and handed out the mugs. One could have been forgiven for mistaking this pair for two of the thousands of music school graduate trying to scrape together a living by performing in pubs and clubs around the city - forgettable names, forgettable faces, forgettable music. But Michael had not merely employed two regular musicians. Olivia and Alex had been scouted for their skills of improvisation and composition. They had not mentioned, in their unassuming British way, that the 'gig' they had just come from was at the Royal Albert Hall.

They chatted for a while, draining their mugs, or waiting for them to cool and forgetting them entirely. They asked about Japan, New York, the best places to eat in London, filling in the gaps left in their last conversations, and opening up new and unfinished trails of thought which were abandoned and went cold, only to be replaced with someone else's interjection.

"Would you give us a demo," Maurice asked, "since you have your stuff this time?"

"Oh, absolutely!" Olivia seemed delighted, Alex rather less so. She dug him in the ribs playfully. "He's just moping over Jim still."

Olivia took out her violin and Alex settled himself down at the piano. "Okay, you got to give us a tune." She nestled the violin under her chin, the bow poised over it.

"You must know a song, Hamida." Maurice was now perched on the arm of the chair she had sat in.

Hamida tilted her head to one side, trying to recall. "Oh, I know. They used to have us sing songs in school. 'All things bright and beautiful, all creatures…'"

"Great and small!" Alex and Olivia both chimed in and laughed.

"Oh wow, I haven't heard that since primary school! They made you sing that in India?" asked Alex.

"It's a hymn," added Olivia. She finished off the verse, "All things wise and wonderful, the Lord God made them aaallll." She gave a mock bow. Alex clapped.

"It was a missionary school," Hamida told them.

"Oh, well that makes sense. Indoctrinating the kids of India with the message of Jesus Christ!" Alex laughed, and then stopped abruptly. "No offense." He sounded as though he might be asking whether he had caused any.

"Idiot." Olivia prodded him with her bow in an attempt to disperse any possible tension.

Hamida was not sure why she should have taken any offense. The Mission made no secret of the fact that they aimed to spread the message of the gospels amongst those who had not yet been touched by the light; a mission she regarded as mere words, misaligned with the harsh treatment the students often faced at the hands of these 'light bearers'. She had picked her way as carefully as she could around the attempts of her teachers to inculcate a Christian spirit in her, taking to algebra, chemistry, and physics in particular, which seemed to represent havens of neutrality, apart from the prayers with which they began and ended every class. It was not so much that she disliked the words, it was that she saw their emptiness, the way they were twisted into nooses and whips, instruments of either punishment or self-flagellation.

"How about giving us a tune instead? Anything you've heard," Alex was saying now.

Hamida thought for a while. There was something. She did not know if it was a tune. She closed her eyes and concentrated. Without opening them, she started humming. She was not sure how long she hummed, but when she opened her eyes, the three of them seemed to be gazing at her.

"Oh wow," said Alex, breaking the reverie. "Well, I've never heard that one before."

"That was beautiful," said Olivia slowly. "You think we can…?"

Alex nodded. "Give me a minute…. Okay, ready."

Olivia settled her chin on the chinrest, placed her bow on the strings, and with a gentle movement of her arm, she played a long shuddering note. Alex's fingers hovered over the piano. As the note quivered in the air, he added a key. Then another, then another. Olivia's arm moved swiftly now, as though painting the air with a new sound with each of her strokes. Together, in a breath-taking harmony, they replicated the melody that Hamida for the first time in her life had hummed aloud.

Hamida was mesmerised. It was as though the room pulsated with a rhythm she had only ever felt inside of her. She closed her eyes, only to open them again abruptly. The darkness beneath her lids had been lit with extraordinary colour. Maurice put his hand on her arm, having seen her jump. She put her hand on his, reassuringly, and then closed her eyes again slowly.

It was as though someone were adding droplets of colour to a swirling glass. They spread, sprouted prongs of lighter shades, danced with the other droplets, each note a colour, each colour a note. Ochre, green, iridescent turquoise, and the brightest of blues.

As the notes rose, the hues gained vibrancy, they played faster and faster and the colours swirled in rings around each other, pulsing, throbbing, until the notes reached a crescendo and the image stood still, hovering, vivid and yet fragile, as though the slightest breeze may blow it away. Then, one by one, the notes resumed, as though the sounds were picking their way down a mountain side, the tints and tones eddying, flowing gently around each other, growing fainter, until with the dying of the last note, the colours faded into darkness.

Hamida opened her eyes. Olivia had lowered her bow, and Alex slowly closed the lid of the piano. No one said a word.

22

June brought with it a warmth that Hamida had desperately missed. The sunlight seemed to soak into her hair until it was almost too hot to touch. It tinged Maurice's with flecks of mahogany and turned his cheeks pink and his forearms a rich brown. They were walking back from the market, their arms laden with the vegetables and herbs they had piled into brown paper bags and blue plastic ones; the tangy, rich scent of the vine tomatoes mixing with the punnets of strawberries Hamida cradled against her chest.

They talked amblingly, side stepping the other pedestrians who filled the hot high street.

"We should get ice cream," suggested Hamida as they walked past the front of a small store, its window filled with patisseries and cakes that looked as though they objected to being in the heat.

"Great idea!" Maurice perched his bags on one of the iron chairs outside the shop front. "I'll go in, you wait here with the bags? What flavour do you want?"

"Lemon."

Maurice headed inside. Hamida sat in a chair next to the bags. She pulled out a strawberry and bit into it, its flesh just the right mixture of soft and resistant, its flavour bursting into her mouth, just the right combination of sharp and sweet. She watched the people walking by. The woman in the sleeveless blouse who pulled a small and reluctant looking dog on a leash, the old man in a grey coat who shuffled along barely lifting his feet from the ground, pulling a battered shopping trolley behind him with a jolting rhythm; the three teenage boys, dressed in black tracksuits who were shoving each other as they jaunted down the road. She hadn't noticed the old woman approach her table.

"Do you mind if I sit here, dear?"

Hamida looked up at her. Her hair was curly and white, arranged in a neat and unmovable shape around her head. She wore a patterned blouse and a pleated cream skirt. She leaned to one side, supported by her cane.

"Not at all," said Hamida, moving some bags off one of the chairs to make room.

The woman lowered herself carefully onto the metal seat. "Gosh, it's good to take the load off your feet. When you get to my age, you can't always handle the weight of your own presence." She laughed, sounding in that moment just like Hamida's grandmother. The similarity caught Hamida in the back of her throat. She smiled, swallowing the sudden surge of longing.

The woman looked up at the bright blue sky. "It's going to rain soon."

"Do you think so?"

"Oh, I know so. I can feel it in my joints. These ones," she ran a finger over the enlarged knuckles of her hand. She nodded.

Maurice emerged from the shop carrying two pots of ice cream. He smiled at the old lady.

"Don't mind me," she said, closing her eyes, soaking up the sunshine and the relief of stillness. Hamida took the pot of pale-yellow ice cream from him.

"Do you like lemon?" she asked the woman, as she held out the pot.

"Oh, I couldn't take your ice cream, dear, you eat it."

"Please, I insist," said Hamida.

The woman's entire face broke out into a smile, "No one's bought me ice cream in a very long time," she said, taking the small pot in ever so slightly shaking hands.

Maurice and Hamida sat with the old lady, sharing their tub of cherry ice cream as she chatted to them about the area. She'd lived here for sixty-two years, she said, and she'd never met a couple as nice as them in all that time. Maurice looked at Hamida, who was scraping out the last of the creamy streaks from the pot and smiled. He knew it wasn't him who had such an effect on people.

"You two better get going before the rain comes if you don't have an umbrella," said the old lady, looking up at the sky again.

"Rain?" asked Maurice, squinting up. "Are you sure?"

"Positive," she replied.

"It was a pleasure to meet you," Hamida said, putting her hand to her chest as she got up from the table.

"The pleasure was all mine, dear," smiled the old woman.

They had barely rounded the corner of the high street when the clouds came rolling in. "Would you look at that, she was right," remarked Maurice as the street was quickly darkened by the shadows. "We better hurry."

They clutched their bags and broke into a brisker pace. They were a few streets away from the apartment block when the thunder cracked, its boom echoing off the tall buildings around them. "*Merde*," muttered Maurice, walking faster.

The rain started with a hiss, which turned into a crackle, and then a gushing as the heavy drops came pelting down, turning all the dimples and furrows in the pavement into dirty grey puddles. They ran as fast as their loads would let them, dodging the other soaking pedestrians, and the walls of water thrown up by cars and buses as they passed.

They arrived at the apartment block panting. The deluge had flattened Maurice's hair to his head, water dripping from the pointed ends of his now straightened curls, his shirt stuck in ripples and ridges to his back. Only his chest was partly dry from the protection of the bags, some of which were now beginning to burst, the brown paper soaked in places.

He had put the bags down in front of the elevator and was digging in his shrivelled pocket for the key.

"I have it," Hamida reminded him. He looked up at her.

"What the...?" He put a hand out to touch her hair. "You're completely dry." He ran his hand over her arm and spun her around to see her back. "How did you...?"

Hamida looked at him quizzically, as though perplexed by his half formed but obvious question. The elevator pinged as it reached the ground floor and its door opened. His mouth was still half open. The doors closed.

He took her bags from her and put them on the floor next to the lift and examined her again. He looked back at the entrance doors. It was still pouring outside, perhaps even heavier than when they had come in.

"Come outside," he said, heading to the doors.

"Are you serious? It's still raining," she said, looking at him worriedly.

"Exactly, and you're bone dry!" he exclaimed. He held the door open for her and then braced himself and stepped out into the street. The rain hammered against his skin, straight through his clothes. He wrapped his arms around himself and turned to Hamida. She was standing there, her feet on the edge of a large puddle that had formed outside the door, looking at him with the same quizzical expression. The rain seemed to be thrashing down around her, and yet there she stood, as dry as she had been before the torrents had begun. He put his hand on her and noticed that he no longer felt the stinging on his skin. He took his hand away, and the pelting resumed. He did it again, and again. Each time, the same result.

If there was a question to ask or a sentence to be said that would have helped him make sense of this situation, he was not sure what it would have been. And yet, at the same time, it did make sense. On some strange level, this was not strange at all.

"Come on," she said, as she pulled the door open, ushering him inside. "You're soaking wet."

*

The kitchen was filled with billowing clouds of steam and pungent aromas. The condensation dripped down the small windowpanes that looked out over the park, still battered by the summer storm outside.

"You need to cut the eggplant a bit smaller," Hamida called over the loud hiss of the onions she had just thrown in the pan.

"*Oui, chef*!" replied Maurice, saluting her with his knife as he chopped finer.

She stirred the other pot on the stove. She enjoyed the quiet concentration, the artistry of cooking. Her grandmother had taught her the importance of attention to food. The blending of colours, scents, flavours, textures, the respect for the integrity of each ingredient, the way of reading the readiness of fruit with your fingers, the sequence of recipes from smelling the spices blend. She wondered what her grandmother would think were she to wander into the kitchen and see her, standing over a stove next to this foreign man, whose apron she had tied and whom she was teaching to cut vegetables like an artist wielded her brush. Hamida turned to the door, almost expecting to see her standing there. The doorway was empty. She turned back to the stove, and watched the onions slowly turn translucent, catching colour at their edges. She showed Maurice how to add the tomatoes. He caught the colour in her cheeks as she explained now how to wash the lentils and could not help but kiss her. She laughed at him, and then made him wash them again.

They laid the table together, bowls on top of plates, knives, forks, spoons, glasses, napkins, spread out like a mandala around the flowers in the vase in the middle. Maurice wished they were not having company. If he had had the freedom to, he would, in that moment, have taken her by the hand, pulled the door closed behind them and jumped into the first taxi to the airport. They would have headed for the middle of nowhere, leaving no trace behind them, shut the door on the world and existed in the other's embrace. Before he could wonder why it was that he didn't, the doorbell rang.

Stefan strolled in as he usually did, scanning the room as if assessing the best angle to position himself in. Kerry came in moments later, her short dark hair falling over her eyebrows as she bent to take off her shoes.

She flicked it off her face with a sharp movement of her head as she stood up.

The guests ate hungrily. The food was of the type that left you both full, and with room for more. Maurice got up and filled the water jug.

"Tell us about your research, Maurice," said Kerry, tearing off a piece of flatbread.

"Yeah, we've told you about ours," added Stefan, pouring himself a drink.

"Are you sure you want to get me started?" Maurice laughed. "You may regret it."

"Nah," said Kerry. "It sounds really interesting."

"Well, just remember it was you who asked!" Maurice helped himself to more of the yellow *daal* and a spoonful of yoghurt. "You know I'm in neurotheology, which is basically an examination of the neuroscience of religion and spirituality. It's a new field, one which gets schtick from both camps, the science crowd and, of course, the religious nuts. My supervisor specialises in mapping neurological responses to worship and religious images."

Hamida listened as she piled two spoonfuls of rice onto her plate. She had heard Maurice describe his study numerous times, every time with a slightly different spin, as though he were discovering something new about it each time he spoke.

"There have been a couple of studies which have done similar things. There's a bunch of scientists who found that intense spiritual contemplation, what you might call prayer or meditation, triggered areas in the brain that meant the practitioners, the people meditating, perceived whatever they were experiencing as real. Tangible."

"Now, see, there's my problem," said Stefan loudly, pointing his fork at Maurice. "Sure, we need more studies and all the rest of it, but what these things are proving is what we've been saying all along. Religion is all in your head. God's in your head." He jabbed his fork as he spoke and then dug it back into the rice.

"What gets me," added Kerry, who had wiped the last of her sauce from her plate with the bread, "is that here we are doing all these experiments to prove God doesn't exist, when the burden of proof is totally on the shoulders of people who say he does! That's how rational arguments work. If you make a claim, you have to prove it. It's not my job to disprove it. And the bigger your claim, the better your proof has to be!"

"Muslims are the worst when it comes to this," Stefan resumed his pointing. "It's like they don't understand what proof even means. I was with this guy the other day, how he got into our PhD group, I'll never understand. The guy's a moron. Anyway, so we're having this discussion about the teleological argument, you know Pailey's Watch, how if you came across a watch in the middle of nowhere you would assume it had been designed by someone, rather than having just appeared?"

"Yeah, yeah," Kerry rolled her eyes, "the argument that something intelligent has to have an intelligent designer."

"Precisely. I won't go into the refutations of the theory but anyway, this guy starts banging on about how the Quran contains complex scientific facts, and how this proves that it must have come from God. And all I wanted to do was say, you idiot, that book you're talking about tells men to hit their wives, what does *that* say about where it came from?"

Hamida collected her dishes from the table and walked towards the kitchen.

"And besides," Stefan continued, "if creation reflects its creator, then whatever made you must be dumb as..."

Hamida put the plates down with more force than she realised. Maurice craned his head to look through the kitchen door. Stefan was still talking.

Hamida came back into the room. She stood at the table, her fingertips either side of her chair. Stefan stopped halfway through his next sentence, and looked towards her.

"It's not reflection," she said, shaking her head. "It's refraction."

"Refraction, what is this physics? Why are you defending that moron?" Stefan asked, frowning.

"You're looking at the wrong thing," said Hamida, taking a glass and placing it at the edge of the table by the lamp. The light hit it and made a pattern of scattered beams across the table. "You're confusing this," she pointed to the glass, "with this." She pointed to the lamp. "And so is your Muslim friend."

Before he could catch himself, Maurice clapped loudly. Stefan snorted through his nose and reached for the jug of water.

"I mean... you still gotta prove there's a lamp."

23

As she lay that night, wrapped in a thin white sheet, entwined in Maurice's arms, their limbs entangled, their chests alternating with the rise and fall of each other's, Hamida dreamt of a trading ship.

The woman at the helm was Maryam uz-Zamani. She wore a headdress made entirely of gold. With her earrings, she could have purchased the crown jewels of Queen Victoria. With a single word, she could have raised an army. She owned a fleet of trading ships and was the richest woman in the world. They sailed now on her ship, Rahimi, which every year carried passengers across the seas to the shores of Arabia from whence they would make their journey to perform the pilgrimage.

Hamida was looking out over the water. All was quiet but for the rolling of the waves, the billowing of the sails, and a melody of chimes she could not quite distinguish. She turned to the deck. The other passengers were moving around slowly. The tinkling sound was coming from them. Each of them, she realised, was made of glass.

The hand on her shoulder was the captain's. The woman in gold. It was time, she said silently. Together, Hamida Begum and Maryam uz-Zamani lowered the body of the woman, shrouded in silk to the water's surface. The passengers had gathered around them. The light, passing through a thousand people, fell upon the shroud now, bouncing off the waves around it.

Hamida watched the waves carry the woman away, past the horizon. Then she looked out over the helm of the ship, still set on its course. She placed her hands on the wheel.

That night, exactly two hundred days after Hamida had departed, her grandmother passed away in her sleep.

*

Hamida had awoken with a sadness; a sense of loss so intense she had run her hands over her body as if to determine whether it was a part of her that was missing. She sat up in bed, suddenly frantic at the realisation that she could not find her beads. Carefully, so as not to wake Maurice who was sleeping beside her, she slid out of bed. She ran her hands under the pillow and the duvet, checked under the bed, her pulse quickening, her breath becoming slowly more audible. She stopped, and closed her eyes, trying to collect herself. Where was this feeling coming from? She tried to turn back the pages of her dream, as if to identify the thread that might explain how this tear had opened up inside of her. She could not remember it.

The doorbell rang. Maurice, his head covered with a pillow, did not stir. Hamida opened the door and saw the woman who had first shown her around the apartment, and a wave of dread washed over her. She had purposely not counted the days and had surrendered all concepts of the passing of time. Only sunrise and sunset reminded her that she would not stay here with Maurice forever.

She repeated the woman's request, as if making sure she had heard correctly.

"Both of us?"

"Yes, that's right. Both of you need to pack and be ready by four thirty, the plane is leaving at seven."

"Where are we going?"

The woman looked at her in surprise, as if she should have known the answer to this question.

"I don't know, I'm afraid. It's just my job to get you on the plane. I'll be back at four."

Hamida walked back into the bedroom and put her hand on Maurice's shoulder, shaking him gently.

"We're leaving."

Maurice turned over slowly onto his back. He had known, in the half-suspended sleep state that he had drifted in and out of almost all night, that tomorrow marked the end of this phase of their journey. He knew they were going back to Cumbria together, and whilst he knew a new chapter was beginning, he could not imagine how anything could compare to the time they had spent together here, insulated, but for the mandatory intrusions of Michael's instruments of immersion. Something in him had wanted to go to sleep that night and simply not have woken up. But sleep is cruel and evades one in the moments they seek it most.

*

"What is this bullshit?"

"Sir?"

"'A sense of otherworldliness', 'humming', 'staying dry in the rain', I thought this guy was doing a PhD in neuroscience, what is he turning into a fucking sap?"

Cooper bent slightly over Michael's shoulder to examine the reports he was reading. Michael tossed them across the desk. Cooper stood back up quickly.

"If he's going to write gibberish, tell him he's fired. I agreed to let him stay but if I get any more of this mumbo jumbo crap, he can kiss his contract goodbye. I want facts not fairy tale drivel. He's starting to sound like a fucking fanatic."

"I'll tell him, sir. I'm sure there's a reasonable explanation."

Michael grunted and picked up the next folder of papers on his desk.

"These are from the cartographer?"

"Yes, from Ordnance Survey. He just needs a final signature from you on the option you've chosen. If you have chosen one, sir?"

"I have. And now, Cooper, I need you to get me in touch with someone from the National Trust. I need exclusive access to this," he slid a map over from the other side of his desk and jabbed at the area he had circled, "for a week. The final week. Tell them it's for a film project. They'll buy it. And…" he said, now rummaging in his desk drawer, pulling out his cheque book. He scribbled down a number and signed his name, "send them this as a donation."

Cooper did not raise his eyebrows at the amount, but very easily could have. He folded the cheque and slipped it into his top pocket.

"I'll get in touch with them right away."

"Priest's Hole," Michael said, pointing again at the map, tapping his finger, "it's up near Dove Crag, Ambleside. I want the area cordoned off."

Michael had picked through the options with meticulous attention, scrutinizing the pictures, visualizing the event: Priest's Hole - a shallow cave gouged into the steep rockface, barely five meters in depth, looking out over the rippling crags, hills and valleys of the area; and the girl - prepared, alone. This is where it would happen. The culmination, the coming together of each step of Hamida's preparation. Here, she would finally be ready for the outpouring of whatever was within her in a moment of intense, isolated concentration, precisely what had really happened with Muhammad. But this time, all on record, every minute, every second, every indisputably human breath. Religion, finally, hoist by its own petard, foiled by its own methods.

Cooper's eyes flitted to the area circled on the map, in the middle of which the name of the cave was inked in tiny round black letters between tight dotted contour lines. "Yes, sir." He folded the map carefully and slid it into the breast pocket of his jacket next to the cheque.

Michael grunted again. How he had existed in the world without the social lubricant that vast sums of money provided, he was not sure. But then, he had not needed to move mountains.

"Right, now is the instructor here?"

"She is, sir. She arrived last night and she's staying in the East Wing."

"And you've checked her out? No religious, spiritual crap?"

"I have. She is a qualified nurse, has a Master's in Nutrition, and is a certified mindfulness instructor. She trained in various meditation practices around the world but does not ascribe to a religion herself. I checked her references thoroughly and ran an in-depth background check on her myself, social media sites, the whole lot."

Michael let out a deep sigh in spite of himself. He still could not shake the heavy feeling of dread that had settled around him like a shroud in the early hours of that morning. The knowledge that each of the remaining components of his plan were slotting into place gave him some relief but did not lift the sensation from him completely.

Cooper watched as Michael flicked through the papers on his desk. His skin looked sallow, and the bags beneath his eyes were grey and heavy. He scanned the room discretely, taking in the glasses on various surfaces, the papers scattered in different corners, the lampshade slightly askew, and the scuff marks on the otherwise highly polished wooden floor, which circled the desk in a large oval ring. He would send in the housekeeper later, and ensure she had a key.

"They'll be arriving in fifteen minutes, sir."

Michael did not answer. He seemed to be staring at the desk, deep in thought. Cooper closed the door quietly behind him.

The Land Rover pulled up outside the cottage, where Cooper and Pippa Sullivan were standing waiting to meet them. Maurice stepped out of the car first, turning around to offer his hand to Hamida who climbed out after him. Cooper noticed the glance that passed between them, the lack of distance as they stood in the warm, buttery yellow sunshine of that summer evening. Hamida looked taller, or perhaps she had filled out. Something in her face had changed. Maurice too. His hair was longer, and he had caught colour in his face, but Cooper had the strange sensation that his features had shifted somehow. He also noted the curious sense within himself that he was pleased to see them both, almost akin to having his own children return home, though he had none of his own. He observed these feelings as if standing outside of himself, peering in at a man he did not quite know.

The woman to his right was small, almost birdlike. She was perhaps in her fifties, although her bright smile and dyed, wiry black hair made it impossible to pinpoint her age exactly. She shook their hands warmly as Cooper introduced them.

Pippa turned to enter the cottage, as Cooper held the door open. Maurice followed her in.

"Mr Cooper, if I may…" Cooper turned to Hamida, surprised to hear her voice. She was still standing a few feet away and hadn't moved. He was sure she was taller.

"Yes, Miss Begum?"

"I'd like to ask what this next phase will consist of. I'd be much obliged if you could tell me."

If Cooper was taken aback at her request, he did not show it. She had not asked in earnest, nor, did it seem, with any sense of anxiousness, but rather an assertion of a right, yet without the slightest hint of a demand. He paused. He had had no instructions to inform her of the details of the experiment and had assumed, given her silence, that she was happy to simply cooperate with whatever instructions she was given. But he also had not been told not to tell her. Looking at her now, this young woman, her hair tied back in a bun at the nape of her neck, in a white blouse, and tan slacks, blending in with her surroundings and yet so starkly different, he saw no reason not to. He took a step towards her and turned his back towards the house; he could not be sure whether Michael was watching.

"Ms. Sullivan is here to instruct you in the art and science of fasting and meditation. She will oversee your progress, monitor your responses, and ensure that you are able to carry out this meditation on your own."

Cooper brought up his head and caught Hamida's gaze. In the same way that passing magnets connect, he felt something inside him suddenly drawn by a powerful pull. He shifted on his feet. He should tell her – he wanted to tell her – the information they had received last night via email from Kolkata. The lawyer who had assisted them with drawing up the contract in India, he had sent them word. The guilt welled in his throat. This, Michael had been clear, she should not be informed of. Under no circumstances should she know of the death of her grandmother. Cooper understood the reasons, and yet, was it not her right to know? He opened his mouth, his objections racing to meet the words he may be about to utter.

"Thank you, Mr Cooper." Hamida smiled and headed inside.

*

"Not even water?" Maurice looked mortified.

"Well, Mr Dufort, you're welcome to follow any schedule you wish, I'm under strict instruction to ensure Miss Begum here follows this regimen." Pippa was stacking glass bottles of water into the fridge and pulling open cupboards to ensure no packets or tins had escaped the ruthless stripping of supplies.

Maurice looked embarrassed. Hamida was not objecting, and he felt foolish for having done so. He knew he could not sit and eat whilst she fasted, he couldn't bring himself to allow her to do this alone, and yet even the prospect of hunger was enough to bring out an animalistic desire in him for sustenance.

"So, explain to me again the regimen," he asked, trying to redeem himself.

"It's a form of intermittent fasting, similar to the Muslim practice, but slightly altered. You'll eat at sunrise, then fast until sunset when you'll eat again, and then you'll eat once more at night."

Hamida was watching them both from her seat at the kitchen table; Maurice, pacing around, animated in his objections to the entire concept, and Pippa, sweeping her arms across every shelf of the kitchen cupboards as she spoke to them over her shoulder.

Hamida was no stranger to hunger. There had been days when money had been scarce, and school was out, and all there was to eat was dry bread and limp vegetables, enough perhaps for half a meal. Her grandmother had always insisted Hamida eat, even if she herself went hungry. It was on those days that Hamida searched the corners of their small rooms whilst her grandmother slept, conserving what little energy she had. She had always found something her grandmother had missed. She remembered the time she had found a bag of lentils hidden under an upturned bowl, and another time she'd found onions hanging outside their door. When she awoke, and Hamida showed her what she'd found, her grandmother had stared at her for a long while. Then she kissed her on the forehead and told her to go and play whilst she prepared food for their aching empty stomachs. Hamida remembered that ache. A constricting inside oneself almost as if the stomach were drawing in its walls around itself to reduce its own emptiness.

Pippa had climbed down off the stool now and was leaning with one hand on the kitchen table. "There'll be no stimulants, no coffee or tea, certainly no cigarettes, although I've been told you don't smoke." She smiled at Hamida. "And no intercourse. You'll sleep in separate beds for the duration of this period."

Maurice spun around. "*Qu'est-ce que tu as dit?*" His eyes were wide with horror. "What did you say?"

"No intercourse, Mr Dufort. You'll sleep in the living room, there's a sofa bed installed, I believe."

"Why do I need to sleep in a different bed? We can still sleep in the same room," he asked with an almost pleading tone.

Pippa gave him a wry smile. "Strict instructions, Mr Dufort."

"*Bordel de merde…*" Maurice muttered as he walked out of the kitchen, running his hands through his hair in exasperation.

*

Maurice paced around the sitting room. He walked out of the door, into the kitchen, came back in again, sat down on the sofa, then got back up.

"It's dark outside already, look!"

Pippa smiled at him, "Just a few more minutes."

Maurice let out something between a sob and a groan. Hamida was looking out of the window. It was true, the sky outside had darkened after their first day of fasting, but the sun had not yet dipped beyond the horizon. As much as she missed London, as much as the memory

216

of the meals and freedom scratched at her insides, she had also missed this view. The expanse. The greenery, and the quiet. She had not seen Cumbria in the summer, and the fading light gave the fields a golden tinge that picked out their softest and richest hues.

"Maurice," she put her hand on his arm as he stood next to her. "It's much easier if you concentrate on something else."

"I can't think of anything else. I'm so hungry." He seemed almost in tears.

"Remind me of the time we got lost walking home from the theatre. And that woman was looking for her cat."

Maurice laughed. "Oh yes, what was its name? Something ridiculous."

"Mr Bumbles," Hamida laughed.

"I couldn't figure out what she was doing, walking around in her slippers, calling 'Mr Bumbles, Mr Bumbles!' How long did we help her look?"

"Two hours?"

"Yeah, something like that. And the whole time the cat was in a flowerpot in her front garden." They both laughed now.

"You know, we had a cat when I was a kid…"

Hamida had heard the story but encouraged Maurice to continue talking. It was working.

"We called it Claude. I'd take him to bed with me every night. He'd always escape when I'd fallen asleep, but I'd put him under my cover and then make sure there were no gaps…"

"It's time." Pippa interrupted them with her singsong voice that masked her otherwise ruthless assiduousness. She had brought a tray into the room. Maurice let out a primal moan and threw himself down on the couch expectantly, peering over the edge of the tray to see the sustenance he had waited far too many hours for.

"That's it?"

"For now," replied Pippa.

"Dates, and water and… what? Soup?" The threat of tears had returned to Maurice's eyes.

"Let's just eat, Maurice. Please?" Hamida had sat down next to him and taken a glass of water from the tray.

She closed her eyes and took a big gulp. She felt the cool liquid rush down her throat and hit her stomach. Maurice did the same. A quiet fell over the room; a sudden tiredness that comes with relief. Hamida lent back into the sofa, her glass still in her hand. She looked out of the window across the room. The horizon was turning a deep red, bordered with an encroaching inkiness as night seeped slowly across the sky. The dying of the day seemed somehow mournful. The sinking of the sun some sort of farewell. Perhaps it had not been her hunger that Hamida had tried to distract herself from all day, perhaps it had been the ache of the day before, the feeling of something missing. For a fleeting moment, she wished she was alone, something she had forgotten she was used to feeling. Perhaps then, in the quiet of absence, she could run her fingers along her thoughts and find what it was that had vanished.

Maurice nudged her arm gently. "Here," he handed her a bowl of soup. "You must be starving."

Maurice sat outside on the bench beside the front door, the cigarette glowing in the dark between his fingertips. The smoke creeping upwards in the warm air of the night. He did not smoke regularly, in fact, he'd only smoked twice during the time he'd spent with Hamida. He lifted up the cigarette and examined the gently crackling embers. The smell of smoke reminded him of his uncle, his nicotine and ink-stained fingers, his grating cough. He wondered how much he knew of this experiment. How much did he himself really know about it?

He was aware of the outline of his role: education, seduction, immersion. But now what? Moral support, he supposed. He knew he could leave any time he wanted now that his contract was officially finished. They'd even drive him to the airport, he was sure. He could go back to his flat in Peckham, order a pizza, crack open a can of beer and get back to life as he'd known it before this… what was it? 'Experiment' did not even feel like the right word anymore, not when the person being experimented on had the same effect on him as sitting next to a fire having come in from the cold, or diving into a pool in the scorching heat of summer. Nothing in the contract had prepared him for the knitting of their lives together. He was supposed to arrive, take her round the world, all expenses paid, give her a couple of bunches of flowers, tell her she looked pretty, hang out in London for a bit, meet some interesting people, bring her back again and then let her get on with whatever it was she was supposed to do in Cumbria. But she hadn't let him. Something about her evaded his attempts to rationalise this, to reduce it to merely a set of social interactions.

The reason he had gone into neurotheology was precisely to give a scientific basis to this idea of 'spiritual', 'religious', 'otherworldly'; to demonstrate its physical groundings in the brain and assist in pulling back the curtain on this universal Wizard of Oz that religion so obviously was. And yet, here he was, experiencing the very same 'symptoms' the subjects of his own research described. He wanted to wire Hamida up to an MRI machine, flick a switch and prove to himself that there was nothing different about her at all, he was just in love with her, it was nothing more than a flood of chemicals rushing through his brain, an ancient mechanism designed to encourage procreation and the protection of children. He knew that's what it was. And yet… it wasn't an act, nor was it confined to moments of prayer, or spiritual practice. Apart from the beads which he'd seen her take to bed with her, she had no rituals, no worship. Whatever it was she was, she was always, without exception. He had lived with her for three months now, they'd shared each other's company constantly, travelled with each other, seen each other at the limits of tiredness and irritation, and she'd not changed. The quiet, the calm, the sense of presence without imposition, the sense of grandeur without grandiosity, the energy without the noise. He almost hated her for it, he almost wanted her to slip up, to turn around and snap at him, to slam a cupboard door when she stubbed her toe, to turn around and yell at the universe for first placing her in the prison of the slums, and then the prison of this experiment. He would have.

He wondered now where this sudden rush of exasperation had come from. Perhaps it was because she was not with him. Hamida had gone for a walk. He'd gone to put on his walking boots to go with her, but she'd laid a hand on his chest and told him she wanted to go alone, that she wouldn't be too long. But she was too long. The moment she left he knew it was too long. He stubbed out his cigarette and went inside. The clock read eleven. He ate the bread and white cheese Pippa had laid out for them, wolfing it down quickly just to spite her instructions to eat slowly. Hunger made him angry.

He heard Hamida come in around midnight as he lay awake on the sofa bed that he'd pulled out and thrown some pillows on. He heard her walk slowly up the stairs. He knew she was trying not to disturb him. But the whole thing disturbed him. The exhaustion, the separation, the repetition, the knowledge that he would have to do the same tomorrow, the same as yesterday, the same as the past three weeks. Hunger, separation, tiredness, irritation, the longing for some image or ideal he could not even quite see. He turned over on the bed, pulling the covers off his hot body. He waited until he heard the creek of her bed frame, and the settling of the silence back in the cottage.

Slowly, he tiptoed up the stairs. She was curled up on the far side of the bed, her back to the door. He lifted the covers and climbed carefully in next to her, sliding his arm around her waist and nestling his face into her hair. He breathed her in, inhaling the scent of familiarity and immersing himself back into the calm. She interlaced her fingers in his, and he fell asleep.

*

In the dark, Hamida lay with her eyes open. She knew she had only a few hours until sunrise, and that if she did not sleep, the exhaustion would only exacerbate the hunger. She had been so sure this would be easy. But her familiarity with deprivation had been eroded by the indulgence she had been immersed in. It was not so much the pain that had troubled her, she could distract herself from it, but the mental yearning for fulfilment. The something that was missing had not returned, and in its place had grown a frustration. She reached out to her grandmother, on the step before the slope into sleep, but she had not found her. She had thought at first it was simply the exhaustion, but after a while, she realised it was something else. The distance between them had increased, and she was having trouble traversing it. Where had she gone? Why had she left her? Had she become so familiar with her absence that she had abandoned her altogether? Her grandmother had sent her here, to the depths of distance, as physically far removed as possible, she had always thought, for a purpose, for her wellbeing. Her wellbeing included her grandmother, and yet, she was out of reach. And here she was, in the arms of a man who could still be withdrawn at any moment. The pain of her grandmother's absence had made this threat even more impossible to bear.

She had walked that evening, though not to escape Maurice. Even with his audible and silent protestations at the idea of fasting and meditation, he did not crowd her with noise. She had walked to try to free herself of her own noise. She felt a cluttering inside of her that was unfamiliar. And she still could not find her beads.

24

Sunrise. Dates. Water. Bread. Walk. Pippa's regimen was rigid, and the rations upon which they were subsisting, they realised, were being systematically decreased. Their blood pressure and vitals were regularly monitored, and Pippa assured Maurice that they were receiving sufficient vitamins, minerals, and calories to sustain them. It didn't feel like it, Maurice reiterated, for the hundredth time.

He tried not to drag his feet as they trekked through the fields and up the hills, through copses and across streams. The lands surrounding the estate were beautiful, and there were times when Hamida would feel as though the entirety of her was filling this expanse, as though she did not know where she ended and the greens, blues, golds, whites, and browns of her surroundings began. Some days she watched the ground as she walked, noticing the tiny flowers and multitudes of different types of leaves that grew in amongst the grass and crept out around the pebbles and grit that lined some of the pathways. Other days she concentrated on sounds, the buzzing of bees, the songs of different birds, some she recognised from the days she'd spent in the fields tending the sheep, others that were new. Some warbled, some chirped, some sang, some cried, squirrels chattered, and sometimes in the distance she could hear farm machinery and the lowing of cows. Sometimes she watched Maurice as he walked, the roll of his shoulders, the rhythm of his body as every muscle and bone cooperated in a wave of motion he was unaware of. She watched Pippa, her deliberate paces, her back straight, the way her arms swung as if instruments in a machine, pushing herself forward. And sometimes, more and more frequently she felt, she was aware of nothing but herself. The expanse inside of her. She wandered about inside of it. The archive of memories she found herself lost in, looking for what it was that was missing, the puzzle board of information and new knowledge she had been presented with; people, their poverty of so many types, origins, endings, absence, presence, facts and truth, truths and lies, gods and man, men and women, women and suffering, pain and pleasure, love and longing, waves and energy, music and noise, frequencies and melodies, sounds and silence.

It was on those days that she felt the hunger the most. A hunger that made her skin feel tender, her mouth dry, her lips crack, and her head hurt. Fasting purged them. She dared not open her mouth in the beginning for fear of her own breath as her stomach churned against itself and the enzymes crawled up and out of her as if clawing for food.

As their rations decreased, the hunger seeped out of their skin. The body sought sustenance within itself, breaking down the fat cells and releasing toxins that had encased themselves like air bubbles in ice or ants in amber. She was glad for the space between them in those moments. She told herself it was because of the odours she was emitting, although in truth they were strongest to herself. But really it was because she did not have enough energy to share herself with anyone. She became sensitive to touch, to the act of making contact with another human being. The intimacy she had once wrapped herself in like a second skin became a threat, the sapping of her energy. Even the memories she had of closeness now seemed uncomfortable to her. She feared that were she to lose her last reserves she might snap, push Maurice away, not because she did not want him there but because she was so protective of what she needed to survive, her sanity, that any encroachment may result in a deficit.

Maurice was struggling in his own way. He had no experience with hunger other than cravings, and the occasional rumble when he had skipped breakfast. Hamida's withdrawal into herself at first worried him, then irritated him, then upset him. He'd try to pull conversation out of her in his desperation for distraction. She would smile and nod, contribute comments, but she became gradually quieter with each day, amplifying the silence and all the thoughts in his head with it. He resented her for the distance, though he knew it was not fair to take when he himself had nothing to give. He craved the strangest things: pizza with anchovies, cherry flavoured soda, green apples, a sushi dish they had once in Japan, milk, something soft like cake, but not cake, but not a biscuit, sweet but not sugary and it had to be with tea. He would lie on the couch, his hand over his eyes, pinching his temples, and sleep to pass the time, wrapping himself in blankets, his body cold despite the warmth of the summer sun outside.

After four weeks of deprivation their bodies stopped protesting; the hunger became a background ache, like white noise. Their stomachs shrank to fit the morsels they were fed. It was as though their organs had surrendered and found a way to subsist on what they were being provided with, but they operated at a reduced capacity. Life was slow, everything was a trickle. The sun crawled across the sky as they crawled languidly through the day. They appeared to each other solely in the moments they ate. In the absence of sunlight and presence of food, they rediscovered each other's company quietly, with smiles, soft words, and proximity, before retreating back into themselves as the next day began.

25

Caudale Beck Cottage was built on the eve of the eighteenth century. It was ringed partly by a low wooden fence connected to a drystone wall which had greened with moss and lichen over the centuries. From the windows, the towering peak of a crag they did not yet know the name of loomed, cutting out a slice of sky with its shades of green and brown. The track leading to it had been tarmacked roughly, making the car shudder as Hamida and Maurice were driven around its bends to the building.

Pippa had arrived earlier that morning and would walk over from the other cottage on Hartsop Hall Farm to meet them that afternoon. As they drove deeper into the Lake District, the peaks, hills, and mountains towered up and around them. If Ravenscroft had been beautiful, the area into which they had driven was magnificent.

They threw their bags down in the hallway, pulled off their boots, a habit they now both did instinctively, and sank into the sofas covered with cream throws. The ceiling was low, beamed with wood so dark it was almost grey. The grate in the rough stone fireplace lay unlit. A soft summer breeze stole in every once in a while through the open windows and played with the hair at the napes of their necks and on their forearms.

The past six weeks had exhausted them and invigorated them with an energy that pulsed at a low but constant ebb, as if they had tuned in to a new wavelength and discovered a fresh rhythm of survival. Maurice rested his feet on the low oak coffee table and Hamida hung hers over the side of the couch, her head in his lap. They were aware they needed to unpack, but the newness of the place and the drone of the car drive had seduced them into drowsiness.

There was a knock at the door. Maurice dragged himself to his feet to open it.

"Well, hello, you two. You made it over okay?" Pippa asked cheerfully without expecting a response.

Maurice had developed a begrudging respect for the woman, the boundless energy she seemed to draw from nothing other than her surroundings and her immovability in the face of his relentless resistance. Her cheerfulness still irritated him, perhaps because he now knew it as a mask for more deprivation.

Pippa walked through to the small kitchen which Hamida and Maurice had yet to explore. She put down two bags and a box she was carrying. "Have you been upstairs?"

"Not yet," said Hamida, who had emerged behind them.

"Well, there's four bedrooms to choose from, one has an ensuite. I'd suggest using that one, there's towels already in there. There's more in the airing cupboard though if you decide to use one of the others."

"Where should I sleep?" Maurice enquired, glad at least that no mention had been made of a sofa bed.

"Wherever Hamida sleeps, I presume, unless you'd rather have your own bed?"

"We can share?" Hamida asked, surprised. She had assumed the rules they'd followed at Ravenscroft would apply here too. The most she had been told was that they were relocating here to embark upon the meditation phase.

"You can, although I must insist that there still be no sexual intimacy." She looked pointedly at Maurice as she said this. "Things are going to work a bit differently here. Let's put the kettle on and I'll explain."

Hamida and Maurice exchanged confused glances; this was the first time they had ever heard the suggestion of tea uttered from Pippa's lips. It sounded almost sacrilegious.

As she heated the water in a cast iron kettle on the hob of the small emerald green aga and emptied the boxes of the tins, packets and fresh fruit and vegetables, stocking the small kitchen cupboards, Pippa explained that their fasting period was complete. They should be careful not to overindulge, she warned them, the mind often craved more than the body was capable of accommodating, and just because they could eat, it didn't mean they needed to. She would arrive promptly every morning to begin Hamida's meditation instruction. They'd spend the day together working on breathing exercises and exploring the surrounding areas. Then they would finish the day with a further period of meditation. Maurice had stopped listening after the mention of food and was watching Pippa intently as she unloaded each item from the bags.

Hamida had questions. What time would Pippa arrive? How long would they meditate for? Were there any rules on what they could and couldn't eat? They would have the rest of the day to settle in, get their bearings, and she'd come back at eight o'clock for their first session, Pippa told her. They were free to eat whatever they liked from what was stocked in the house. It was all local produce. How long they would actually meditate would depend on them, she said, but the sessions themselves should last an hour and a half. She left them with a cheerful goodbye and the suggestion of a nap, if they could, before she returned.

Hamida and Maurice sat at the kitchen table across from each other.

"Hungry?" she asked him.

"You know, if you'd have asked me two months ago if I'd be hungry after forty days of fasting, I'd have called you an idiot. But now, I'm really not," Maurice laughed.

"Well, let's go and explore the rest of the house and put our things away," suggested Hamida, standing up before the urge to stay sitting took hold of her completely.

They unpacked in a peaceful silence, peppered with small exchanges, as they wove around each other in the main bedroom, moving from case to cupboard. They chose the main bedroom as Pippa had suggested. It reminded Hamida somewhat of Ravenscroft with its half-slanted ceiling, cream carpets, and magnolia walls. It smelled faintly of wood varnish, hay, and potpourri.

They emptied the suitcases with a slow systematicity, a rhythm that mirrored the tranquillity of their surroundings. When they had finished, they slid the cases under the bed and collapsed onto the soft cotton sheets. Lying on their backs, Hamida's hands folded on her stomach, Maurice's by his sides, they stared up at the ceiling, at the small bubbles where the paint had unstuck itself from the plaster, at the small cobweb hanging from the lampshade that swung in the breeze. Hamida turned onto her side and placed a hand under her cheek. Maurice rolled onto his and faced her, closing his eyes. Somewhere, a tractor was humming. A dog barked. He could smell the scent of her shampoo and her skin. She pressed her lips gently to his and in the newness each rediscovered the other, the limits they had tightened around themselves lifted, and when they had poured forth into the other and quenched a thirst that reached deep down inside them, they fell asleep.

*

"I'm hungry." Hamida had awoken to Maurice stroking her hair. He laughed.

"Me too!"

They pulled on the dressing gowns they had hung on the back of the bedroom door. The air was warm, but they had slept through the hottest part of the day. The heat that remained was pleasant, as though the fire of the summer sun was now only embers. From the bread bin on the countertop, they pulled out a loaf of seeded bread, and rummaging around in the fridge they found two types of cheese, one cheddar and one which seemed to be goats cheese wrapped in waxy white paper. There were two glass bottles of apple juice in the fridge with rubber stoppers, and a jar of treacley black chutney on the shelf. Grabbing plates and knives, they settled themselves at the table. They tore off hunks of the soft bread with a crust that crunched and crumbled in their hungry grasps, and cut off corners of the cheese. They spooned on smatterings of the chutney, and washed it all down with the cold, tart apple juice, its natural sediment stirring from the bottom of the bottles.

They spoke little, though they no longer felt the silence. When they finished, they paused to examine the wreckage of their ravenousness; crumbs of bread and slivers of escaped cheese scattered across the spaces in between their plates. Hamida pressed her fingertip to the seeds that had fallen onto the table. They stuck to her and she brushed them onto her plate. Maurice drained the last dregs of his apple juice and stacked his plate on top of hers. When they dared to look at the clock, they realised they had two hours until Pippa was due to arrive.

By the time she knocked at the cottage door, both Maurice and Hamida had showered and dressed, and were ready for her. They were going to start in the garden, Pippa told them. There was more space outside. She had three mats rolled up under her arm and they each laid one out on the grass near the cottage.

The first thing they would do was a body scan practice. They lay on their backs. The idea was not to empty their minds, Pippa told them, but to concentrate fully on a single thought or sensation. They should start at their toes, feel each one of them. If it helped to move or clench them, they could do that, but they should focus only on each toe in turn until she told them to move on. Observe the feeling, she instructed them. Were they conscious of the muscle movements, the skin, the feeling of their socks against them? If passing thoughts crossed their mind – memories, or associations – they should observe them, but not indulge in them.

"Our thoughts may come from us, but they are not us; we are in charge of them, not held hostage by them." Recognising this was a key to mindful practices, Pippa told them.

The timbre of Pippa's voice lent itself to a lulling sensation, almost as though she was not instructing but subduing them, a wave beneath the boats they felt they were lying in, bobbing gently in the last of the evening rays. From their feet, they progressed up through their calves, knees, thighs, and pelvis to their stomachs. Here they paused for longer. What was happening here? Pippa asked. The stomach often told a person much about their emotional state. Was it tight, nauseous, clenched, uneasy? The chest too, told them much about how they were feeling. Could they feel their chests rise and fall? Could they feel any constriction? Was there anything that quivered somewhere around their hearts and lungs? Hamida focussed on the sensation of rising and falling. With her eyes closed, she could hear her heartbeat, and she realised if she concentrated without overexerting her effort, she could visualise her heart beating in her chest, the ventricles throbbing and pumping blood around her body without her lending the process a single thought. She watched it for a while. The purpley-red flesh pulsing, pushing the blood through the veins with power and speed, indifferent to her emotions; its only response was to beat faster or slower. The clutching she had felt had no physical manifestation, and she wondered why it was that she had sensed it here when she knew her thoughts came from her mind. Was it still there? The tightness? She scanned her chest as Pippa was instructing them. It was. As though she was trapped in a rope that wound around her tighter the more she writhed to try and release herself.

They moved upwards, through the shoulders, which they relaxed, the neck which they stretched, to the jaw, which Hamida had not known she had been clenching. She let her teeth separate from each other, relaxing the muscles in her cheeks. She focused on the muscles around her eyes and unknit the eyebrows she did not realise she had furrowed. Hamida waited for Pippa to move to the brain, to think about what was going on in their heads. Perhaps she could help unravel the tightening threads that seemed to have knotted themselves inside of her mind. But she didn't. She asked them to breathe – seven deep breaths, in through the nose for seven seconds, and out through the mouth for another seven – and then to open their eyes. When they felt ready, they could sit up.

As they rolled up their mats slowly, Hamida felt frustrated although she was careful not to show it. Pippa had felt the session went well, and Maurice seemed bright and enthusiastic, better than he had felt in a long time. Hamida, once again, wished that she was alone. She told Maurice she would come upstairs to bed, she just wanted to put the dishes away in the kitchen.

She pulled each one slowly out of the rack, drying the remaining drips with a tea towel. To describe her as absent minded in that moment would have been inaccurate. Hamida may not have been concentrating on the task of unloading the dishes, but her mind was in no way absent. If she had to describe how it felt, she may have said it was churning, swirling violently with strands of thoughts that caught and pulled on each other, dragging her deep into the undercurrents of her consciousness.

What her grandmother had taught her in the absence of utterances, others had forgotten in the silence. This silence came from a multitude of places. She had seen it in New York, in the distraction of lights and the frenzy to claw a way up from the ground where reality lived. She had seen it in Houston, where the silence had been filled with words which meant nothing in churches as big as stadiums, in Japan where silence was an indifference, a decision to live without, and in Maurice's friends, whose silence was filled with anger. Her grandmother was silent now too. Where was she? Hamida knew she knew the answer to that question. But she also knew she could not admit it.

She did not hear Maurice come down the stairs. She was not aware of his presence at all until he found her standing at the sink, staring out of the window and placed a hand gently on her arm. He did not know where she had gone, but he knew it was somewhere inside of herself. It was not sadness or sorrow, but a depth he simply did not have the words for. He wrapped his arms around her beneath the soft cotton sheets, in the hope that wherever she was, he might bring some of her back.

26

On the other side of sleep, Hamida found herself by a fountain. The water trickled into it gently from a marble carving in its centre. She reached down to touch its surface and it rippled. She watched the rings reach out to the furthest edges. As the surface settled, she realised that the face reflected on the surface was not her own. The woman's hair was white. And she was smiling. She turned from the fountain to see her grandmother.

The tears in Hamida's eyes formed the question. Her grandmother's smile gave her the answer.

They walked along a marble pathway, along a stream that fed into the fountain behind them, to a garden. In the garden was a ring of peacocks, circling. They parted as Hamida and her grandmother neared the circle, then closed around them again.

From somewhere both in the distance and inside of her, Hamida heard a low thrumming, like the beating of a thousand wings. The sound had a rhythm, the rhythm had words, but she could not make them out. The peacocks were circling faster now, their golds and resplendent blues becoming a blur. The thrumming became louder, Hamida closed her eyes. When she opened them, her grandmother was standing before her. She had two chalices in her hands: one of ruby, one of pearl. She held them between her fingers and offered them to her granddaughter. Hamida took the pearl chalice and drank.

The thrumming stopped. When she lowered the cup, Hamida saw she was standing in a ring of women. Each dressed in royal blue. On their heads, each wore a golden crown. Hamida looked at every face in turn.

She recognised her own in each one of them. If she had counted, she would have found that altogether they numbered twenty-nine.

The Empress of Empresses placed her hand on Hamida's brow. Another placed her hand on her shoulder. One by one, each of them placed their hand on her, and they began once again to move in their circle. The humming now started again. They moved faster and faster and faster, as if binding and unravelling her in the same movement.

Their colours blurred, their faces merged, until they moved so fast that all Hamida could see was light. And then… nothing. Just a humming. It was everywhere and nowhere. Audible and silent. Inside of her, just as she was inside of it.

From the everything and nothing, her grandmother stepped forth. Into the palm of Hamida's hand that had always been outstretched, she placed something cold. She closed Hamida's fingers over it, and kissed her on the forehead.

When Hamida awoke in the middle of the night, and opened her palm, she found her beads inside.

*

Pippa arrived early the next morning. The three of them sat on chairs in the dewy grass, their bare feet against the blanket of droplets that had settled overnight. It was important they place their feet fully on the ground, their hands on their knees, relax their shoulders and loosen their jaws. Pippa wanted them to pick a sound and listen to it. It could be the birds, their own breathing, the sound of the tractor in the distance. It didn't matter if the sound was not consistent. If it disappeared, they simply had to wait for it again. It was important, she told them, just to listen. If they found themselves distracted, all they had to do was bring themselves back to the moment and listen again.

Maurice picked out the sound of a nightingale that was busying itself somewhere nearby. Pippa herself focused on her breathing, the steady, rhythmic hiss and rush of her breath as it was inhaled and exhaled through her nose and into her lungs. Hamida chose the humming.

*

Priest's Hole had been cleared of the litter intrepid climbers had left over the years; the spare cans, the extra bedding, empty bottles, things they told themselves that if they left the climb down would be easier. In their place, a web of interconnected wires and instruments had been discretely installed around the cave walls and at its wide gaping mouth. There should be no flashing lights, or sounds of any type, Michael had insisted. There were cameras craning from behind rocks at all angles, sound and motion sensors, heat sensors, temperature monitors, infrared equipment, and radio wave detectors. A flat wooden surface had been laid in one corner, covered in foam mats and foil sheets, the type that racers are wrapped in when they collapse at the finish line. Provisions had been made for basic sanitation, a lock box had been fully stocked with food and water. In the middle, facing the mouth of the cave, was a dense foam block, a cube, covered in thick cream leather such that it could be picked out when only the light of the moon shone in. Here, Hamida would sit, facing the mouth of the cave, Pippa explained.

"A week?" Hamida asked her, without taking her eyes off the mouth of the cave. She was standing with her hands on the drystone wall that blocked some of the entrance of Priest's Hole, built by unknown hands to keep out at least some of the elements. It did not obstruct the view. From where she stood, Hamida could see for miles across the rugged undulations of mountains and hills, valleys, and ravines of the Lake District; the greens that looked yellowed from this distance and that seemed to change colour imperceptibly every day, slopes with gaping gashes of grey rock exposed by the clawing of time against the hillsides, shadows that danced around the peaks throughout the day.

Hamida looked down towards the steep gravelly path up which they had climbed that morning when the horizon had still been pink and had not yet completely cast off its covers of darkness. The sky now was growing in brilliance, dying itself brighter shades of blue in indistinguishable increments. It was not the blue of Kolkata, one that burned almost white, but Hamida knew if she followed the horizon, the dust would eventually rise to meet her.

The cave was around four miles from the cottage as the crow flies, and it had taken them several hours to make the trek. Maurice was sitting on a rock by the path below, swinging his feet and throwing small pebbles. He had not said a word when they had entered the cave, and Hamida had not noticed him leave.

"That's what I've been told, yes. A week."

Hamida nodded. "And who will be watching?" She gestured her head towards the craning cameras that Pippa had pointed out.

"Your benefactor will be monitoring you. I'll be periodically checking your vitals to make sure you're okay."

Hamida nodded again. She suddenly became aware of the coolness of the stones beneath her fingers and felt a shiver. The day was getting hotter but inside the cave was cool. She ran her hands along the rough rocks, feeling the jagged bumps nick against her palms and fingers.

"Any more questions before we leave?"

"What if something goes wrong?" Hamida asked, finally turning her body away from the mouth of the cave towards Pippa.

"Well, we'll be able to see what's happening on the monitors, and we'll get a rescue team up immediately. But everything has been thoroughly checked. The area is cordoned off so no one will disturb you, and there's an emergency phone by the generator outside if you absolutely need it."

Hamida looked up at the unblinking eyes of the cameras and nodded slowly, wondering if she was already being watched.

They lingered only moments in their goodbyes. Pippa was cheerful, patting Hamida's arms as though to check she were completely put together before leaving. Maurice was quiet. He embraced her only briefly for fear of feeling her already slip away inside of herself. It was painful enough that he had to leave her, he did not want to sense her leaving him. From the mouth of the cave, Hamida watched them both pick their way carefully down the path, shrinking as they descended until finally they disappeared completely.

With her eyes still fixed on the wide intensities of blues and greens, she pulled the beads out of the back pocket of her trousers and rolled them between her fingers.

They were warm from the heat of her body. Other than the low breathing of the wind, their faint clicks as they brushed past each other in her palm were the only sounds she could hear.

It must be well into the afternoon, she thought, taking note of the sun which had passed its zenith now. She leant against the wall again. The scene was beautiful, achingly so; the type of untampered naturalness that inspired a painful, overwhelming awe, all framed, amplified, by the dark stone ring of the cave's mouth. The sun felt hot on the backs of her hands as it crept its way inside the cave now. A bee settled on a clump of clover on the other side of the path.

The human capacity for internal contradiction is universal and perhaps most pronounced in moments of freedom. As Hamida stood facing the unending view and the seven days that stretched out before her, she felt both a profound and weighty calm settle over her, and an acute needle of fear pierce her chest. The prospect of undisturbed solitude, she had not realised, was something she had longed for. The opportunity to sit with herself, to take each of her thoughts in turn and piece them together, cut them apart, examine them and rearrange them again was something for which she needed quiet. Not the comfortable quiet she enjoyed in Maurice's presence, for even in their silence they were always communicating. She needed the quiet that only the silence of solitude could provide. Only then could she listen and respond. And yet, she was afraid, when she finally listened, of what she might hear. What was it that she was saying? What was it that was being said?

Hamida turned away from the horizon. The cool shadows of the cave invited her into their depths. It was at once a safe and terrifying place, cavernous yet close as though its sides pressed against her when she was not looking like the walls of a womb. The light was constantly moving, as if searching for something hidden in the jagged cracks, the dark crevices, under the slabs of rock that made up the uneven floor. How many eyes had cast their searching glances over the stones? How many souls had sought shelter in these rough walls? Had they found what they were looking for? Hamida picked her way carefully over the rugged surface towards the cream block. What had they seen? What had they heard? On a makeshift seat facing the mouth of the cave, her beads in her hand, Hamida sat and closed her eyes.

*

"What is she holding?" asked Michael, peering at the screen. The image was clear and the sound quality so crisp he could hear Hamida's footsteps on the loose stones. But whatever it was she was clutching he could not make out.

"I'm not sure, sir." Cooper, behind him, could not make out the object either.

"Get Maurice in here as soon as he's back. I want to know what's in her hand."

"Yes, sir."

Michael checked the screens and monitors the engineer had installed in the room next to his office. Hamida was sitting in the centre of the cave, her eyes closed. A slight crackling came through the speakers. Michael looked up at the equalizer bars, the coloured columns indicating the presence of noise. They rippled slightly with the low sounds they were detecting. It must be the breeze, he thought. He loosened his tie and undid the top button of his shirt, and settled back in his chair, watching the screens.

Hamida felt a breeze blow into the cave, stroking her across her cheeks and collar bone. She began with her noise. Similar to the process of sifting through lentils, she began by picking out the stones from her thoughts. What would happen when this week was over? She imagined herself on a plane, watching the green of England grow fainter beneath her as it eventually gave way to ocean, and then to clouds. She imagined running through the streets of the slum, dodging the crowds of people, gathering dust on her shoes that had never known Kolkata dirt and finding her grandmother sitting outside the breezeblock hut, washing tin plates. She felt something swell in her chest as she imagined embracing her. But what about her dream? Her grandmother had not said anything in it, and it was just a dream. She'd had dreams before, the manifestations of her fears in various forms, or the presence of loved ones who had appeared to comfort her in times of uncertainty. It was just a dream. Her grandmother was alive and waiting for her, and Hamida was desperate to return.

But reunion came with the cost of separation. Maurice's face swam before her in the crisp clarity of temporal proximity which she realised her grandmother's face no longer had. She had to work to remember her grandmother's features, and she felt guilty for it. Maurice she could recall as if he were standing right in front of her, but her grandmother's edges were blurred, her features fuzzy. Her presence she could summon, but her outline alluded her.

Hamida breathed deeply. A tension spread from her jaw, through her neck, her shoulders, and wrapped itself tighter around her chest again. The woman who had sent her here was disappearing, and not only was she becoming fainter but returning to her now meant leaving something else, someone with whom her own outline seemed intertwined. Could she put Maurice on a plane, ask him to live with her in the middle of a mass of human squalor? Could she ask her grandmother to come and live in the lap of luxury? That would be easier, and yet if her grandmother could have come, surely she would be here. She had stayed and sent Hamida away. Had Hamida fulfilled whatever it was she had been sent here to achieve? At least, she was sure, that whatever her grandmother had received by way of payment would at least ensure them a better future. Perhaps they could move, perhaps she could come here after all, perhaps there was a way to unite these two disparate parts of her, knit them together around her so she would not have to lose any more of those she loved ever again. Perhaps.

She felt the tightness loosen then tighten again. Was that all she was here for? A financial reimbursement? To take part in some program for some rich someone? Hamida could not believe that her grandmother would have done it for mere financial compensation. Their bond was too important to have been severed solely for monetary reasons. She knew her grandmother believed that. She knew her grandmother believed her to be special, but was this what she had in mind? To be shipped off to be part of some experiment? Surely, this did not make her special. Surely, any one of the girls who she had been at school with could have been chosen. They were all poor, they had learned English, they needed the money and, in fact, they were desperate to escape, unlike Hamida had been. She knew what her grandmother would have told her; that it was her imperial blood – the blood of the generations of women from Persia to the furthest reaches of the Mughal Empire that ran in her veins – that made her special, that marked her out for whatever it was that had been promised. But Hamida knew she was not the only descendent of the Mughal line, and the empire had died generations ago. She knew the history her grandmother did not tell her. She knew how their lands had shrunk, how their battles had been lost, how the kingdom they ruled had dwindled to a province, then a palace, and then a name, and then to dust.

"I'm not special," Hamida said in silence. "I am not special." There was no empire. There was no throne. She was here, in a cave, alone. She could not leave. Where would she go? How would she ever get back? And what would happen to her grandmother if she did? Would all of this have been in vain? Could she look her grandmother in the eyes and say aloud what she'd said all along? She was not special. And yet still her grandmother had sent her away. She sent her away. She sent her away.

"You sent me away!" Hamida screamed this inside of herself. "You sent me away! Why did you get to choose? You didn't send me to freedom, you sent me to a prison. A place of rules, of enforced indulgence and deprivation, a cold exposure to the indifference of people the world over, their obliviousness, their poverty and their greed, their knowledge and their ignorance."

She felt hot tears stream down her face. "The least you could have done was keep me with you. Now, I don't even know how to get home." Her sobs were audible now. Her shoulders shook, and her tears poured between her fingers as she covered her face and bent her head to her knees. She was not sure how long she cried. But when the shaking stopped and the scalding stream of grief and anger had poured out of her, Hamida found herself utterly exhausted. Making her way slowly to the hard flat surface that had been laid out as her bed, she curled up under the blankets and fell into the oblivion of sleep.

By the time she awoke, darkness had fallen. She sat up on the mats and pulled the blankets around her shoulders. Night had brought with it a coldness and strange assortment of sounds. Hamida listened to the fullness that the dark seemed to bring. A sliver of moon illuminated the clouds that cloaked it in a luminous grey, every now and then breaking through the inkiness of the sky and casting a creamy light over the tips of the mountains which caught on the corners of the rocks at the mouth of the cave and stole its way inside.

A new kind of quiet descended. Though the sounds from outside – the chirping of crickets, the whistle of the gentle wind around the hills – were louder than those she had experienced during the day, the noise she had brought with her inside the cave had somewhat cleared. She felt with her hands around the edges of the cave, the stone surface an unpredictable journey of jagged edges, smooth worn surfaces, and crumbling crevices. There was a smell she had not noticed before, amplified perhaps in the lack of light. An oldness, a mixture of damp and dry, and centuries of existence, the odour of the inside of the earth.

She found the water bottle, twisted open the lid and drank. Fumbling with the clasp, she pulled out one of the energy bars from the lock box, tucked the wrapper into the compartment at the side, and stepped carefully back to the block in the centre of the cave floor.

27

"You cannot simply throw together the ingredients and expect to produce a dish."

Dufort was sitting on an armchair in Michael's office. His trench coat, which by now Michael had realised must be a permanent fixture of the man's existence, was open and hung loosely by his sides. His deep-set eyes were staring intently at Michael who stood at the window, swilling his drink slowly, the late afternoon light bouncing off the edges of the cut glass and through the amber liquid.

"Dufort, I did not invite you here at this crucial point of the experiment, six days in, to criticise."

"I am not criticising, *mon ami*. I am merely... cautioning. Preparing you for what may be... disappointment. This has never been done before, and the idea that one experiment will produce the extraordinary results you are hoping for..."

"What results am I hoping for, Dufort, do remind me?" There was an edge of sarcasm in Michael's tone; a challenge to a man who himself had barely come to terms with his own ineptitude in the face of the same enemy.

Dufort had met with too much spite in his past to be moved to irritation by Michael now. He could see his slowly emaciating form, the rings on his desk from innumerable glasses, the lack of sleep evident from his greying skin and the reds of his irises. Hope was not enough to produce results, but neither was anger.

"You want to have created a modern-day antichrist, the antithesis to religion using its own methods. You submerged this girl in the substance of science and hope that she will eventually sing a hymn to atheism. You wanted to use religion against itself. And all I am saying is that…"

"I don't have time for your doubt, Dufort."

"Doubt? Doubt is the language of religion, *mon ami*. I do not bring doubt, I bring a reminder of scientific reality. Experiments require repetition, honing, meticulous reworkings to ensure that all the components are present and in their correct quantities."

"I have been meticulous. Every step has been monitored. Every action observed. Every component precisely worked out."

Michael turned his back on Dufort and looked out of the window. The bracken, the fields, the endless expanse. All it would take was one match. One spark. A single flame. And it was about to be lit.

*

Back in the monitoring room, with Dufort's doubts still stinging the edges of his consciousness long after he had left, Michael banged his palm on top of the speaker. "Fucking piece of junk! Cooper!"

"Yes, sir." Cooper emerged swiftly into the room.

"Call the engineer and ask why this fucking interference is still coming through on the speakers."

"I called him on Monday, sir, the first time you asked. He assured me the equipment was in perfect working order, and he ran a systems check on all the sound equipment."

"That was six days ago. Call him again!"

"Yes, sir."

Michael looked back at the screen, and the image of Hamida sat so still he wondered if maybe the cameras had stopped working. The digital time stamp in the corner reassured him that they were still running.

"And the storm, sir?"

"What?"

Cooper's voice was calm, despite Michael's barbed tones. "The storm. There are reports of a heavy storm on the way, hitting tonight, within a few hours. I wonder if we should…"

"She doesn't move." Michael swung around on his chair to face Cooper. "No one interferes with this, do you hear me? No one! I didn't come this far to be scared of bad weather," he spat.

"Yes, sir." Cooper closed the door behind him. He pulled the mobile phone from his pocket, opened up the last email Maurice sent that morning, and quickly typed his reply.

*

The early evening breeze blowing into the cave now lapped harder at Hamida's still form. Where she had needed respite from her thoughts in the first few days in the cave, now she had found a rhythm within them. The clutter had cleared, the flotsam of fears and anger that had floated on the surface of her consciousness now seemed like distant memories. She was not sure how long her eyes had been closed, nor, when she did open them, whether she had been awake or asleep. Though she had ceased to count them, the sixth day was coming to a close, folding in on itself, the orange light of sunset deepening into violet. Hamida did not notice. Her eyes were still closed.

It was scenes that came to her now in the quiet, beneath her lids, in the depths of herself, fed by the cadence of her breath. Galaxies flying by as she leaned back against the chair in the theatre, the rushing of a billion stars pulsing as they passed, the heartbeat of the lamb she had held moments after it had been born, the purring of the cats that had laid in her lap. Vast expanses of sea beneath the plane as they had crossed between continents, the endless ripples of waves, and how the wind had the same effect on the swathes of grass that rolled out wherever she looked. The sheep, and their ceaseless rituals, their differences and their similitudes. The dead lamb, lying in the straw, saturated in the life its mother had tried to give it. The rain in London, the incessant hiss as it hit the ground. The sound of thundering footsteps, running down narrow alleyways, getting louder and louder, ringing in her ears, the mobs, the faces of faceless men, their differences and their similitudes, their anger and their pitifulness, their malice and their wretchedness as they pillaged for pride and raped for righteousness. Their greed and their poverty. The homeless man rummaging through the bins in Times Square, his half-gloved hands, his half-shoed feet, his half-formed face, his half-lived life. The lights followed. The reds, ambers, blues, greens, flashing and whirling, the faces they illuminated, looking up, looking down, eyes open, eyes closed, it didn't matter, none of them seeing. All of them missing. Missing something.

Outside the cave, the sky, now black, trembled. Thin and distant veins of lightning cut jagged flashing cracks through the darkness. The thunder echoed its warning, resounding off the hills. The wind moaned and swept around the cave, seeking shelter. The storm was close.

Hamida breathed deeply. Her eyes were still closed. She was back in the butterfly house, the wings of the delicate creature fluttered before her, an iridescent blue. It became brighter as it burst now into the colours she had seen dance with the music of her mind, played on quivering notes in a room she had once known. The colours swirled before her, the lines leaching into each other until the reds became yellows, the blues became greens, the browns became golds, and they glowed, brighter and brighter and harsher and faster, blazing and burning… They mixed with the sounds – the rumbling, hissing, cracking. Louder and louder they became. The heat, the cold, the light, the dark. Brighter and brighter they blazed. Faster and faster and faster they churned.

Hamida's chest tightened, and as the colours spun themselves into a frenzy of light inside and around her, they pressed against her from without and within, squeezing until she thought she might disappear. Until suddenly, in a piercing burst they exploded before her. And everything stopped. Hamida opened her eyes, gasping, desperately trying to breathe.

28

"No!"

Michael slammed his hands on top of the monitor. The screen had just gone black. The high-pitched crackle from the speakers – which had grown to such a peak he himself had clamped his hands over his ears – abruptly stopped. There was no image. No sound. Nothing. Not even the lights of the machines were working.

"No!" Michael slammed his hands back down on the equipment. "No, no, no!"

Cooper burst into the room just as Michael was about to sweep his hands across the desk and send the equipment crashing into the back of the door.

"Sir!" Cooper was of breath, as if he had run down the corridor. Michael turned back to the screen, his heart still pounding fiercely in his ears, and throbbing behind his eyes.

"It must have been the storm that knocked out the signal. It's over the cave now, sir," Cooper panted, fumbling with his phone, attempting to show Michael the angry, pulsating mass of the storm moving over the map of the area.

Michael let out a moan of the likes only deep despair could cause, and swiped Cooper's phone out of his hand, sending it spinning through the air. He sank into his chair, his hands pulling at his hair.

"All this… all this… months of preparation, months, months ruined by rain at the very end?" He thumped his fist down on the desk. "And nothing, nothing to show for it. She said not one damn word! Nothing!"

Cooper stood in the corner of the small room, looking not at Michael who sat slumped before him, his eyes glassy, his nails dug into the leather arm of the chair, but at the small screen in his palm. The amoebic mass of digital clouds was thinning, the pulsating heart of the storm shrinking as it trailed off the screen and away from the blinking red dot on the map.

"The storm is passing, sir."

Cooper looked up at the oval of thin grey skin at the crown on the back of Michael's head. The man did not move. He had not moved for the entire hour that the storm had raged. Beyond the rooted figure before him, Cooper was sure the dead screens flickered. He took a step towards them, peering. A faint glow was spreading across the monitor. Slowly, the infrared image of the cave crystalized back into sight.

The sharp light from the screens stirred Michael from his stupor. He looked up at the monitor. A wave of energy bristled through him. He sat rigid, his eyes darting, suddenly alert. He scanned the screen. He grabbed the keyboard. Hammering quickly at the keys, he flicked over to another camera angle, and another, and another. Each one showed the same image of the gaping bowels of the cave.

He swung around to face Cooper.

"Where the *fuck* is she?"

29

Maurice had slid backwards down the stony path to the cave, slick with the streams of water that were rushing down the sides of the mountain. His hands were bleeding, and his knees were cut and bruised. The flashlight he had strapped to his head flooded the path before him with a beam of bright light but the rain beating down relentlessly made it hard to see more than a foot in front of him. He had not waited for Cooper's reply to his urgent messages. He had set out that afternoon when he had seen the clouds closing in. Experiment, he seethed. No money in the world, no fortune or cause could excuse this. This was torture, a violation of basic human rights. It was inhumane. She was eighteen in a cave in the middle of nowhere with the worst storm of the summer about to hit. He clawed his way up the final stretch of the path and ran towards the cave, bellowing Hamida's name. There was no reply. He reached the mouth of the cave and clambered over the rocks inside, the beam swinging wildly around the cave walls as he searched.

"Hamida!"

And then he saw her – lying, curled up, in the centre of the cave floor, the block next to her overturned, shaking, trembling uncontrollably. He threw himself onto his knees and ripped off his coat, dripping wet, and then his thick sweater beneath. He wrapped this around her, cradling her in his arms, stroking the damp hairs, slick with sweat, away from her face. The thick beam of the flashlight, cast aside, cut a sharp angle across the dank darkness. She was freezing cold, and her eyes were still closed. Maurice wrapped his arms tighter around her and in the middle of the cave, in the middle of the storm, he cradled her, beseeching his warmth to reach her.

He did not know how long he knelt with her, perhaps seconds, perhaps minutes, perhaps hours. Outside, the storm was passing. The thunder rumbled fainter, and the sheets of rain had thinned. Maurice looked from the dark opening, illuminated now only by distant bursts of lightening, and back to Hamida. Slowly, she opened her eyes. With Hamida still in his arms, Maurice climbed carefully to his feet and carried her out of the cave.

*

Michael had retreated to his office. He had wrenched out the wires from all the equipment and had yelled at Cooper to get rid of it. He had walked the few steps to his office and slammed the door behind him. He was not sure how long he sat there, looking out of the window seeing nothing at all, nor did he care. What had started as despair, transformed into rage, and then contorted into a steely conviction was now just numbness. An empty nothingness. He heard nothing, felt nothing, wanted nothing. If he could have ended his existence then without the slightest effort he would have. But he had no energy left to make such an effort, and so he sat, staring out of the window.

The early rays of grey morning light trickled across the sodden fields beyond the window. The trees and plants shivered and huddled, animals cautiously sniffed at the cold, wet air now calm again. The search parties Cooper had sent out had picked their way carefully over the waterlogged ground towards the cave and had confirmed what they had seen on the screen. The cave was deserted. The only traces of human life the empty food wrappers tucked neatly into the side of the lock box, and a string of beads. It was over, his entire experiment, thwarted by a storm. And Hamida was nowhere to be seen.

*

When Cooper knocked at the door three days later, Michael did not hear him, nor did he hear the key turn in the lock. Only when Cooper shook his shoulder did Michael emerge from his stupor.

"Sir, I think you should see this…"

Michael looked at the face before him blankly. Cooper cleared his throat.

"I went through the tapes before dismantling the equipment." The words fell on Michael like news of a distant burial, the interment of a dream.

"It seems," Cooper continued cautiously, "that the speakers did catch something when the cameras went out." Michael stared hollowly at Cooper without moving. "Except it wasn't words… at least, not at first…"

Cooper took a small machine from his pocket and placed it on the table. "You see, sir, I kept replaying the recordings and, at first, it did just sound like noise, the interference we heard. But then, I noticed a pattern. A pattern of some sort, as though there was something beneath the noise."

Michael frowned at him, the glassy sheen of his eyes told Cooper he was tapping into the last sliver of himself willing to engage with any mention of this entire endeavour.

"So?"

"So, I called in a favour. I sent it to an old military friend of mine who now works at the UK Space Agency. I thought perhaps it was a signal of some sort."

"You sent it? Without my permission?" The edge in Michael's tone could have cut glass, his gaze sharpened, and the beginnings of fury crept across his face. He may have turned against the very thing into which he had invested so many months of his life, not to mention his hopes for revenge and the prospect of a definitive victory, but this did not mean his failure was now free for anyone else to observe. He opened his mouth again to pour out the boiling anger, but Cooper, undeterred, continued talking.

"He said it was some sort of a signal, but they'd never seen anything like it. He worked on decoding it and filtering out the interference over the past couple of days. And this morning, he sent me this."

With a sharp click, Cooper pushed his finger down on the button of the small black recorder.

The room filled with a hissing and crackling, the same noise Michael had heard in the monitoring room on the very first day Hamida had sat on the block and closed her eyes. Despite himself, he listened. Ten seconds passed… fifteen… twenty…

"Is this a joke, Cooper? This isn't words." His voice rose again, his posture stiffening.

"Just wait." Cooper held up a finger, as the sound rose higher and higher into a piercing hum. Michael looked from the small machine to Cooper's finger, his mouth open as if to object again. Cooper's finger quivered. "Wait. They're coming..."

By Our light when it is refracted

Desecrated

Forgotten

Redacted

By Our light as it travels across cosmic veins

Exploding with novas

Cascading with solar winds

Arriving within neurons of thirsty brains

Thirsty for dust

Thirsty for Us

Thirsty to become

And by her final words

The words she whispered into his ear:

> *Forgive me for not joining your war*
> *Forgive me for not sharing your fear*

The light he is trying to erase

Is here.

Michael slammed his hand down on the recorder. Cooper jumped. The sound came to an abrupt stop, Michael's hand frozen over the device as though trying to blot it out from existence. His breathing was heavy, his eyes wide, his entire body rigid, as though he had been struck.

"Sir?" Cooper ventured. Michael seemed not to hear him. "Is this… what you were expecting, sir? Do you know what it means?"

"No one else knew…" Michael's voice emerged hoarse, barely above a whisper.

"I'm sorry, sir?"

"No one else knew." He turned his gaze slowly to Cooper, whose expression was now tense with concern. Every drop of colour had fled from Michael's face, his pupils yawned wide, rimmed only with a thin line of grey. "Not a soul."

"Knew what, sir?"

"What she said to me. No one else heard those words. No one."

"Who, sir?" Cooper leaned forward, his eyes darting to the recorder, still invisible, clamped beneath Michael's palm. Michael's breaths shuddered out from him.

"My wife," he whispered. "Celeste."

If you loved *'The Celeste Experiment'* please consider reviewing it on Amazon or Goodreads.

Read on for a sneak preview of Omar Imady's next novel...

Catfishing Caitlyn

I

There is a certain sadism to the search for knowledge. A streak her father neither possessed nor understood. It was why she had done a PhD in the first place. But now that was over, and the chasm it had filled lay achingly empty.

Try as she might, Caitlyn could not get through to her father. It was not for lack of trying; he simply did not have the processor needed to appreciate what it was that made her tick. To be fair, he had done his research and, as far as he could tell, his daughter's career prospects fell into very specific categories: intelligence, government, or academia. She could join the CIA, or even the NSA. They'd practically start a bidding war over someone fluent in Arabic with an in-depth knowledge of the history and politics of the Middle East that surpassed many of their so-called 'experts'. Or she could pretend she was a born-again Christian and join the Zwemer Center, and be showered with research funds to come up with ways to meet their relentless goal of converting Muslim heathens back to Christ. He was less a fan of the latter, which he threw out more in jest than any seriousness, but still, it was money, and position, and a job, for goodness' sake. At the very least, she could pursue a career path in her field at Yale. They'd be desperate to keep her, of that her father was both sure and reassured by one of his many friends-in-high-places, though he did not share this little nugget with Caitlyn for fear she would reject it merely because it seemed to be such low hanging fruit. It didn't even have to be Yale, he told her. What about NYU or Columbia? He didn't mention the fact that he'd just purchased a house in Long Island and the thought of having her near him staved off the looming sense of crippling loneliness that seemed to grow with every passing year.

Bob O'Keefe was approaching seventy, though he fought the gravity of age with a rigorous fitness routine. The years had claimed his color, but his shock of silver hair, he felt, had given him a swank edge, so he'd steered clear of the box browns and blacks so many of his friends had not so subtly resorted to. With his electric blue eyes, he liked to think he looked like an Irish Paul Newman.

He was comfortable financially. More than comfortable, really, and not just because of the eyebrow-raising sum he had inherited from his father, and definitely not because of his long career as a senior editor at Scarecrow Press, from which he had reluctantly retired. It was because he was always careful with money, as he was with everything else in his life. Bob was prudent. With finances, with investments, with choices, and with emotions. He trusted this trait as much as he hated it. He was convinced now it was the reason Caitlyn's mother had left him for their impulsive, unpredictable, and at least in Bob's eyes, perfectly hideous, dentist. The kind of person who bought a jet ski and talked about it at dinner parties or with a fist in the gaping holes of wide-mouthed patients. So suffocating Bob's prudence must have been, that his wife had left not only her husband of more than a decade, but also their beautiful three-year-old daughter, as though wanting to expunge any and every memory of him and the eleven years she had spent in his organized, meticulous, prudent prison.

"Dad, listen to me. I want something else. I need something else. None of these excite me. I need excitement, Dad. Something that will take over my days, my nights, my life. Something that makes me want to get up in the morning and actually keeps me up, way after all the professors and desk spies and government cogs you want me to be like have fallen asleep. The career equivalent of nicotine, Dad, not Nytol."

His smile filled her with a mixture of frustration, anger, and pity. And then guilt. She tried again, though the futility was obvious.

"I want something riveting, Dad, I want something more…"

If it hadn't been her father she was speaking to she might have described the rush she was really after. Something far superior to nicotine, something she'd only ever described to her therapist in the confines of the cream room with oak blinds, muted tones, and sensible plants selected solely to inject a hint of life other than one's own.

"Something even more sensational than burying my head between the legs of a first year. More intense than listening to her moan as she experiences her very first orgasm with a woman. Something even more dramatic than walking out of her life, even as she pleads for me to stay."

Her therapist, who matched the subdued tones of her clinical confines, implied that her sexual orientation was probably linked to her subconscious anger at her mother, and her distrust of heterosexual relationships following her parents' divorce. That was, of course, bullshit. In Caitlyn's mind, she was like this because she was like this. She didn't need a reason.

The therapy sessions were a gift and a curse. Paid for by her father once Caitlyn hit puberty. She went, reluctantly and religiously, once a month, driven solely out of a sense of duty, a desire to assuage her father's own personal sense of guilt, which he could never admit to, but which was written all over his face and the expensive gifts he bought Caitlyn on every possible occasion. She'd give the other gifts away, but the therapy she could not avoid, though she'd made it quite clear to her father she really did not want or need a surrogate mother.

As affectionate as he tried to be, her father was always rationally beyond her reach. A man who never slept a minute beyond six, who faithfully attended church every Sunday, and whose idea of a wild time was to watch *Dirty Harry* as he swigged down a few bottles of Heineken, could never, Caitlyn had resigned herself to realizing, understand the gaping, growing, desperate void inside her that she knew if she did not fill, would soon swallow her whole.

*

The final submitted version of Caitlyn's dissertation was, to her, not a testament to all she had researched, compiled, constructed, and analyzed, but a testament to everything that had not made the cut. The hours upon hours of carefully crafted paragraphs, citations, translations that had been cast aside like the contents of a vacuum cleaner, dumped out, unceremoniously on the trash heap of unpublished work.

Footnotes had been the final frontier. Like hell three thousand was too many, she'd argued. According to whom? It was her dissertation, her topic, her argument, surely she should decide. But her advisor disagreed. Of course, he would. It didn't matter that she knew far more than he ever dreamed of knowing about the history of the ancient Middle East. It didn't matter that she had mastered Arabic, Hebrew, Syriac, and almost Greek, which her footnotes reflected. What mattered was that his name was on a door in the department and hers wasn't. They reached a compromise, excruciating for the both of them, Caitlyn because she had to excise over nine hundred punctiliously crafted and referenced footnotes, and her advisor because he still had to read the remaining two thousand.

The Concept of Religious Authority in Late Antique Arabia. The title of her dissertation was a mere guise for Caitlyn's obsessive indulgence in fifth to seventh century sources from the Middle East and its borderlands, from the edges of Byzantium to Bukhara, from Constantinople to Central Asia. Caitlyn luxuriated in history, in the excavation of ink, the dusting off of aged tomes, splitting open their secrets and extracting information that no one else had read for over a millennium, like one wheedles out a walnut from a carefully cracked shell. She reveled in the language, running her fingers over the words looking for loose threads and pulling with the satisfaction of unraveling the stitch on a woolen cuff, watching a structure reduced to the essence of its fabric, ready to be made again into something new. More than that, she loved the links. The links that could only be found at three in the morning, in the amber light of a library lamp, with eyes itchy from insomnia and dust, links that had never before been made by a living soul, links that denoted explosives hidden deep under the arguments of some of the most prominent figures in her field, living and dead. The satisfaction was greater if they were alive, of course, the floundering for a response was a delight to watch, less so if they were dead and their defense was left to their living lackies.

It was both with and without a sense of irony that her fellow doctoral students christened her 'Bint Qutayba', after the ninth century judge, encyclopedist, and polymath – master of fields as implausibly diverse as botany and exegesis, astronomy and legal theory – and a prolific writer, whose influence reached as far as *The Economist*:

"There can be no government without an army,

No army without money,

No money without prosperity,

And no prosperity without justice and good administration."

And no thesis without fucking footnotes.

Such was Caitlyn's notoriety for mining not only the mantle but the inner core of manuscript archives that she was often surreptitiously contacted by major-league names for 'assistance with locating sources' – confessions, in other words, of their ineptitudes in a field in which she had already outstripped them. It felt powerful to be asked. Seductive to be sought out. There was a salivatory satisfaction in the knowledge of how much painstaking thought had been put into ways to avoid asking her in the first place. It was the same feeling she experienced watching the baffled faces of conference attendees when she divulged discoveries in places no one else had even thought to look. Talismans in the margins of ancient recipes, riddles, mysteries, and missing links hidden in treatises on animal husbandry, sightings of Alexander the Great carved into tombstone inscriptions. She listened to their 'more-of-a-comment-than-a-question's with the intoxication of an Olympic gold medalist. It was the same feeling she experienced when a first year would sidle up to her table in the common room and ask, doe-facedly, whether she could help them decipher a fragment of their freshman assignment. *She was very busy. Did they realize she had deadlines looming?* But, she supposed, she could maybe give them five minutes if they met her for coffee after dinner in the campus cafeteria. She imagined their eyes held much the same look as those of a person whose captor had just uttered the words 'I'm not going to kill you'; a gaze that ran the gamut of wide-eyedness, from pleading, to terror, to gratitude.

She'd let them talk afterwards, deadlines could always wait, though they didn't know that yet. Talk about themselves, and inevitably her. They'd all heard about her, she was told for the hundredth time. She was famous in the faculty. *Why didn't she teach a class?* Easy pickings, she'd sigh.

They'd read her articles. They always had questions. *What was it like to work with all those dusty old men? How did she bear all the port and tweed? And didn't she just hate Professor X, Y, and Z?* She'd watch their faces as she'd open departmental cupboards to reveal the cigar-smoking, drunken, fumbling, freshman-fucking skeletons, and listen to them titter as she recounted the recountings of women – who'd gone on to leave the field far behind – about how these Jurassic geriatrics fared between the sheets, and how they'd mumbled their thanks and regrets in the same sentence at the end of their next awkward encounter.

Did she ever…? Hell, no. Museum exhibits were not really her type. She was into… well, a stroke of the thigh said it all really.

She could have graduated in half the time. But then, she would have had half the fun. Being a PhD student was a ticket to places, projects, and people inaccessible to those outside the realms of senior studenthood. And, though she would never acknowledge it, the looming prospect of judgment, of brutal examination, of a chance to verbally spar with the panel she herself had handpicked, she would not find anywhere but in a doctoral program. She had not wanted it to end. Not the library access, not the common room conversations, not the constant influx of distractions in fresh, young, female form, the unjaded, inexperienced, vernal vivacity and libidinous eagerness that permeated the corridors, seminar rooms, library columns, courtyards, and cafes that was unique to a university. It almost had a scent, the sweet suffusion of sex and scholarship. There really was no place like it anywhere else. Of this fact, Caitlyn was painfully aware. And so, she stayed. Signing up to every possible research project and seminar series, plucking grants from every possible branch until she had under her belt more publications and presentations than most professors could dream of.

It was only recently, to her surprise and dismay, that Caitlyn had discovered the stash of manuscripts stored away at the Digital Vatican Library. This was bound to be a treasure trove and she kicked herself for not finding it sooner, before the final twenty-four-hour countdown to the end of her university access had begun. She took a seat in the far corner of the canteen, pulled her laptop open and slid her headphones on. She had a five hour stretch before her meeting with her now former, emancipated, advisor to discuss a proposal she had put forward for a postdoctoral research project. Ornately inked manuscripts stared up at her from the screen. She sipped her coffee, cracked her fingers, and clicked.

Three hours passed before she noticed her tea had gone cold in its cardboard cup, and another passed before she realized that she had drunk it anyway. The unsung side of archival excavation was elimination, the separation of the wheat from the chaff, the dirt from the bones. One could spend hours chipping away at a document only to realize there was a reason no one had read it in centuries. Some days were spent discovering only this fact. Today seemed to be one of those days. Caitlyn tried not to give in to the feeling of frustration. Perhaps she could ask a colleague in the department if she could borrow their login information when hers ran out at 23:59 that night. But then they would have access to her search history… so scratch that. She'd ask her advisor again. Maybe.

Caitlyn leaned back in the wooden chair, her spine pressing against its scalloped back, designed purposely to torture students who tipped chairs onto their two back legs, teetering like rearing cavalry and daring gravity to topple them. The lunch rush had begun. She slipped her headphones off her ears and around her neck like some sort of futuristic ruff. The babble and chatter of the common room was rising; chairs scraping, the rustle of plastic and paper, and the chatter of amateurs discussing other people's ideas.

The first-year students were always so obvious. The men more so. Less men than boys, really. From the untidy scruff they sprouted and convinced themselves was passable facial hair, to their bags laden with library books containing a handful of pages for an assignment they did not realize they would have been better off taking a photograph of to read on their phones later and save somewhere sensible. They generally looked and smelled the same, a fetid mélange of testosterone, confidence, and teenage redolence. The only variation was the opposite end of the cool kid binary, the geeks who smelled less of confidence than of crippling insecurities and the wet-dog scent of air-dried clothes.

The women, on the other hand, fell along a spectrum. A spectrum not so much of scents as of flavors. There were the self-assured daddy's girls, who had never been told they had any reason to doubt themselves, they melted. Like butter into toast, they gave way under the heat of an exchange and disappeared. Then there were the sharp, citrusy ones. The ones who walked not with a languor but a shock in their steps. The ones that changed the taste of one's own saliva for hours afterwards. There were the licorice ones, with an aniseed afterglow, and a dark bitterness that permeated the movement of their fingertips, even if it did not show on their faces. The ones that tasted like Christmas cake Caitlyn liked the least, though the initial nutmeg and cinnamon tingle was enticing, they quickly became too sickly, and she always felt she needed to wash them down with something strong and smokey. If she had to guess, Caitlyn imagined she herself might be likened to cardamom coffee, the type that frothed in small copper pots over hot coals, that always burned your tongue at the first taste.

Caitlyn smiled at the young woman who had approached her table and asked if she could share it, glancing around at the packed room in earnest justification of her plea. She was a dark redhead, with a smattering of freckles across her ovaline face, not pretty by conventional standards, but striking. That's what you called women who weren't pretty but whom you could not take your eyes off all the same. She had a ring in her nose. Caitlyn had a strange certainty she'd taste like sage.

With a heave and sling of the bag over one shoulder that Caitlyn had carried out daily for the past ten years, to the extent that she was sure her right trapezius was permanently concave, she surrendered her seat and strode over to the other side of campus to collect her mail. Lasts are perhaps even more poignant than firsts. Difficult emotions always seem to leave a more indelible mark on one's memory than the fleetingness of exuberance and novelty. Perhaps this explains the desperate scramble to record a loved one's last words, when their first are celebrated but so quickly forgotten. The first sip of wine might be appreciated but the final drops are savored. Caitlyn would have liked to savor the experience of slowly pulling out the mail from her thin wooden pigeonhole, tucked away between O'Brian and Okotie, but by the time she had leafed through the junk, she realized she had only minutes to make it up the five flights of stairs at the other side of the courtyard to Professor Bernheim's office. Even for someone who ran at least a mile most mornings, making this journey was a feat. She arrived flushed and annoyed, her forehead and upper lip prickling with sweat. She shoved the remaining envelopes and flyers she hadn't realized she was still holding into her bag as she knocked on the heavy wooden door.

Caitlyn always forgot how short Bernheim was. His height, or lack thereof, took her by surprise at their every meeting. She was not much taller than average and yet she seemed to tower over the figure who looked as though he may have once inhabited a hole in Middle Earth. She prepared herself with three mandatory deep breaths and steeled herself for the long pauses and objectless stares that peppered their every interaction.

Bernheim invited her to sit in one of the leather armchairs worn thin by a thousand twitchy asses and fidgeting elbows. She sank into it, now accustomed to the familiar though still somewhat disorienting sensation of sitting with one's knees higher than one's hips. She eyed the lines of books with their calligraphic spines, embossed in gold, their elaborate titles written in Arabic from right to left, brocaded with intricate designs – twelve volume sets, fourteen volume sets, twenty-six volume sets. They were all available online of course, and she was not interested in the easily accessible, but still, she would love to line her shelves with such collections, just to be able to run her fingers over the covers, and occasionally rummage around in their footnotes for forgotten gems.

Bernheim cleared his throat and in his horsey whisper broke the news.

"Wait, what do you mean the committee rejected my application?"

Her proposal had been a work of art. She had identified three major overlooked areas of scholarship, pinpointed the sources she would need to examine, outlined all the ways it could contribute to knowledge, jumped through every fucking hoop they'd laid out in the application guidelines. It had taken weeks to write.

"'Demonstrable impact outside the field?' What does that even mean?"

Apparently, the department was being criticized for its 'insularity', and 'lack of engagement in knowledge exchange and impactful contributions to academia beyond its own walls'. What kind of Orwellian horseshit was this? What did they expect her to do? Solve global warming while she was at it? The department was being reviewed and needed to submit a report justifying its funding and outlining ways in which they would meet the university targets during the coming year. Who wrote this crap? It was *Big Brother* on speed.

"What happened to knowledge for knowledge's sake? What happened to being bastions of world class scholarship?"

Bernheim looked down at his desk, doing nothing to allay Caitlyn's suspicions that he was reading from a crib sheet. He had no answers to her question of whether the committee would accept a revised proposal, and she left with nothing but the distinct impression that Bernheim had been less her advocate at that meeting than a dwarven town crier, tolling the bell of his own insecurities and fatigue. There might be a position with Professor Fischer in Germany, he murmured. Fuck Germany. And fuck Fischer. Caitlyn purposely left the office door open after her in the hope that a strong gust from the drafty corridor might send the stacks of papers flying, along with Bernheim himself.

Perhaps it was the ardency, the frustration, the desperation in the face of fleeing seconds that made Caitlyn's return to the Vatican archives just as fruitless as her morning session of searching. It was with the franticness of the hunt for a dropped needle in the pile of thick carpet, a lost passport on the eve of departure, an incriminating sliver of evidence with the police outside the door that Caitlyn tore through manuscripts of Latin, Arabic, and Aramaic with a manic tapping, the uncontrollable twitch of an addict desperate for a fix as the blade of the 23:59 guillotine drew ever closer.

The measure of an addict's obsession is the point at which their pride comes into play; how far they are willing to push before they come up against the wall of their own dignity. Caitlyn closed her laptop at 23:49. With the resignation of a death row inmate, she made her way unfeelingly, unthinkingly down to the common room vending machine, fed the greedy black bowels her coins and punched in the numbers for a Diet Coke. She sank into the slightly sticky gray sofa, the shape of sensibility and minimal comfort, and waited for midnight to pass as she felt the cold, sharp, thistly fizz against her tonsils and the carbonated sting at the back of her nose.

The redhead from the canteen was sitting at a desk in the corner of the room, scribbling furiously on a large pad of paper. Caitlyn had made it a principle never to be the one to initiate an approach. She felt a voltaic surge creep down from the back of her tongue, spread tendrils across her chest, and then run a finger right below her navel. She took another stinging swig of Coke.

Caitlyn liked to think of how her therapist might have analyzed a situation, precisely to come up with her own counter theory.

> *Theory A - The Therapist's Theory: Caitlyn was afraid of humiliation. She would not approach the woman because there would be a chance she could turn her down, thus compounding her own sense of rejection.*

> *Theory B - Caitlyn's Counter: The satisfaction of uninitiated seduction would soothe her sense of fury at the imbecility of this institution far more than a desperate attempt to seek some first year's attention. If she had to ask, it wasn't worth it.*

Caitlyn threw her empty can into the bin in the corner from her seat on the sofa and lay back, closing her eyes. The woman looked up at the clatter.

The difference between men and women when it came to sex was in the object of their pursuit. Men wanted the explosion, the guttural gasp at the finish line, the torsion of the body at the climax, the so-called summit of sex. Their mistake lay in thinking women wanted that too. For women, the pleasure of sex came with the climb, the agonizing anticipation, the slow ascent, the combination of being at once melted and electrified, the gratification of delayed gratification. Caitlyn had mastered this art, reading the signs of the body beneath her, the tautness of thighs, the tightening of lips, and knew precisely the point at which to withdraw to draw out the exquisite torture of unfulfilled expectation, and then to gently resume the climb.

The redhead reached her peak disappointingly soon and irritated Caitlyn with her assumption that the prelude had been the finale, much the same as one might pity a person who fills up on appetizers. She climbed the ladder from the wide bed that constituted half the ceiling of her studio flat and washed her hands and face to reset. She suggested to the girl that she do the same. Caitlyn straightened the bedsheets, cracked open the window.

"Let's try that again."

Red freckles were different to brown, the constellations across the back of the body lying next to her were almost translucent, as though the spattering of paint that was once sprayed across her had been worn away. Caitlyn watched the woman's chest rise and fall gently. It helped, she had found, to synchronize her own breath with the women she slept with, helped to calm her, stem the inevitable tide of thoughts that would come rushing back in the moments of undistracted quiet. No two bodies were the same. Not just in height or build, but in texture. With a finger, she carefully slid a rebellious strand of hair from where it was curled below the woman's ear, pulling it over her shoulder until it slipped back onto the pillow. There was something magnificent about a person's neck. Caitlyn ran the back of her forefinger over the soft down behind the woman's ear that thinned gradually into her ivory skin, dappled with freckles. It reminded her of corn fields in the wind, the ways hair grew, tides meeting each other in disparate waves. She touched the outer edge of the woman's ear, feeling the unique bumps of the cartilage beneath, and the dimples of her empty piercings.

The woman breathed heavily and rolled over onto her front, pulling the blanket with her, and stretched out her legs from the sheet beneath. Caitlyn leaned back to allow her room to cool. The rise and fall of the woman's shape transported her to sand dunes, the mountains of deserts, layered against an unreachable horizon, ever shifting imperceptibly, distinguishable from the inky darkness beyond them by the way they caught the light of a fierce moon. If you listened carefully, Caitlyn knew, you could hear them speaking. In hushed tones they whispered to each other. Every night, the sand dunes shared their dreams.

The young woman's hips were angular, and her thighs long and narrow, and Caitlyn could see the veins, blue, purple, and almost green, through the skin on the backs of her knees. The skin on her thighs was different to her back, which along with the spatterings of freckles, was pockmarked with tiny scars and miniscule craters, pink, brown, or simply hollow. Her thighs, though visibly smooth, were slightly rough to the touch, Caitlyn had noticed, much like her own, where the hair she had shaved that morning was resuming its growth. Her calves were mottled with an assortment of inexplicable bruises. She often tried to imagine them into clearer shapes, much like as a child she'd looked for images in clouds. The softest skin, Caitlyn always found, lay at the backs of women's knees. She stroked the skin there gently. Then, laying her head by the woman's feet, she pushed her own under the pillow, and watched her chest rise and fall, as she tried again to match the woman's breathing.

Her exhaustion kept at bay the fitfulness of anxious sleep until five the next morning, at which point Caitlyn awoke with a nauseous jolt and clambered quickly down the ladder to her bag. With the acidity of nervous energy pumping through her, she pulled out her laptop and set it down heavily on the desk. There was a chance, just a slim chance, that the university had not canceled her library access. That somewhere some glitch had occurred, some secretary had overlooked a button, that an automated system had been mercifully misprogrammed and the keys to her castle would not be confiscated.

She pulled open her laptop. The subtle severing of the magnetic pull between screen and keyboard caused the envelope tucked between them to flutter up and slide onto the floor under her desk. Crouching down to reach it, Caitlyn realized it was not an envelope at all but a single piece of oblong ivory card. It looked like an invitation. She slid herself out from under the desk with the slip between her fingers and sat back in her chair, the fibers prickling against the backs of her thighs. She turned over the card.

www.CaitlynMOKeefe.com

Was this some kind of a joke? A ploy to sell webspace, or some new alumni recruitment stunt? Right on the eve of her cascading off the cliff edge of studentship into the abyss of the job market, someone thought it was okay to set up a website in her name? That would be the first thing anyone found now if they looked her up. Who in the hell…?

She hammered the website into the search bar, already composing the furious email she would send to whoever had thought this was a remotely good idea.

The page that appeared was black. The white writing small but stark.

Welcome to the Game, Caitlyn.

Password required

"You've got to be shitting me." Caitlyn postponed her thoughts on the fate of the little IT punk that designed this, and clicked the small question mark beside the password box.

Hint: If you're not smart enough to guess the password, you're not smart enough to play.

Who the fuck did they think they were? Not smart enough? Caitlyn leant back in the chair, the initial sting of the insult subsiding. They'd got her right where they wanted her. They'd know it, and she knew it. So, sure, she thought, let's play.

To continue reading Catfishing Caitlyn,
sign-up to receive advance notice for pre-orders,
discounts and promotional offers at
https://villamagnapublishing.com/newsletter/

Join the conversation and follow us!
Instagram @publishingvillamagna,
Twitter @VillaMagna_pub,
and Facebook @VillaMagnaPublishing.

CPSIA information can be obtained
at www.ICGtesting.com
Printed in the USA
JSHW062215110523
41610JS00003B/140